Praise for Jennifer Sturman
The Pact

"Sturman's debut is a rare delight, and her sharp, sassy writing is wonderfully addictive. Sturman is as adept at detailing a career gal's search for a good man as she is at crafting a clever mystery, making *The Pact* a great choice for chick-lit fans and readers who enjoy their amateur sleuthing with a dash of romance."
—*Booklist*

"*Sex and the City* meets Agatha Christie! Jennifer Sturman is an exciting new voice in mystery fiction."
—Meg Cabot, author of *The Princess Diaries* and *Every Boy's Got One*

"Why is this debut so thoroughly enjoyable? Perhaps it's because Rachel is such a winning detective: she sifts through clues at the reader's pace and does so with wit and pluck. The novel's mise-en-scène—successful, attractive Ivy League graduates at a lakeside mansion—makes for escapist pleasure, and well-placed cliffhangers, a careful distribution of motives and unexpected twists promise readers light, satisfying suspense."
—*Publishers Weekly*

"Great mystery, super characters!"
—Michele Jaffe, author of *Loverboy*

"This mystery is a fresh and terrific new addition to the chick lit genre. Most of the traditional chick lit elements are here—the heroine's love life, career and friendships—but the whodunit is an excellent and welcome twist. Debut novelist Sturman delivers great characters, a dash of humor and a mystery that keeps you interested—and guessing."
—*Romantic Times*

4P

JENNIFER STURMAN

THE
JINX

**RED
DRESS
I N K**

THE JINX

A Red Dress Ink novel

ISBN 0-373-89540-2

© 2005 by Jennifer Sturman.

www.RedDressInk.com

Printed in U.S.A.

This book is dedicated to Michele Jaffe.
Have I mentioned that you're my best friend?

Acknowledgments

I benefited from the support of many friends
and colleagues in writing this book.

Laura Langlie offered her usual mix of kind wisdom
and unflappable calm while continuing to humor my
theory of jinxing. Farrin Jacobs, Margaret Marbury
and the team at Red Dress Ink expertly shepherded
the manuscript to publication, improving it
with every step in the process.

Friends Anne Coolidge, Michele Jaffe and
Rulonna Neilson supplied invaluable encouragement
and solidarity. Cameron Poetzscher provided a
much-needed refresher course in corporate finance,
and Holly Edmonds and Daniel Allen graciously
assisted in reacquainting me with
Boston and Cambridge.

My parents, Joseph and Judith Sturman,
my brothers, Ted and Dan Sturman, and my
sister-in-law, Lindsay Jewett Sturman, remain
remarkably restrained in their discussions of the
path my career has taken—in fact, they've even
been enthusiastic. Finally, my nieces, Miss Edith
(Edie) Michael Sturman and Miss Cecelia (Cece)
Esther Sturman, kindly allowed me to borrow
their names, although they've been far less
forthcoming with their Pirate's Booty.

Thank you.

Prologue

A homeless man found the body.

It was New Year's Day, and George Lawrence Fullerton IV was up early, rooting through a Dumpster in an alley near the Cambridge Common, searching for any item of value that could be exchanged for a nip of something to seal out the cold. He generally stuck to the tonier neighborhoods across the river in Boston for his treasure hunts—Beacon Hill, Back Bay—but he made a tradition of starting the new year in Harvard Square, close to the familiar red bricks and cupolas of his alma mater.

He poked through the trash using an elegant ebony walking stick. The stick had been an exceptional find, requiring only minor repairs to make it whole. He had reattached the handle with black electrical tape, a neat fix that was barely noticeable to the casual observer.

Skillfully, he swept the top layer of trash over to the side of the Dumpster, revealing a woman's foot, shod in a red high-heeled sandal, protruding from a heavy-duty brown garbage bag. The lifeless flesh was so pale it looked blue. The toenails were painted gold, but the chipped polish needed touching up. Tacky, tacky, tacky, George remarked to himself. His nanny had always said that good grooming was a mark of good breeding. The garbage bag was nestled between a pizza box (empty) and the shell of an aged television set (worthless).

George stopped his digging to consider the foot. He was not shocked—years spent sorting through other people's rubbish had schooled him well in the seedy ways of the world. He often thought that he could write a book about the things people discarded. A modern anthropologist. He imagined himself holding forth from a lectern, an audience of students entranced by his brilliance. And, of course, his dapper demeanor and flashing wit.

He used the tip of his walking stick to lift the edge of the bag and peer in for a better look at its contents. The bright winter sunshine illuminated a woman's body, folded at the waist and clad in a small dress of one of those synthetic materials that George refused to have anywhere near his own skin. Her head was pushed against her knees, and George wondered at the dead woman's flexibility. He couldn't even touch his fingers to his toes when he did his morning calisthenics. Her platinum-blond hair gave way at the roots to a coarse brown, and the sliver of profile George could see was garish with makeup.

George cast an indignant look around him. No matter what he did, this body would be the cause of great inconvenience in the neighborhood, inevitably disrupting his routine as soon as the sanitation men came around. The police knew him and the handful of others who made their livings from the area's refuse. He would be an obvious first step in their investigation. After all, the others had neither his degree of intellect nor his well-spoken manner.

The discovery of this body was likely to attract even greater attention than sordid events like homicide usually did. It was the seventh body of a prostitute to be found in a Dumpster in Cambridge in the past year. And there were rumors that the responsible party was connected to the Harvard community in some way. The bodies found previously had been strangled, as had this one judging by the bulging eyes and protruding tongue. He wondered if the forensic team would find the telltale crimson-and-white fibers from a striped wool Harvard scarf around the neck of this victim, as well.

George mulled over his options. In such situations, he generally thought it best to go on about his business and let the police come find him when they got around to it. But on a bitterly cold day like today, a trip to the police station to answer some questions might not be so unpleasant. Some warm coffee, maybe a couple of doughnuts (a plebian treat in which George occasionally indulged), some quasi-civilized conversation. Indeed, the police would be around eventually to see if he or any of the other local residents had seen anything of interest. He might as well make the most of the misfortune.

He straightened up, brushing off his coat (cashmere from Brooks Brothers—the lining was ripped and the elbows quite worn, but it had still merited rescue from the garbage of Beacon Hill). He adjusted his hat (a perfectly good deerstalker that he'd found in a trash bin the day after Halloween) to its customarily jaunty angle. With purposeful steps, he ventured forth to the nearest police precinct.

He did have a soft spot for doughnuts.

One

I live a very glamorous life. At least, that's what you would think if you didn't know any better.

You've probably seen my type before—striding briskly through airports with a cell phone clasped to my ear, settling into first class as the gateway doors shut. Power breakfasting at New York's finer hotels with men in expensive dark suits and silk ties. Or perhaps reading the *Wall Street Journal* in the back seat of a Lincoln Town Car, heading south on the FDR Drive toward Wall Street.

You may even have seen me on a recent cover of *Fortune* magazine, posed in a crisply tailored black Armani with several other Yuppie-types under the caption "Wall Street's Next Generation: They're Young, They're Hungry, and They're Women."

My father had a copy of the cover blown up to poster-size and framed; it hangs on the wall of his office, incongruous next to his numerous academic degrees. The article also inspired a long-distance lecture from my grandmother titled "You don't want to be one of those career girls, now, do you?" This was actually a welcome change from her usual repertoire, which includes such popular hits as "Have you met anyone nice?" "My dentist has the most handsome new associate," and (my personal favorite) "I just want to go to a wedding before I die."

I am an investment banker for the new millennium. Forget the movies you've seen—Michael Douglas with his hair slicked back in *Wall Street* or Sigourney Weaver in *Working Girl*. This is a kinder, gentler era. We talk to our clients about managing the transition to a global economy and relationship-driven banking. The partners at Winslow, Brown, the firm I've called home for the better part of a decade, espouse diversity and teamwork.

This doesn't mean that it's all fun and games. My life is far less glamorous than it appears. I have worked into the early morning hours on more nights, canceled more weekend plans and slept in more Holiday Inns in small industrial towns than I care to count—standard practice in the business of mergers and acquisitions. Entire months of my life have passed in a fog of caffeine, numbers, meetings and documents.

So why, one might ask, do I do this?

Fresh-faced, newly minted MBAs ask me this question frequently, and I tell them how rewarding it is to counsel top executives on issues of critical strategic importance and to work with sharp, highly motivated people in a collegial environment.

These might be the reasons I joined the firm when I was a newly minted MBA. Why I'm still here, despite the grinding work and red-eye flights, is much simpler.

Greed.

I know it's not an attractive answer, but the oversize year-end bonus checks and their promise of financial independence are the only thing that can make hundred-hour work weeks palatable. For me at least. There is the occasional deranged individual who truly loves finance, the thrill of closing a deal and the illusion of power it bestows.

One such individual is Scott Epson, a Winslow, Brown colleague who was sitting next to me this Wednesday afternoon in early January. We were on the Delta Shuttle, bound from New York to Boston, on our way to participate in an annual ritual at Harvard Business School known as Hell Week, when all of the major investment banks, consulting firms and other corporate recruiters compete to lure the most promising students to join our respective companies upon graduation. An advance team from Winslow, Brown had completed an initial round of interviews during the first half of the week, and second rounds were to take place on Thursday and Friday.

I was not sitting with Scott by choice. I had seen him in the waiting area, gesticulating wildly on his cell phone with his customary air of self-importance. I thought that I had crept by unseen, but I was only a few feet down the gateway when I heard his nasal voice behind me. "Rachel! Rachel! Hey—wait up!"

For a split second I'd toyed with the possibility of playing deaf, but remembering my New Year's resolution to be a nicer person, I turned around, feigned surprise and gave Scott a big fake smile and wave.

He was weighted down by a bulging briefcase in one hand, a stack of file folders under his opposite arm and a garment bag suspended from his shoulder. His suit jacket hung loosely from a scrawny frame, and his striped shirt was almost completely untucked. If it weren't for the rapidity with which he was losing his mouse-brown hair, it would be easy to mistake Scott for a high-school student dressed up in his father's clothing. I knew from a good source that he needed to shave only a couple of times a week.

"Hi," I greeted him when he'd caught up to me. "How are you?" I gave myself a mental pat on the back for the warmth I'd mustered in my tone.

"Busy, busy, busy," answered Scott with an exaggerated sigh. "We were up all night running the numbers on Stan's new deal. The client has completely unrealistic expectations as to how quickly we'll be able to close, but of course Stan told him we could get it done."

Stan Winslow is the head of Winslow, Brown's Mergers and Acquisitions department, or M&A. Scott spends a great deal of time trying to ingratiate himself to Stan. This can be highly amusing to watch, because our trusty leader is largely oblivious to much of what goes on around him. His attention is usually focused on his next golf game, his next martini and his new, significantly younger wife. The primary value Stan brings to Winslow, Brown is his surname (which is, in fact, related to that on the firm's letterhead) and his over-stuffed Rolodex, the product of an adolescence enrolled at an elite New England prep school and a young adulthood engaged in drinking, puking and otherwise bonding with future leaders at Yale.

Scott and I advanced down the gateway together, and he blustered on about his incredible deal and how incredibly pivotal his role in the entire endeavor truly was. I prayed that the flight would be too full for us to possibly sit together. Alas, an empty row beckoned right up front. I slid into the window seat and Scott took the aisle. We put our coats and briefcases on the middle seat as a silent deterrent to anyone who might be interested in sitting there. Not that I would have minded a buffer between us in the form of a disinterested third party, especially since Scott was all ready to settle in for an amiable chat.

"So, Rach," he asked, "how goes it with you? What have you got in the hopper?" I hate being called Rach by anyone but a close friend, and even then I'm ambivalent.

"Oh, the usual." Unable to resist the opportunity to prey on Scott's insecurities, I mentioned a couple of high-profile deals in progress. "And then there's the entire HBS effort. It's a big time commitment but Stan did ask me to take it on—I couldn't say no. You know how it is when the partners really want you to do something." I gave Scott my most winning colleague-in-arms smile.

Winslow, Brown was growing rapidly, and to fuel its growth we had intensified our efforts to recruit new MBAs. When Stan asked me to head up the process, I had mixed feelings. On the one hand, it was a prestigious role that offered significant exposure to the firm's partners. On the other hand, I resented that it seemed always to be the few female bankers at the firm who were asked to spearhead such activities as recruiting and training. However, I knew that Scott had been angling for the honor himself, probably because he derived so much of his identity from his own Harvard MBA. It didn't help matters that Stan seems to enjoy setting the two of us up in competition.

He eyed me with an expression that was either jealousy or indigestion and straightened his tie. It was a nifty little number featuring white whales on a navy background. "Well," he harrumphed. "I guess women have a special knack for that sort of thing, what with all of this emphasis on 'diversity.'" The way he said *diversity* made it sound like a curse word, which I guessed it was if one had the misfortune to be born a white male.

"Oh, definitely. We really do have a knack for these things," I agreed innocently. "Well, I wish I could spend the whole flight talking, but I need to catch up on a few things. Do you mind?" I asked, indicating my briefcase.

"Oh, me, too. I'm just incredibly busy. Just an incredible amount of stuff going on."

I pulled some papers from my black leather portfolio, hoping that he didn't notice the copy of *People* poking out from the inside pocket. Eager to demonstrate his equal if not superior level of busyness, Scott started punching numbers into his calculator.

I began flipping through my papers, but it was hard to concentrate on facts and figures, much less a stack of student résumés. I had more on my agenda for this trip than recruiting. The best part was Peter, my boyfriend of nearly five months. Peter ran a start-up in San Francisco, but he would be joining me in Boston to attend a high-tech conference. To my utter amazement, not to mention that of my friends and family, I seemed to be in a successful relationship for the first time ever. The New Year's we'd just spent together had been pure romantic bliss—a remote ski cabin, very little skiing and lots of snuggling in front of roaring fires. This was in stark contrast to New Year's with boyfriends past, particularly the New Year's Eve Massacre three years ago, when my date had taken me to a nightclub and forced me to listen to live jazz as he explained that he'd decided to marry his college girlfriend. Of course, the Valentine's Day Massacre of two years ago completely trumped the New Year's Eve Massacre. My date had shown up with his mother, whom he'd surprised with a dozen red roses and a Tiffany heart on a delicate chain. He gave me a pair of mittens.

With Peter, I'd finally stopped waiting for the other shoe to drop. I'd even stopped worrying that I'd jinx everything by referring to him as my boyfriend and making plans more than a week in advance. And I had an elaborate theory of jinxing, one that wasn't easily discarded. To feel secure, particularly in a relationship with an attractive man, was to invite the wrath of the Jinxing Gods, a nasty pantheon watching from above, taking note of any occasion on which I became too sure of myself and gleefully ensuring that I was punished with an appropriately confidence-depleting blow.

But Peter was honestly what he seemed to be—smart, funny, handsome, considerate. He even smelled wonderful. The time I'd spent with him had thoroughly vanquished the Jinxing Gods. I'd sent them packing, assured that I was no longer their plaything.

The only drawback—there had to be one—was that Peter lived on the opposite side of the country. I'd managed frequent trips to San Francisco for work, and he had made a number of trips to New York. We'd spent the holidays together—Thanksgiving with my family and Christmas with his—and everyone had gotten along wonderfully. Still, being with him was bittersweet, always knowing that it wasn't long before one of us would have to get on a plane.

At least this time I'd have him with me for the better part of a week. He was due in Boston that night and would be staying on after the conference for my annual reunion with my college roommates, which we always held on the second weekend in January. This year Jane, who lived in Cambridge with her husband, Sean, was the designated host. It was convenient for me since I already had to be in the area. Emma purported to live in New York but had been spending most of her time of late with Matthew, a doctor who worked in South Boston, so it suited her nicely. Hilary, a journalist, didn't really live anywhere, but she was working on a new project and had said that Boston was exactly where she needed to be for her research. Luisa would be flying up from South America and had recently ended her relationship with her girlfriend of three years; she seemed eager for an excuse to flee any continent on which Isobel lived, regardless of the distance she'd have to travel.

I nearly purred with contented anticipation. Peter and my

best friends, all in one place, for an entire weekend. It would be perfect.

The only thing I had to worry about was recruiting. And Sara Grenthaler.

The next day, I planned to skip the morning's schedule of interviews to attend a memorial service for Tom Barnett, who had been my client and the CEO of Grenthaler Media. He had suffered a heart attack the previous Friday and was pronounced dead on arrival at the hospital. That evening I had plans to dine with Sara Grenthaler—Tom's goddaughter, Grenthaler Media's largest individual shareholder, and a friend of mine. I was uneasy about the dinner—I sensed that Sara was distraught about more than Tom's death when we spoke, by phone earlier that week, and she'd been insistent that we meet, sooner rather than later. But when I pressed her, asked her what was wrong, she simply said that it would be better to discuss things in person. And I was hardly in a position to disagree.

I wondered why she felt so strongly about seeing me that night.

I shared a cab with Scott to the Charles Hotel in Harvard Square. The ride passed painlessly enough, although it occurred to me that perhaps I should worry that I evaluated so much of my life in terms of pain avoidance. I made polite responses to Scott's various attempts to one-up me, and he didn't seem to notice that I wasn't feeling one-upped. Fortunately, he had some business of his own to attend to, so he didn't even try to tag along for dinner.

I stowed my bag and briefcase with the hotel concierge and then headed up Eliot Street toward the restaurant where I was meeting Sara. On the way, I pulled out my cell phone and called Jane.

"Hey, there! Are you in town?" Her greeting was warm.

"I just landed half an hour ago. I'm on my way to a dinner, but I wanted to say hello."

"Great. Hilary's already here, and I spoke to Emma and she's at Matthew's, as usual, and Luisa's getting in tomorrow morning. It looks like everyone's on schedule—wait, Hilary wants to talk." I heard the fumbling noise of the phone changing hands.

"Rach! Is Peter here, too?"

"Not until later tonight. His flight gets in around ten, I think."

"As if you don't know the exact time it gets in and haven't calculated to the second how long it will take him to get to the hotel," she pointed out, no small trace of amusement in her tone.

I had, of course, but I knew better than to admit it. Hilary's talent for mockery was finely honed, and I had no desire to supply her with ammunition. Instead, I changed the subject. "What's the new project you're working on? I can't wait to hear about it." Asking Hilary about Hilary was a guaranteed way to divert her attention.

"It's a book," she told me with enthusiasm.

"A book?" I asked. "What happened to journalism?"

"This is journalism. It's just like a long-form article. I'll tell you all about it on Friday, but it's a true crime book. I figure I'll write it, it will be a bestseller, I'll sell the movie rights for a fortune, and then I can stop chasing all over the globe for random stories."

Knowing Hilary, it probably would be a bestseller, so I didn't bother to question her lofty expectations. "I thought you liked chasing all over the globe for random stories?" I asked.

"I'm getting a little sick of it, to tell the truth."

"Don't tell me. Your nesting instinct is finally kicking in."

"Well, I wouldn't go that far. But it would be nice to have

a fixed address. What are you—" I heard more fumbling, and then Jane came back on the line.

"Hilary's decided to use us as her fixed address for the time being," she said, her voice neutral. When Jane's voice was neutral, you knew that she was actually freaking out.

"Has she given you any sense of how long she's planning on using your guest room as her base of operations?"

"Nope," she answered with false cheer.

"Well, you know Hilary. I'm sure she'll move on quickly."

"Uh-huh." She didn't sound convinced.

"How much luggage did she bring with her?"

"Enough."

"Oh."

"Oh is right. Anyhow, I know you're busy with work and Peter, but we'll see you on Friday for the kickoff dinner, right?"

"Absolutely. Is there anything I can bring? Anything I can do?"

"Don't even start, Rach. We're not going to let you cook."

Two

Upstairs on the Square was new to Harvard Square since my student days. The space it occupied had been a bar and restaurant called Grendel's when I was in college and business school. I'd spent a lot of time there, particularly as an undergrad, and mostly in the cellar bar, which had been a low-budget affair with scarred wood tables and rickety chairs. The restaurant above hadn't been much better, so I was unprepared for the grandeur of its current state.

The walls of the foyer were now a deep lacquered red, and I checked my coat at a polished wood counter. I'd opted for the Monday Club Bar on the first floor for dinner, which was more casual than the Soiree Room upstairs and slightly funky, with zebra-striped carpet and red-cushioned gilt chairs. I was a few minutes early for our seven-thirty reservation, but I let the hostess lead me to a corner table, ordered a glass of Pinot Noir, and wondered again why Sara had been so anxious to see me tonight.

Sara's company, Grenthaler Media, had become a Winslow, Brown client due to the efforts of Nancy Sloan, the firm's first female partner. Nancy had been a mentor to me, a dynamo of a woman with tremendous confidence. I'd learned a lot from her about not letting myself get stepped on by the wingtips and tasseled loafers that roamed Winslow, Brown's halls.

Two years ago, at the age of forty-one, Nancy met an artist, fell in love and quit the firm. She and her artist now lived in Vermont with their year-old baby boy, and Nancy divided her time between the baby, managing her stock portfolio and writing the business column in their local newspaper.

She'd bequeathed to me several of her clients, including Grenthaler Media. Sara's father, Samuel Grenthaler, founded the company in 1958 with the launch of a groundbreaking journal on international affairs. He went on to introduce several other magazines, ranging from the obscure and erudite to more popular weeklies, and he became an American success story in the process—a Holocaust refugee who had worked his way up from nothing. In the late 1970s, he'd met Anna Porter, a graduate student studying physics at M.I.T. Anna was the blue-blooded, bluestocking daughter of Edward and Helene Porter, scions of Boston society. Their marriage had been an unlikely one, given their differences in background and age, but by all accounts it had also been a happy one.

Seven years ago, the couple died in a car accident on icy roads. They had been en route to their ski house in Vermont, where their eighteen-year-old daughter was to meet them for the Christmas holidays, when their car skidded off the road, tumbled into a ravine and burst into flames, leaving Sara a very wealthy orphan.

Tom Barnett, Samuel Grenthaler's best friend and business partner, stepped into the role of CEO. While Tom proved to be a visionary leader and a superb manager, he viewed himself as a caretaker of his friend's company, and he began grooming Sara to take over. During her vacations from college, she worked in a variety of roles at Grenthaler, and after college, she spent two years at a management consulting firm before enrolling at Harvard Business School. She'd spent the previous summer as an intern at Winslow, Brown, learning the essentials of corporate finance to supplement her formal business education before returning to HBS for her second and final year.

Sara had been assigned to one of my deal teams that summer, and the two of us had hit it off immediately. We had certain things in common—including a love of bad teen movies from the eighties. I loaned her my copy of *Valley Girl*, and she returned the favor by introducing me to *Tuff Turf.* But while we had forged a close friendship and our conversation frequently ventured beyond company affairs, I still was surprised that she would want to see me on the eve of Tom's memorial service. I doubted that I would be among the first people she'd turn to at a time of personal grief.

Seconds after a waitress delivered my glass of wine, I saw Sara framed in the doorway across the room and raised my arm in greeting. A tall woman, she had the slight slouch of someone who was both self-conscious of her height and reluctant to attract notice. But she was striking, and not a few people turned to watch as she made her way through the maze of tables to where I was sitting. She had her mother's fine-boned features and her father's piercing dark eyes and luxuriant black hair, and the unusual combination worked.

I rose from the table and gave her a hug. As she settled into the chair across from me, I noticed with concern how thin she'd become and how tired she looked despite the warmth of her smile. She had dark circles under her eyes, and the charcoal-gray of her sweater emphasized her pallor.

I repeated the condolences I'd offered when we'd spoken by phone, and we made small talk about the details of the next day's memorial service until after we'd ordered. As soon as the waitress departed, we settled down to business.

"I'm glad that you could make it tonight," Sara began, fidgeting with her place setting in an uncharacteristic display of nerves.

"Of course," I reassured her. "I know that Tom's death must be hard for you."

"It is," she admitted. "My grandparents are wonderful, and I'm so lucky to have them, but Tom was like a second father to me. And it was quite a shock, too. After he had his first heart attack a couple of years ago, he went on a total health kick. He'd been exercising and eating right and everything. He told me how pleased the doctor was with his blood pressure and cholesterol. And he'd lost a tone of weight."

"He looked terrific the last time I saw him." I'd almost been inspired to go on a health kick, too, but a good dose of Diet Coke and chocolate had quickly banished that thought.

She paused, and I could tell she was choosing her next words carefully. "I need your advice."

"Whatever I can do," I told her.

"I had breakfast with Tom last Thursday morning, the day before he died. He was worried—very worried—about something at the company."

"I was scheduled to speak to him on Friday afternoon, but I didn't know what it was about. He made the appointment with my secretary."

My dealings with Grenthaler Media had been fairly limited of late. I'd assisted with the sale of a set of trade magazines the previous year, but it hadn't been a particularly complex transaction, and I'd shepherded it to closing with no major problems. I'd appreciated that Tom had trusted Nancy Sloan and her faith in my ability to handle the deal without more senior supervision from Winslow, Brown. Many of our clients felt that they deserved to see a little more gray hair on the bankers who would be collecting hefty fees from the transactions they handled.

"I know. He thought you might be able to help."

"Help with what?"

"Tom thought that someone might be buying up our stock in the market. He'd noticed the price had been up a bit—even though there had been no recent announcements that would explain any movement."

I thought for a moment before responding. "I noticed the price increase. But the market as a whole has been pretty volatile. And even if Grenthaler hasn't made any announcements, announcements by competitors or suppliers or a whole host of other factors could account for the uptick." When a company announced shifts in strategy or operations, it could alter the public's expectation for future performance, thus causing swings in the stock price. Moves by a competitor or a supplier could affect the price as well.

"I told Tom that it probably didn't mean anything. But he was also concerned about the volume of trading. He thought it was unusually high."

"Given that less than half of Grenthaler's stock trades publicly, even a small bit of trading looks like a major increase in the number of shares changing hands," I replied.

Sara controlled thirty-one percent and Tom Barnett controlled twenty percent of Grenthaler's four million shares outstanding. Only the remaining forty-nine percent—about two million shares—traded publicly. Each share was worth approximately $250, which valued the company as a whole at one billion dollars. The relatively small number of publicly traded shares meant that only an incremental few thousand shares had to change hands to create a spike in the usual trading volume.

Sara nodded in agreement. "I know that it's hard to draw conclusions from the trading volume, but Tom was still concerned."

Now my curiosity was officially piqued. "That somebody might launch a takeover?"

"No, it wasn't that. I mean, nobody could gain control of the company without buying shares from either me or Tom. He was just worried about someone else becoming a significant power in the company—even with a minority stake somebody can still start changing the composition of the board and influencing company strategy."

"That would have to be a pretty significant minority stake," I pointed out. "The investor would need to have at least twenty or twenty-five percent of the company to exert that sort of influence, and he would have to make a public disclosure to the Securities and Exchange Commission regarding his intentions once he reached five percent. Nobody's reached that threshold." But even as I was saying this, I began to wonder if Tom had been right to be concerned.

"That's true. But it still makes me nervous. Especially now that Tom is dead."

I had the feeling I knew where she was heading. "Would Barbara sell Tom's shares?" Barbara was Tom Barnett's widow.

"I don't think so, but I'm not sure. When they read Tom's will on Monday, she seemed surprised that he had only left her half his shares and that the other half reverted back to me. I thought she already knew that was the arrangement Tom made with my father years ago, before the company went public. But she's always wanted Adam to be more involved in the business, and maybe she was hoping that if she had more control she could make that happen." Tom had adopted Adam, Barbara's son from her first marriage, when he married Barbara.

"What do you think?"

"I think that Tom didn't want Adam to work at Grenthaler. He and my father agreed that I would take it over one day, and he didn't think Adam would be a good fit there, anyhow. He's much better off where he is." Adam had worked for an investment company in Boston but had recently opened his own firm. I would bet that he was a superlative number cruncher, but I doubted he had the strategic vision or management skills to lead Grenthaler Media.

"What does Adam want?"

"Who knows what Adam wants? He's so weird. At least he's given up on trying to date me."

I had to laugh. "Adam tried to date you?" Tom had invited me to dinner at his house while I was in town working on Grenthaler business, so I'd met Adam on a couple of occasions. He'd struck me then as a quintessential dork, the sort of guy who was more likely to spend his free time playing Dungeons & Dragons than man-about-town. He and Sara would have made a highly improbable couple.

"I know, it's ridiculous. But he finally got the message. I wouldn't be surprised if Barbara put him up to it—she has a blind spot where Adam's concerned. She thinks he's a genius." I'd met Barbara, too, at those dinners, as well as at Grenthaler board meetings, and she was a piece of work, to put it mildly. Her most distinguishing feature, in my eyes at least, was that she'd been Miss Texas in the early seventies, and a close runner-up for the Miss America title. Thirty years later, she still had the perky blond looks and theatrical presence of a pageant contestant, although her aesthetic sense seemed to have stopped evolving at some point in the late eighties. Her marriage to Tom had always been a bit of a mystery to me—she seemed too ditzy for him, and he too staid for her—but she seemed to adore him, and by all appearances he'd been a good husband to her and a good father to her son.

"Does Barbara need to sell her shares? Does she need cash?"

Sara shook her head. "I can't imagine that she would need anything. The dividends from ten percent of the company should provide a sizable income. She has more money than she could ever begin to spend."

"Have you spoken to her about it?"

"No. Monday didn't seem like the right time, and things have probably been so hectic for her, planning the memorial service and everything." She hesitated again. "I was actually hoping that you might talk to her for me, to see what her intentions are."

"What if she wants to sell?"

"Then I want to buy," Sara replied without missing a beat. "My father trusted me with this company. It's all I have left of him, and I refuse to let it go out of my control. In fact, even if Barbara doesn't plan to sell, I want to figure out how to acquire another ten percent so that I will be the majority shareholder."

"You would have to raise one hundred million dollars to do that," I reminded her.

"I know. I thought you could help me figure it out. I have a trust fund from my parents, but it's nowhere near big enough to help much."

"Let me talk to Barbara. Maybe the two of you can work something out that would allow you eventually to own her shares without us having to find the cash up-front." I wanted to talk to Barbara about as much as I wanted to go out with my grandmother's dentist's handsome associate, but Sara was a friend as well as a client.

"Thank you, Rachel. Maybe I'm overreacting—I hope I'm overreacting—but I can't relax if I know that the company might get away from me somehow. I can't let that happen." Her gaze locked on mine.

"I won't let that happen," I promised her.

★ ★ ★

Exchanges like that sometimes made you forget that Sara was only twenty-five years old. She spoke with the focused confidence of the CEO she would one day become. However, once we had finished discussing business it was almost as if she switched that side of herself off. She was still far more self-possessed than most people her age, but as we talked about her classes and her friends her voice took on the casual cadences of her peers.

She described the tension that was gripping the campus now that Hell Week had descended upon it.

"Is there anyone I should look out for who's interviewing with Winslow, Brown?" I asked Sara after I'd convinced her to order dessert.

"I'm glad you asked—I'd almost forgotten. One of my suite-mates, Gabrielle LeFavre, is trying to get a job in investment banking. I think she had her first round of interviews with Winslow, Brown today. She's been talking to all of the usual suspects—Goldman, Morgan Stanley, Merrill. She has her heart set on this."

"What's her background? Does she have any finance experience?"

"No, not really. She was an accountant before business school. She'd put herself through college at a state school down South, and then she went to New York and tried to get a job in banking, but you know how it is—the big firms only recruit people out of college from Harvard, Princeton and Yale for the most part—nobody even gave her a chance."

"That must have been tough. So she went into accounting?"

"Yes. She had earned her CPA at night when she was in college. Anyhow, she's a bit of a stress case, but she's really ambitious, and I think she'd work like a fiend if she were hired."

"I'll keep an eye out for her." I made a mental note to myself, but from what Sara had said, her friend sounded like the sort of high-strung perfectionist who would fall to pieces the first time a partner yelled at her.

I turned the conversation to a lighter topic. "Now, what else is going on with you? How's your love life? Besides Adam, of course," I added with a smile.

"Nice."

"Sorry. Couldn't resist. But seriously, anything of interest?"

"Hardly," she responded with a grimace.

"That good?"

"I was sort of seeing this guy before the holidays, but it didn't go anywhere. I mean, he's sharp and good-looking and everything, but we just didn't click. It's awkward, because he seemed to be really into it. We'd only been out on three or four dates and he was practically ready to propose. It was bizarre—we barely knew each other." She looked up at me. "Actually, I think you might know him. He was an analyst at Winslow, Brown before business school."

"Who?" I asked, not anticipating what the answer would be.

"Grant Crocker. Do you remember him?"

My heart sank as I tried to keep my expression even. I remembered Grant all too well, having had the misfortune of working with him several times during his two years at the firm, likely due to yet another of Stan's none-too-subtle plots to torment me. Grant was unusually cocky in an industry where arrogance was nearly a prerequisite. He'd spent several years in the Marine Corps after college, so he was closer to my age than Sara's, and the military seemed to have trained him well in various forms of chauvinism. He had difficulty following directions from a woman, and he more than once almost derailed a deal due to his reluctance to do the grunt work that fell to the most junior person on a team. Several of the secretaries had complained about his condescension and suggestive statements that came just short of overt passes.

Most of the men in the department would have described him as a "great guy" and a "real go-getter," and he was the star of the department basketball team, but the women in the department had their own nickname for him—Too Much Testosterone Guy—which was quite an achievement in our testosterone-rich environment.

Sara was waiting for my reply. "I remember him slightly," I hedged. "I didn't really know him very well."

"To complicate matters more, Gabrielle has a massive crush on him. As far as I'm concerned, she's welcome to him, but he won't give her the time of day. And she seems to be taking her frustration out on me. She's barely said two words to me since we got back from winter break."

"That must make for fun times back at the dorm," I said sympathetically.

Sara shrugged in response.

"How's your other roommate—Edie, right?"

"Edie Michaels. She's from L.A., and she wants to go back there and work in entertainment after graduation, so she's not all caught up in the Hell Week hysteria, like Gabrielle. It's nice to have at least one sane voice in the suite. Anyhow, enough about me. What's going on with you? How's Peter?"

"Peter's wonderful." I couldn't keep the grin off my face. "Absolutely wonderful. In fact, he's meeting me here tonight. He has a conference to go to this week in Boston."

"How convenient," Sara said dryly but with a smile. "I hope I get to meet him."

"I hope so, too." It was getting late so I signaled for the check and handed my credit card to the waitress. "Are you still rowing?" I asked. Sara was passionate about the sport, and she worked out regularly on the Charles River in her single-person scull.

"Every morning, before class. Fortunately the river hasn't frozen over yet. Usually it has by this time of year."

"It must be really cold. And dark." The entire proposition sounded unpleasant to me. Exercise was bad enough at a gym, with music and television and the option to skip the treadmill and go straight for a post-workout massage.

"It feels good. I think I'm addicted."

"Better you than me."

"You should try it. You might like it."

"I might like beating myself over the head with a blunt object, too, but I don't think I'll try that, either."

She laughed. "Well, if you put it like that…"

I signed the bill, and we retrieved our coats and walked out into the cold night. I accompanied Sara along JFK Street toward the bridge that led across the Charles to the business school campus. A bitter wind was blowing off the river. When we reached Eliot Street, where I would turn to go to the hotel, I gave her another hug. "Try not to worry," I said. "I'll look into what's happening with the stock. And I'll talk to Barbara."

"Thank you, Rachel. I really appreciate it."

"No problem. Sleep well."

I watched for a moment as she walked quickly toward the bridge, a lonely dark figure wrapped in a long wool coat.

Three

The hotel lobby looked like an advertisement for Brooks Brothers, thronged with men in dark suits and silk ties, their hair cut conservatively short and accessorized with briefcases and cell phones. Here and there I spotted a token woman or minority in the forest of navy. I'd been so distracted by my conversation with Sara that I'd forgotten to steel myself for the jungle that was the Charles Hotel during Hell Week. It was the preferred venue for recruiting, and most people stayed at night in the rooms that they would use for interviews during the day. Hence the Yuppie invasion.

I retrieved my bag and briefcase from the bell desk and threaded my way through the crowd toward reception, catching snippets of people's conversations as I passed. A group of large men with loud ties was debating in even louder voices about which bar to start their evening. I guessed that they were probably traders, generally acknowledged as the most uncouth employees of investment banks and treated by those in corporate finance as a necessary evil, even during years when they contributed the bulk of their firms' profits. Traders were the ones who spent most of their time yelling "buy" and "sell" into the phone with cigars clamped between their teeth. At the Winslow, Brown Christmas party in December a fight had broken out between a renegade group of traders from the Latin American arbitrage desk and their counterparts in corporate finance. Security had arrived before any real damage was done, but my money had been on the traders, hands down.

A Calvin Klein-clad woman was questioning someone intently over her cell phone as she made her way to the elevator. "Did you double-check all the numbers?" she asked anxiously, smoothing the knot in her Hermès scarf. "I want you to check them again, and then rerun the model using the higher discount rates. Fax me here when you're done." Somewhere a novice banker had just been sentenced to a sleepless night.

I checked in, collecting a pile of faxes and a packet from Winslow, Brown's recruiting administrator that was waiting for me. The man at reception gave me an apologetic look. "We're booked so full that all we have left is a suite. I hope you won't mind."

I assured him I wouldn't, trying to hide my jubilant smile. Four nights in an expense-account hotel room with Peter was enough of a treat; four nights in a suite was more than I could have dreamed of. Sharing a hotel room with a boyfriend always made me think of *Love in the Afternoon,* one of my favorite movies (aside from bad teen flicks from the eighties). Audrey Hepburn, Gary Cooper, Maurice Chevalier, champagne and gypsies playing "Fascination." Nothing could be more romantic. Of course, with my red hair, I was no Audrey Hepburn, and Peter was a couple of decades younger than Gary Cooper, and we would both be swamped with work during all of our afternoons here, and it would probably be hard to find a band of gypsy violinists for hire in Cambridge, but knowing all this did little to dim my anticipation. I found myself unconsciously humming "Fascination" under my breath as I headed for the elevator.

On the way, I ran into two separate acquaintances from business school who were also here to recruit fresh blood for their respective firms. I paused to exchange news and gossip and took some good-natured teasing about the *Fortune* cover. It was nearly ten by the time I'd shut the door of the suite behind me, happily taking in the cozy living room and nice big bed, all furnished with the Shaker furniture and blue-and-white fabrics that were the Charles's trademark décor. I made quick work of kicking off my shoes and hanging up the clothes in my suitcase. There was no message from Peter, but he was probably still in transit. If all went according to schedule, he'd arrive by eleven. I ran a bath and poured a glass of wine from the well-stocked minibar before undressing and lowering myself into the steaming water, taking care not to splash the faxes I'd brought with me to review.

One of them was from Jessica, my assistant, who had kindly transcribed the voice mails that had piled up for me that afternoon and noted which calls she had already responded to on my behalf.

I scanned the list. Jessica had grouped the calls by subject matter and urgency. Fortunately, nothing seemed to demand immediate attention. Her last notation made me laugh.

No messages from the Caped Avenger. He's been strangely quiet. Can we hope that he's transferred his affections elsewhere?

As if. The Caped Avenger's real name was Whitaker Jamieson, and there was nothing I'd like better than to see him transfer his affections, but I held out little hope. I sighed and took a healthy sip from my wineglass. Whitaker was the bane of my existence. Or, at least, one among many. He was an old chum of Stan Winslow (Stan seemed to know a lot of people with last names for first names) and was known in the business as a "high net-worth individual." This was a polite way of saying that he was loaded. Generations of inbreeding among extremely wealthy families had culminated in the production of Whitaker more than seventy years ago. He had a personal fortune of several hundred million, much of which was invested with Winslow, Brown's asset-management group.

Rather than sitting back and collecting his dividend checks, however, Whitaker fancied himself a mogul-in-the-making. All too frequently he would have a "fabulous idea" for a business he should acquire. He would swoop into my office, wearing his trademark cape over a natty custom-made pin-striped suit, and park himself in my guest chair for hours at a time. His breath reeking of gin, he would regale me with the details of his latest scheme, which he invariably described as a "fabulous idea. We simply must do it. It will be too fabulous." When I was out of the office, he would pepper Jessica with calls, nagging her relentlessly about my whereabouts. She had developed a fierce antagonism toward Whitaker.

Of course, none of Whitaker's "fabulous ideas" actually came to fruition. In the past year alone, I had analyzed the profitability and prospects of a fire-hydrant distributor, a failing women's apparel chain and a producer of diet olive oil. An acquisition of any of these businesses would have been disastrous, and I managed to gently curb Whitaker's enthusiasm.

I had no doubt that Stan had first steered Whitaker in my direction to torment me. I wished I could say that I had since developed any esteem for the Caped Avenger, as Jessica and

I referred to him, but unfortunately I still found him just as pompous and tedious as the day I met him. I also had a secret hunch that he wasn't that serious about any of his proposed acquisitions but had another agenda altogether. While Whitaker's wardrobe and mannerisms screamed gay, he'd proved himself to be not only straight but lecherous to boot. When he wasn't invading my office, he tended to favor small dark restaurants for our "meetings" and would encourage me to sit next to him on the banquette, rather than across the table, downing martinis while plying me with wine. I was always sure to order two cars to take us each home separately after these meetings so that there would be no question of any after-dinner activities. I would have loved to be rid of him altogether, but he was far too important to the asset-management group and relatively harmless when handled correctly.

Silence from the Caped Avenger should probably have made me nervous—who knew what he could get up to on his own? But I was glad of the respite, even though I was confident it would be only temporary. I tossed the faxes onto the bath mat next to the tub and turned to the packet the recruiting administrator had left for me.

A team of ten associates had already been at the Charles for three full days conducting the first round of interviews, and my packet included the results, as well as a schedule for the second round of interviews that more senior bankers like Scott and I would conduct over the next two days.

I checked the lists to see what had happened to Sara's suitemate, Gabrielle LeFavre. Sure enough, she'd had her interviews that morning—two back-to-back forty-five-minute sessions. Judging by the evaluation forms the interviewers filled out, Gabrielle had not fared too well in the process.

"Seemed extremely nervous and on edge," one interviewer had written. "I was worried she might start crying," another had added. Apparently she had frozen during her first interview when she had flubbed a fairly basic question about an item on her résumé. Things had gone downhill from there. Unfortunately, the comments were too consistent from both interviews for me to resurrect her for another chance.

I placed the recruiting packet on top of the faxes, ran some more hot water into the tub, and gave thanks that I was long done with business school and all of its associated stress. I'd loved college at Harvard, and after I'd completed two years as an analyst at Winslow, Brown, Harvard Business School had been the logical next step. I was lucky—I knew I'd return to Winslow, Brown after graduation, so I never had to go through Hell Week. But it had been hard not to get caught up in the competitive warfare that was a constant undercurrent of daily life on campus and erupted to the surface during recruiting season.

Harvard College prided itself on attracting a well-rounded class rather than well-rounded students. Thus, most of the undergraduate student body was extreme in some way. The person sitting next to you in class or at the adjoining table in the dining hall was likely to be the junior world chess champion, or a budding novelist, or a future Nobel Prize winning physicist. Harvard Business School prided itself on its diversity, as well. My class had boasted students from more than thirty countries ranging in age from their early twenties to a woman in her late forties. Demographics aside, however, the place was relatively homogenous, which made sense since everyone there wanted to pursue a career in business. And to pursue it aggressively. My college roommates had always teased me about my Type A personality, but at business school I'd felt practically passive in comparison to the other students.

The water was cooling again, and my fingertips had begun to resemble raisins, so I pulled myself out of the bath and dried off, wrapping myself in a plush terry robe. I padded into the living room with my soggy papers and dialed into voice mail to leave instructions for Jessica. With a thrill I checked the bedside clock—nearly eleven, and Peter would be here any minute.

It had been just a few days since I'd seen him last, when he'd put me on the plane after our New Year's ski trip in Utah, but it felt like an eternity. It was hard to believe that I had only known him since August. Our meeting had been less than auspicious, taking place during a disastrous wedding weekend. Peter was supposed to be the best man. But Richard, who was to marry my old roommate, Emma, ended up dead before the ceremony could take place. By the end of the weekend, I'd managed to fall in love with Peter, decide he was a murderer, turn him into the police, realize I was completely wrong about him being a murderer, and force a confession from the actual killer, who'd tried to kill me twice.

The entire series of events hadn't cast me in my most attractive light, but Peter hadn't seemed to mind. The past five months had been nearly perfect, marred only by the difficulties inherent in a long-distance relationship.

I heard a knock at the door, and I rushed to throw it open. There he was, in the flesh.

He enveloped me in a long hug accompanied by a delicious kiss. "Mmm. You smell good."

"I just took a bath. You smell good, too."

"You smell better." He kissed me again.

"No, you smell better."

"No, you do." Another kiss.

"You do."

"Let's not fight about it. We both smell really good."

"Agreed." And yet another kiss.

"Can I come in?" We were still standing in the doorway.

I laughed. "Absolutely." I waited impatiently while he put

down his bags and tossed his coat over the back of a chair.
He looked so cute in his standard Silicon Valley wear—
khakis and a navy sweater, his sandy hair slightly mussed from
the long flight. I hurried to pour him a glass of wine from
the half bottle I'd opened. He took it from me, set it on the
coffee table and pulled me down on the sofa next to him.

"Good trip?" I asked.

"Fine," he said, running his hands through my hair. If I
were a cat, I would be purring.

"Four nights," I said.

"Four nights," he replied with a grin. "And a suite. How
did you pull that off?"

"I have my ways."

"You definitely do," he said, moving in for another kiss.
And then his cell phone rang. "Crap. I should take this." He
jumped to his feet and dug the phone out of his coat pocket.
"Peter Forrest."

He was silent for a moment, listening. "That's great, Abigail. Thanks for letting me know…yes…no…sure…I agree."
He began pacing as he talked.

I stood and crossed to the window. The room had a view
across the small park to the river, which was still and dark in
the moonlight. A vague feeling of unease settled over me as
I listened to Peter's one-sided conversation. Peter had hired
Abigail to be his head of business development a few months
ago, and even though I was more secure in this relationship
than any I'd ever been in before, it was hard not to feel a tiny
bit threatened by the knowledge that my boyfriend spent
most of his waking hours with a woman who was brilliant,
accomplished and bore more than a passing resemblance to
Christy Turlington.

Peter finished his call after a few minutes and came to stand
behind me, wrapping his arms around my waist and resting
his chin on the top of my head.

"What's going on?" I asked, leaning back into his embrace. "Is everything all right?"

"Um, yeah. It's just that we're, uh, trying to sign up a new client. They'll be at the conference."

"That's good, right?"

"Yes. The only problem is that there are a couple of other companies trying to beat us out, and they'll be at the conference, too. Abigail and I have been working pretty hard on our pitch—it's going to be a hectic few days."

"How's Abigail?" I asked, striving for a casual tone.

"She's great. A real firecracker. Hiring her was one of the best decisions I've made in a long time. She's been instrumental in going after this new business."

"I'm glad," I said, trying to sound like I was. But I would have been a lot more glad if I didn't know what Abigail looked like. Or if she'd been a man. Or gay. Or, at the very least, only brilliant and not beautiful.

"Anyhow, enough work talk. I brought you something."

"A present?" I spun around to face him, thoughts of Peter's brilliant, beautiful, model-material colleague nearly forgotten. "Where? What is it?" I loved gifts. Especially surprise gifts.

"Don't get too excited. Just a little something from the airport." He unzipped his suitcase and began rummaging through it, extracting a paper bag. He handed it to me.

I shook it. "Hmm. It doesn't rattle."

"Good. It's not supposed to."

I opened the bag and withdrew an oversize bar of Ghirardelli chocolate. "Yum." Peter had known me long enough to recognize that I considered chocolate to be one of the four major food groups, along with caffeine and alcohol. I always forgot what the fourth one was. "Should we eat it now or later?"

"I'm thinking later," he said, a gleam in his eye. He had

hold of the dangling end of my bathrobe's belt and was pulling me toward the bedroom.

It occurred to me that perhaps I should be annoyed that Peter's gift hadn't shown much forethought, but instead had been picked up at the newsstand on his way to catch the plane. But he quickly put any such peevish thoughts right out of my head.

Four

I was sleeping like the proverbial baby, sweetly tangled in Peter's arms, when he gently untangled himself and got out of bed.

"Where are you going?" I asked, still half asleep.

"Shh. I didn't mean to wake you."

"Then come back."

"I can't. I have to meet Abigail before the conference starts. We need to go over the pitch we're making one more time."

"But it's dark out." There was only the faintest glimmer of murky light coming through the windows.

"It's nearly seven. I'm supposed to meet her at the convention center at eight."

"She won't mind if you're late."

"Yes, she will. And I will, too, if we don't get this client signed up. The company we're pitching is hot."

"But how can you even be effective if you're sleepy?"

"I can't be sleepy when I'm this stressed."

"You're stressed?" Peter? My calm, unflappable, good-smelling Peter was stressed?

"A little. Nothing to worry about." He leaned down and kissed my forehead.

"I know an excellent way to relieve stress," I offered, holding out my arms.

"I'm sure you do." But he was already out of reach. "I'm just going to jump into the shower."

I leaned back against the pillows. "Don't hurt yourself."

"Funny."

"You can't expect great wit in the middle of the night."

"It's not the middle of the night," he protested, then thought better of trying to argue with me before I'd had any caffeine. "Never mind. Go back to sleep." I heard the bathroom door shut behind him and the sound of the shower running.

I rolled over, trying to recover the nice dream-state I'd been in, but it was no use. I was awake, and there was no going back. I sat up and swung my legs over the side of the bed, bending down to pick up the bathrobe I'd discarded the night before. I wrapped it around me, tying the belt tightly around my waist, and ran my hands through my hair to restore some semblance of order. Perhaps I should call room service for breakfast, I thought. At least I could make sure Peter was well fortified for his stressful day.

Then I had a better idea.

I knocked on the bathroom door but received no answer, so I pushed it open. Peter was in the shower, whistling an unrecognizable tune. I let my robe slip to the floor, pulled the shower curtain aside and stepped in behind him.

Between the running water and his whistling, Peter hadn't heard me come in. When I reached around him he gave a shout of surprise.

"Jesus Christ! Are you trying to give me a coronary?"

His hair was lathered with shampoo, standing up in a sudsy Mohawk.

"That would be counterproductive," I said. "Your hair looks cute like that. May I have the soap?"

He laughed. "Allow me."

The shower took longer than Peter had expected, so he was racing around the room, frantically getting dressed, when his cell phone rang. "Peter Forrest," he answered, holding the phone with one hand while he awkwardly tried to buckle his belt with the other. "Oh, hi, Abigail." He listened for a moment. "You're kidding." He listened some more. "I knew they'd be all over this. Listen, I'm out the door right now. I'll be there in twenty minutes. See you soon."

"Problem?" I asked.

"Hamilton Tech trying to outmaneuver us. Nothing we can't handle. Abigail just saw Smitty Hamilton having break- fast with the head of the company we're trying to—I mean, that we're pitching."

"Don't worry. I'm sure they'd much rather hire you than anyone named Smitty."

"I hope so." Peter pulled a dark green V-necked sweater over his head.

I reached up to smooth his damp hair, and he gave me a quick peck on the lips. "I've got to get going." He picked up his overcoat and briefcase. "I'll see you later?" he asked.

"Definitely," I said, wrapping my arms around him for a hug.

He returned the hug but let go way too soon. "I need more affection," I said. "That was completely insufficient to sustain me for a whole day." He sighed and hugged me again, tightly, but I kept holding on after he let go.

"Rachel," he said, trying to extricate himself. "Really. I'm not that great."

I laughed and relinquished my grasp. "Go get 'em, Sparky."

So much for a romantic hotel-room morning and leisurely breakfast.

I dried my hair and put on the black suit I'd packed for Tom Barnett's memorial service. I wasn't due at my recruiting meeting until half past eight, so I took a Diet Coke from the minibar and called into voice mail to clear out any messages that had accumulated.

It had been only nine hours since I had last dialed in— hours when normal people were asleep—but I already had five new messages. Four were from colleagues in our Asian offices. The last message made my heart sink. It was time-stamped 2:00 a.m., never a good sign. It was from Gabrielle LeFavre.

"Ms. Benjamin," she began, her voice betraying her Southern roots. "This is Gabrielle LeFavre, a student at Harvard Business School. Sara Grenthaler may have mentioned my name to you. I had my first round of interviews with Winslow, Brown, and I'm concerned that I was not able to convey the full extent of my capabilities, or my commitment to a career in investment banking. I know that it's very unusual to reconsider the results of an interview, but I strongly believe that if you would allow me to try again, I could convince you that I would be a valuable asset to your firm." She left her contact information.

I hung up the phone, annoyed. Between the time Gabrielle had left her message and the precision with which she'd spoken, it sounded as if she'd spent hours carefully scripting what she'd say. Turning people down was one of the things I disliked most about recruiting. There were always a couple of candidates who wouldn't take no for an answer and would besiege the recruiting team with phone calls, letters and, in a few instances, gifts. Dealing with these cases was always uncomfortable, and the fact that Gabrielle lived with Sara made the situation even more so. I would have to talk to this woman sooner or later, and I was not looking forward to it.

I took another Diet Coke from the minibar. Something told me that I would need even more than the recommended daily allowance of caffeine to get me through the day, what with a memorial service and the inevitable unpleasantness of my recruiting duties to look forward to. I popped open the can and crossed to the window to check out the weather, wishing it was evening already and time to meet Peter for dinner.

The morning light showed the view off in a way that I hadn't been able to appreciate the previous night. The sky was gray, in keeping with the forecasts, which called for lots of snow. Still, the air was clear, and across the river I could see the familiar red bricks of the business school campus to the south and Soldiers Field Stadium to the west, nestled in the slush-spotted green of the athletic fields. In the foreground, a traffic jam was taking place on Memorial Drive. Its source appeared to be a flock of police cars parked at the junction of the drive and JFK Street, at the foot of the bridge.

I pressed my nose against the glass for a closer look.

There was a crowd surrounding the Weld Boathouse, home to several of Harvard's crew teams. A bright stripe of yellow crime-scene tape held back onlookers, while uniformed policemen clustered in front of the building.

I wondered what could have happened. Some sort of crew team prank, perhaps, gone awry? One never knew what sort of hijinks rowers could get up to. I'd had the misfortune to date a rower my freshman year, and I'd never been so bored in my entire life. Our relationship consisted of lots of long, tortured conversations about his rowing, usually conducted over dining-hall meals with his teammates. I would watch in awe as they consumed enough food to feed small developing countries. I still vividly remembered my boyfriend commandeering an entire loaf of bread, loading it onto the toaster, slice by slice, then using up two sticks of butter, packet upon packet of sugar and a shaker-full of cinnamon to make cinnamon toast. He'd eaten it all in one sitting. And later that night he'd ordered in pizza. He was the only guy I'd ever gone out with who made my eating habits seem birdlike.

I pulled my attention from the view and my gluttonous ex-boyfriend and gathered my coat and purse. It was time to get going.

Winslow, Brown had set up its recruiting headquarters in a suite identical to my own but one floor down. I arrived a few minutes before the meeting was to start. Cecelia Esterhazy, the administrator from Human Resources, was already there, setting out name tags and schedules on a side table. While I was the titular head of the recruiting effort, most of the actual work fell to Cece, who had the unenviable job of liaising with the Career Services office, scheduling information sessions, reserving blocks of hotel rooms and cajoling unwilling bankers into showing up to interview eager students. Fortunately, she had an unflaggingly sunny disposition, and her fresh good looks ensured that most of my male colleagues were easily persuaded to do their part.

"Hi, Cece. How's it going?"

She gave me a look that managed to be both harried and good-natured at the same time. "The usual. Three interviewers have already canceled on me. But I overbooked, so everything should be okay." While recruiting was vital to Winslow, Brown's future, it didn't generate fees, and fees were the lifeblood of the firm. It wasn't uncommon for bankers to decide at the last minute that whatever deals they were working on took precedence over a commitment to participate in recruiting.

"I'm sorry. I'm not making things any easier for you by cutting out this morning."

"You, at least, have a valid excuse." I'd told her about the memorial service earlier that week, and she'd been sympathetic.

"You're doing great," I reassured her.

She rolled her eyes.

"Courage," I said. She rewarded me with a smile.

Colleagues from Winslow, Brown began trooping in, descending upon the breakfast buffet like vultures, most of them simultaneously talking on their own voice-enabled Blackberries. I helped myself to a bagel and cream cheese and another Diet Coke and found an empty chair. We needed to wait for a quorum to get things started, so I used the downtime to scroll through the accumulated e-mails on my own Blackberry before pecking out a quick message to Peter, wishing him luck with his pitch. Scott Epson was among the last to arrive. Today he was wearing a tie that put yesterday's to shame—green silk dotted with little red golf tees. If he had been anyone else, I would have suspected sartorial irony.

When the room had filled, I cleared my throat and called the meeting to order. "I'd like to thank you all for being here. I know how busy everyone is, but we have an ambitious hiring goal this year, and your participation is very much appreciated." I said a few more words by way of introduction, reminding everyone of the qualities Winslow, Brown deemed desirable in its prospective employees, and then turned the meeting over to Cecelia to explain how everything would work over the next two days.

I ate my bagel and listened while she smoothly ran through

the day's logistics. "We need everyone back here at five o'clock for the roundup session. Please don't be late—we'll try to finish up as quickly as we possibly can." With that, she began handing out name tags and schedules.

No sooner had she finished than the first students began trickling in for their interviews, neatly turned out in aspiring Wall Street wear. Cece efficiently matched them up with the pairs of bankers to which they'd been assigned and sent them off to the interview rooms. By ten past nine, she and I were the only ones left. I was relieved—Scott Epson hadn't seemed to notice that I wouldn't be interviewing that morning. If he had, I was sure he would waste no time in letting Stan know in some backhanded fashion that I was shirking my duties. My absence that morning could be easily explained, but I'd rather not have to explain it. The partners at Winslow, Brown had strange ideas regarding how one should prioritize one's various commitments. The memorial service for a client seemed to me to be an important event, but firm lore was sufficiently rife with stories of bankers being called back from hospital beds, bar mitzvahs, honeymoons and graveyards to make me hesitant to publicize the trade-off I was making.

I exchanged a few final words with Cece, thanking her and assuring her I'd be back by noon. Moments later I was in a cab bound for Trinity Church in Boston.

Five

The taxi turned from Eliot Street onto JFK Street, passing the police cars that still swarmed around the Weld Boathouse. We crossed the bridge over the river and made a left onto Storrow Drive.

"What happened back there?" I asked.

"Dunno," the driver said. "But whatever it is, it's sure screwing up traffic."

Unenlightened, I pulled out my phone and dialed Emma's mobile number. I'd talked to her the previous day, on my way to the airport in New York, but she was my best friend, and we usually talked daily, at least.

It took several rings before Emma picked up, and when she did, she sounded distracted. "Hello?"

"It's me."

"Oh, hi, Rach. I'm glad you called. Did you get into town all right?"

"Yes. I'm in a cab on Storrow Drive right now, heading into Boston. Are you at Matthew's?"

"Yes. He just left for the clinic, and I was about to start on some sketches for a series I've been thinking about." Now I understood the distracted tone. When Emma was starting a new series, her existence bifurcated into two worlds, one filled with ideas and shapes and color, and the other filled with reality. Needless to say, the former usually eclipsed the latter. Emma was a gifted artist, the daughter of a world-famous painter. After a difficult summer, during which she'd narrowly escaped an unfortunate marriage via a set of even more unfortunate circumstances, she seemed to be back on an even keel, happily dating Matthew and climbing to new heights of artistic success.

"Anything interesting?"

"Maybe. It's too soon to tell." I could almost feel the effort it took for her to pull her thoughts away from her work and back to our conversation. "But did you say you were going into Boston? I thought you were supposed to be at Harvard, interviewing. What's in Boston?"

"A memorial service. A client of mine passed away last week."

"It seems like a lot of people are dying lately," she mused.

"Like who?"

"Actually, not a lot, I guess. It's just that a patient of Matthew's was found murdered yesterday, in Cambridge. And then hearing about your client. It just feels like a lot."

"What happened to Matthew's patient?" I asked.

"I don't know, but the police want to talk to him today. She had an appointment at the clinic a couple of days ago. It probably hasn't made the New York papers, but there have been six or seven prostitutes murdered in the Boston area over the last year—the police think Matthew's patient might be the most recent victim." Matthew worked at a free clinic in a particularly seedy neighborhood in South Boston, so it didn't surprise me that a prostitute was among his clientele.

"Matthew's being interrogated by the police?" I commented, amused. Matthew was a skilled doctor and one of the kindest people I knew, but he bore more than a passing resemblance to Shaggy from *Scooby Doo,* and the mental image of him confronting hardened police detectives was an entertaining one, although he'd managed it with aplomb the previous summer.

"Yes, I know. His second time in six months. He must be getting good at it by now." Emma laughed at the thought. "On to happier topics, did you have a nice time with Peter last night?"

I thought about last night. And the morning's shower. "I always have a nice time with Peter."

"You sound like you're blushing. Is he still too good to be true?"

"Absolutely," I sighed blissfully.

"Well, I'm glad to hear you say it. Usually you're so worried about jinxing everything that you refuse to admit you're actually happy."

"You don't want to mess with the Jinxing Gods." To tell Emma I was rid of them was a bolder statement than seemed safe. It was one thing to have vanquished them in my mind— it was a wholly different thing to say so aloud.

"There is no such thing."

"Okay, now you're just tempting fate."

"I don't know if I believe in fate, either."

"I'm going to pretend you didn't say that. Next thing I know you'll be looking for ladders to walk under." The cab turned off Storrow at the exit for Back Bay. "I should let you get back to work," I told Emma. "And I'm nearly at the church. But we'll see you guys tomorrow night, at the kick-off dinner, right?"

"Sure. I'm getting there early to help Jane cook."

"I wasn't invited for that part."

Emma laughed again. "Gee. I wonder why not."

The taxi deposited me in front of the weathered stone and brick of Trinity Church a few minutes before ten. I joined the slow-moving queue to sign the guest book and then found a seat in one of the ornately carved pews halfway down the nave. The church was packed, which was fitting given Tom's prominent role in the community. I could barely make out the tops of Barbara's and Adam Barnett's heads in the first pew.

The service began, and I alternately stood, sang and sat as directed. The formal rituals that accompanied death always left me numb, and I had a bad habit of automatically tuning out during any sort of lecture. My eyes wandered, taking in the crowd. I recognized both the mayor of Boston and the governor of Massachusetts, along with one of the state's U.S. senators. Several other faces were familiar to me from Grenthaler board meetings. I looked for Sara, wondering how she was holding up, but I didn't see her, which wasn't surprising given the masses of people in the church.

As the minister rambled on, I thought again about Tom and Barbara and their unlikely union. They really could not have been more different—even if you accepted that opposites did, in fact, attract. Tom was descended from a long line of erudite and genteel New Englanders. He had joined the staff of Grenthaler Media as a graduate student in international affairs, intending to work part-time as he pursued his doctorate. Soon he had dropped his classes and joined the company full-time, becoming Samuel Grenthaler's partner and a significant force in the growing enterprise.

Nancy Sloan theorized that Tom had been slow to marry because he was secretly in love with Anna Porter, the wife of his best friend and partner. He was nearly forty-five when he met Barbara. By then, she'd left her pageant days and an unsuccessful first marriage behind and had moved to Boston with her young son to take a position as the host of a local daytime talk show. A statuesque blonde, perfectly coiffed with the signature big hair of her home state and always dressed in bright Escada or Chanel suits, she was a surprising success in a town that prided itself on its intellectual heritage. But she retired from show business shortly after marrying Tom to dedicate herself to home and family. Nowadays her skin had the tight shiny look that betrayed the attentions of a plastic surgeon, and she maintained her size four with a fierce devotion to exercise and diet, but she was still a stunning presence. Every time I saw her I felt dwarfed and frumpy by comparison and immediately noticed that my stockings had a run or that my nails were a mess. She was also an aggressive extrovert, invariably peppy and talkative and with a Texan drawl that coated her words like syrup.

Her son, Adam, was in his late twenties now, tall and lanky and completely lacking in his mother's charisma. Tom had formally adopted him soon after he and Barbara married, but there was something nervous about him, as if he never felt that he really belonged. He was a bit of a mama's boy, too, and he still lived at home, in a third-floor apartment that Tom and Barbara had fashioned into a bachelor pad. I doubted, however, that the pad was seeing much action. I was amazed that he'd actually gotten up the guts to try to romance Sara. It seemed obvious to me that she was way out of his league.

I spied Grant Crocker across the aisle and a few rows up, recognizing him from the rigid set of his broad shoulders and the military-short brown hair. Yet another man who didn't seem to realize that Sara was way out of his league. He turned and met my gaze, as if he'd felt my eyes on his back. He gave me a friendly but subdued nod before turning back around. I wondered, and not for the first time, how such a handsome boy-next-door face could belong to such a domineering jerk.

After a eulogy from an old friend of Tom's and a final benediction, the service drew to a close. The guests were invited to the Barnetts' house for a reception directly following the service. Tom's body had already been cremated, per his request. The congregation stood to let Barbara and other immediate family pass before we filed out.

Barbara's blond head was bowed, and she had linked her arm through Adam's, who guided her dutifully up the aisle. Several older couples followed, whom I imagined to be assorted relatives. Edward and Helene Porter, Sara's grandparents, were among the group, a stately white-haired pair I'd met at Grenthaler board meetings. Then the other rows began emptying out. I still didn't see Sara. I wondered if maybe she'd left through another door, wanting to avoid the crush outside.

I'd turned to walk up the aisle when Grant Crocker materialized at my side. "Rachel," he greeted me, his voice appropriately hushed to reflect our surroundings. "What brings you here?"

"Tom was my client," I explained, "and Sara Grenthaler and I worked together when she was a summer associate at Winslow, Brown. And I needed to be in town for recruiting, anyhow. How are you, Grant?"

"I'm fine. But this is a sad day." He put his hand on my elbow as we made our way up the aisle. He'd always been quick to go through the motions of chivalry—opening doors and offering to carry stacks of heavy client presentations—but from him they'd always rankled, knowing as I did that the flip side of his chivalry was chauvinism. And his sanctimonious tone made me wish somebody else was there to hear it, so that we could joke about it later. "I felt it was important to be here," he added. "For Sara. Since they were so close." He said Sara's name with a proprietary air, which I thought was odd given what she'd told me the previous night.

"Have you seen her anywhere?" I asked.

"No. In fact, I was just about to ask you the same thing."

"We probably missed her in this crowd," I replied as we emerged from the church into the crisp air. A few flakes of snow had started to fall, precursors of the major storm that was expected that weekend.

"Probably," he agreed. "Are you going to the reception?"

I made a quick decision. My presence among the several hundred who were likely to descend on the Barnett house would hardly be missed. Nor would it be an appropriate time to discuss Barbara's ten-percent stake in Grenthaler Media. "No, I've got to get back to the Charles. We're doing the second round of interviews today and tomorrow."

"I guess I'll see you at the Winslow, Brown thing tomorrow night, then." I'd almost forgotten that Winslow, Brown was hosting a cocktail party Friday for the candidates we were asking back to New York as well as previous analysts, like Grant, who had offers outstanding to return to the firm after graduation. I stifled a shudder at the thought of once again having to work with Grant on a daily basis.

"I guess so," I said, striving to be polite. There was nothing technically wrong with anything Grant had said or done in our brief exchange, but just being around him seemed to rub me the wrong way. I said goodbye, glad to extract my elbow from his grasp and be at least temporarily done with him, and walked down Boylston Street in search of a cab. I found one idling at the corner of Clarendon Street and got in, asking the driver to take me to Harvard Square.

I felt apprehensive, and I tried to figure out why. Clearly, a memorial service was not the most soothing event, nor was it comforting to think about Grant Crocker being back in my life full-time should he return to Winslow, Brown in the fall. But there was something else. I realized that I would have felt better if I'd known for sure that Sara had been at the church. It was strange that neither Grant nor I had seen her. And I couldn't imagine that she would have missed the service.

I busied myself on the trip back to Cambridge by calling my office to check in with Jessica. I also tried Peter, just to say hello, but his cell phone went straight into voice mail. I left a message then leaned back in my seat, staring out the window. The cab rounded a final curve, zooming past the business school campus to the left and the familiar red brick buildings and cupolas of the undergraduate campus across the river. We turned off Storrow Drive and made a right-hand turn onto the bridge and into an unmoving line of cars.

The driver braked abruptly, cursed at the traffic and added his horn to those that were already honking. After several minutes during which we traveled only a few feet, I paid him and got out. I'd get to the hotel faster by walking. The driver happily pocketed my money and made an illegal U-turn, tires squealing, to return to Boston.

I turned up the collar of my coat against the harsh wind and made my way across the bridge. At its foot, the yellow crime-scene tape remained with its accompanying flock of police cars. Those rowers must have been up to some serious hijinks.

Curious, I stopped to ask one of the uniformed policemen what had happened.

"A young woman was attacked this morning," he told me.

"Attacked?"

"Uh-huh. In the boathouse. Really early."

Suddenly, I knew why I hadn't seen Sara at the church. I felt the blood drain from my face.

Six

I rushed up JFK Street to Mount Auburn, hung a right and sprinted the remaining block to Holyoke Center, which housed University Health Services. The run on the uneven brick sidewalks was no easy feat, dressed as I was in a skirted suit and heels, and the mere act of passing through the building's entrance instantly brought back unpleasant memories of the times I'd gone there as an undergrad, nursing a bladder infection or something equally embarrassing, but these concerns were eclipsed by my concern for Sara.

Flu season was in full gear, and the clerk at reception was busy with other visitors, but I guessed that Sara would be in the Stillman Infirmary on the fifth floor, so I headed for the elevator bank, punching the call button impatiently. Nobody ever seemed to stop you when you gave off the air of knowing exactly where you were going.

The elevator arrived, and I jabbed at the button for the fifth floor, and then the button to close the doors. The elevator rose at a glacial pace, ticking off each floor with a beep. When the doors finally parted, I strode to the nurses' station. "I'm here to see Sara Grenthaler," I announced in my most authoritative tone. While UHS was probably less strict than a normal hospital, I worried that visitors would be restricted to family, of which Sara didn't have much.

"And you are?" asked the nurse behind the desk.

"I'm Rachel Benjamin. Sara's cousin." If you were going to lie, I knew that the only way to do it was simply and with confidence. And there was, after all, a small chance that we were distantly related—her father's family and my father's family could have lived in the same Russian shtetl, many generations back, being persecuted by the same Cossacks. It wasn't a complete lie.

My bluff seemed to work, or it may have been completely unnecessary, because the nurse consulted her computer terminal. "She's in five-oh-six, ma'am." I ignored being ma'amed—now was not the time to get hung up on concerns that I'd become prematurely matronly. Instead I hurried off in the direction she'd indicated, counting off the room numbers on either side. The door to Sara's room was ajar, and I gave it a gentle knock before going in.

She was lying in one of the two hospital beds, and she looked awful. Her head was wrapped in white gauze, and she was hooked up to a variety of tubes and monitors. Her eyes were shut, and her skin was nearly as white as the gauze that framed her face. I let out an involuntary gasp.

"It's okay. The doctor said she's going to be all right." I turned, startled, to the corner, where a young woman rose from a chair. "I'm Edie Michaels," she said, proffering her hand.

"The roommate," I answered, putting the name to the face.

"Well, one of them."

"I'm Rachel Benjamin. From Winslow, Brown."

"Oh, sure. You had dinner with Sara last night."

"Yes. So what happened?"

Edie sank back into the chair, running a hand through her mass of curly black hair. Her big dark eyes were worried in her olive-skinned face. "Well, you know how Sara rows every morning?"

I nodded, perching myself on the second, unoccupied bed. "We were just talking about it." The previous evening suddenly seemed very far away.

"Apparently, she did her workout, and she was putting her scull away when somebody hit her over the head with an oar. A homeless man saw the whole thing—he'd come in to use the bathroom in the boathouse."

"Did they catch the guy who did it?"

"No, he ran out when he realized he'd been seen. And the homeless guy was too busy checking that Sara was all right to follow him. He's the one who called the ambulance and the police. All he saw was somebody wearing a ski mask and a big coat with a hood—it was still pretty dark out, and he wasn't even sure if it was a man or woman."

"And what did the doctors say?" I asked anxiously.

"They think she's going to be fine. She has a bad cut on her scalp, and she had to have stitches. They did X-rays and everything, and there's some swelling, and they said she might have a slight concussion, but they didn't think too much damage had been done. She was conscious when they brought her in, but she didn't remember seeing anyone. They gave her a sedative after the stitches, and it knocked her right out."

"So she really was attacked," I said in disbelief.

"I know. I can't imagine who would have done such a thing. It's so…gritty."

"Maybe it was a vagrant of some sort? Maybe she surprised somebody who was hiding out there?" There was a pretty sizable and less than mentally stable homeless population in Harvard Square, and I could easily imagine one of them using the boathouse as a temporary shelter and freaking out that his space had been invaded.

Edie shook her head. "I thought that, too, at first. But I've been sitting here, trying to figure it out, and I don't think that makes sense."

"Why not?"

"If somebody were hiding out there, she would have surprised him when she went into the boathouse in the first place, to get her scull. And if he were going to attack her, why wouldn't he have attacked her then? But she was attacked when she was leaving."

"Sort of like someone was waiting for her when she came back from her row?"

"Exactly. Especially when you think about the ski mask. I mean, what sort of random attacker would come equipped with a mask? That sort of thing just screams premeditation." I recalled Sara mentioning that Edie planned on finding a job in entertainment, and going by her dramatic choice of words, it seemed that she would be well-suited to it.

"And you're sure it wasn't the guy who said he witnessed the entire thing?"

"I don't think so. George, the homeless man, is sort of a fixture around Harvard Square. There's a shelter at the University Lutheran Church, and both Sara and I have volunteered there. He knew Sara and had talked to her—I mean, it's not like he's the most sane person you'll ever meet—in fact, he's a total nutcase—but he has no history of violence. If he'd run into Sara, he would have just tried to engage her in conversation of some sort. He thinks he's a real intellectual, and he's always trying to debate philosophy or literary theory or whatever with students. He wouldn't hurt anyone. Bore them to death, maybe, but that's as bad as he gets."

"That's funny. I think I might remember him from my college days." I hazily recalled a shabby man who would sit in on my English lectures, occasionally posing an interesting and clearly well-informed question.

"Yeah. He's a bit of a legend around here. Anyhow, the hospital called our room, and I picked up the call and came right over."

"So it probably wasn't George."

"No. I'd be really surprised if it were."

"Then I wonder who. And why."

Edie was quiet for a moment. I had the sense that she was taking my measure, wondering if she could confide in me.

"There's something else, isn't there?" I asked.

She nodded. "Look, I feel sort of uncomfortable talking about this, but I know that Sara trusts you. And looks up to you."

The idea of anyone viewing me as a role model was a bizarre one, and coming so soon after being ma'amed, it made me wonder if the time had come to ask my doctor about Botox. "Well, I don't know about the looking up part, but she can definitely trust me. And you can, too."

"Okay." She seemed to make up her mind. "Sara's been getting these strange letters."

"Letters?"

"Yes. Like love letters, but sort of sinister. I mean, they're all flowery and gushy and go on and on about how beautiful she is. But they're never signed, and there's no return address or even a stamp or postmark on the envelopes, and they show up in the weirdest places—not just her mailbox at school, but slipped into her bag or a notebook. She once even found one on her bed."

"Creepy," I said.

"And invasive. I mean, the letters seem harmless enough—really badly written, but harmless. But when they show up in her personal space, it's really disturbing. I know it sounds like a cliché, but it's like she's being stalked."

"Does she have any idea who might be sending them?"

"No. Not a clue. We've been over and over it, but we just can't come up with any likely suspects. It would be hard to imagine any of the guys at school writing anything like them, much less giving them to her."

"But it must be someone who has access to the school—otherwise, how could he get the letters to her? How could he get into your dorm?"

"Well, it's not like security is that tight. Anyone who looked like he could belong on campus could probably walk around without too much difficulty. And people are always letting people into the dorm, even though they shouldn't."

"What about Grant Crocker?" I asked, remembering the odd, proprietary way in which he'd spoken of Sara earlier that morning.

"Sara told you about Grant?"

"Yes. And I knew him from when he worked at Winslow, Brown. He was at the memorial service this morning, and he was asking me if I had seen Sara." It would be a great way to deflect suspicion from himself, I thought—acting like he was perplexed not to see her at the church, even if he knew exactly why she wasn't there. My distaste for him made me more than willing to cast him as a creepy violent stalker.

"We talked about it maybe being Grant, but it's hard to picture. If you could see the letters—they're not a Grant Crocker type production. I mean, he's an ex-marine and a fanatical weight lifter—he even takes those weird supplements that build muscle or whatever. But this stuff is really lovey-dovey, and also sort of pretentious with all of these esoteric quotes from various poets. We just couldn't imagine that Grant had it in him. He's been a total pain since Sara broke things off with him—he still calls all the time. In fact, he called last night when you guys were having dinner, and he practically had a jealous fit on the phone. But these letters—they're just not his style."

"Do the police know about the letters? Did you tell anyone about them? Did Sara?"

"Actually, she did. Just yesterday. I'd been urging her to go to campus security, but she was worried that she'd be overreacting. And the letters weren't threatening, really, except for being anonymous and showing up in strange places. So she decided to show them to her section leader and get his advice."

The business school class was divided into sections of about ninety students each. During the first year, students took all of their classes with their sections. It was an interesting arrangement. On the one hand, it allowed students to become comfortable with their peers and thus, in theory at least, more willing to put forth unconventional opinions. On the other hand, by the end of the first year you could pretty much guess what any one of your section-mates would say in answer to any question before he opened his mouth, and you spent a lot of time hoping he wouldn't open his mouth. A professor was assigned to each section as its leader, acting as an ombudsman of sorts.

"That's good. What did he say?"

"Professor Beasley said he would take a look and help her figure out whether she should report the letters to campus security."

"Professor Beasley? Is he new?" The name sounded familiar, but I couldn't remember a Professor Beasley.

"I think he's been around for a couple of years."

"Well, given what happened this morning, it seems like he should definitely tell the police."

"I think so, too. I was going to go see him later, but I don't want to leave Sara right now. I called and left a message but he was in class."

"I'll tell you what," I said. "Why don't I go talk to Professor Beasley?"

"Would you do that? I'd feel so much better if I knew somebody was looking into it, but for all I know, he doesn't even know what's happened to Sara yet."

"Well, I'll make sure he knows."

"That would be great," Edie said, visibly relieved. "I'd just hate to leave before Sara wakes up."

We exchanged cell-phone numbers so I could call her after I'd spoken to Professor Beasley and she could let me know when Sara awakened.

I called Cecelia back at the hotel as I left UHS, explaining what had happened. It was just after noon, and interviews wouldn't resume until two o'clock. I hoped that I could get to Professor Beasley's office, talk to him and make it back to the Charles in time for the afternoon's interview schedule. I also tried Peter's cell phone again.

He picked up this time, but he sounded harried.

"Hi, it's me."

"Oh, hi, Rachel. What's up?" His greeting was warm but rushed.

Just as I was about to relate the morning's events, it occurred to me that given how busy he was, and how stressed, unloading on him right now was probably not the most considerate thing a supportive girlfriend could do. "Nothing," I said lamely. "Just wanted to say hello."

"Great. Hi." I heard a voice in the background, and a trill of female laughter. "Listen, I'm sort of in the middle of something right now. Abigail and I are at her hotel, refining our proposal for this pitch. Things are really heating up. Could I give you a call back later?"

"Um, sure," I said.

"Okay. Talk to you later."

I started to ask him about our dinner plans, but he'd already hung up.

I know it was irrational, but I felt annoyed, even while recognizing that there were plenty of times when Peter called me and I couldn't talk. But the laughter I heard tapped into some well of insecurity in my heart, and the thought of Peter and Abigail working closely together in a hotel room wasn't a particularly welcome one.

Stop it, I told myself. It's Peter. You have nothing to worry about. He's just busy.

With his gazellelike business associate, a mean little voice in my head reminded me. In a private place with a big bed. I shushed the voice, but not before registering a flash of jealousy so intense it made my stomach churn.

I'd reached the river and was passing the boathouse once more. There were only a couple of police cars left now, but the yellow crime-scene tape was still up. I crossed the bridge, leaning into the wind coming off the water and burrowing my hands in my pockets. I tried to take my mind off Peter and Abigail, and instead imagined what Professor Beasley would be like.

Old, I decided. Very old. With a walking stick, bow tie and lockjaw, like the professor in *The Paper Chase*. But imagining the decrepit Professor Beasley did little to quell the anxiety that my truncated conversation with Peter had stirred. I crossed Storrow Drive to Harvard Street and then took a left onto the business school campus, still wrapped in insecurity and fretting about Peter's strangely distant tone.

The grounds of the business school looked more Harvard than the college campus on the other side of the river. Here there was even more red brick, and more ivy, with patches of green grass broken by stone paths. A large endowment from corporate donors and successful alumni ensured that everything was maintained beautifully, and every time I came here a new building had risen, doubtless graced with the name of one of those donors. A couple of students walked by me, dressed in suits and overcoats. Judging by their clothes and serious expressions, they were on their way to interviews at the Charles.

I mounted the stone stairs to Morgan Hall, which housed most of the faculty offices, checking the directory in the foyer for Professor Beasley's office and quickly finding the listing—Beasley, J.—on the third floor. I heard the swoosh of the elevator doors opening behind me and dashed to catch it.

And collided, head-on, with the love of my life.

Seven

"Oof," I said.

The impact sent me sprawling, and I lost my grip on my shoulder bag. Its contents spilled out to surround me on the cold stone floor. My Blackberry ricocheted off a wall, and a lipstick rolled into a distant corner, but my first thought was of my nose, which felt like it had suffered some serious damage from its run-in with the man's chest. He must have been made of steel—either that or he was wearing a bulletproof vest.

"Are you all right?" The voice was rich and deep and it sent a shock of recognition down my spine. Along with a delicious tingle that made me promptly forget about any need for an emergency rhinoplasty. The man knelt down beside me, and with a strange sense of destiny I looked up and into Jonathan Beasley's blue, blue eyes.

Suddenly I was eighteen all over again, sitting across from Jonathan in English 10 (A Survey of English Literature from

Chaucer to Beckett) and wondering how such perfection was possible in one human being.

I had worshipped him for the better part of a year. He was a senior when I was a freshman. He was brilliant. He was beautiful. He played varsity ice hockey. He was the Ryan O'Neal to my Ali MacGraw. Except that he never actually spoke to me, and if he had, I would have been tongue-tied, completely unable to conjure up a comment that managed to be both clever and alluring at once. Then he graduated, and I never saw him again. I went on to form other unhealthy and unacted-upon crushes from afar, but Jonathan had been my first, and on some level I'd never forgotten him.

"Are you sure you're all right?" he asked again as I stared at him, openmouthed.

"Y-yes," I stuttered. "I'm fine, thank you. And I apologize. I was in such a rush that I wasn't watching where I was going." Think of something witty to say, I implored myself. Please, please think of something witty to say.

"Don't worry about it." He smiled—how I remembered that smile! "Here, let me help you." He began gathering my spilled belongings and putting them back in my bag. He handed me my Blackberry and gave me a quizzical look. "I think I know you from somewhere. From college, maybe? Across the river. An English course, right?"

I nodded, speechless, as he extended a hand to help me to my feet. What would Ali MacGraw do in a situation like this?

"I thought I'd seen you before. It's been a long time. I'm Jonathan. Jonathan Beasley."

"I'm Rachel Benjamin." I covertly looked him over, taking in the blue shirt that set off his eyes and dark blond hair and the slightly battered tweed jacket that stretched over his shoulders. He'd been beautiful a decade ago, and the years since had treated him well. My knees were shaky, and while I could blame their condition on my fall, the warmth I felt in my cheeks could only be blamed on simple, old-fashioned lust. He seemed to be having even more of an impact on me now than he had when I was eighteen.

He leaned against the wall. The elevator had long since come and gone. "So, what are you doing here? Are you a student at the business school?"

"No, at least not now. I graduated years ago. I work in New York. At Winslow, Brown. And you're a professor?" Now I knew why Professor Beasley's name had sounded familiar, but somehow the title of professor had managed to blot out the less-than-professorial associations I had with the name Beasley. This Professor Beasley was a far cry from the bow-tied, lockjawed curmudgeon I'd imagined.

"Believe it or not. Organizational behavior. Incentive systems, things like that. I put in some time on Wall Street and then went to Columbia for a Ph.D. I've been teaching here for three years now."

I remembered, with great difficulty, why I was there. "You know, it's funny, running into you like this. I was actually on my way to see you. Only I didn't realize it would be you, specifically. I didn't realize that you were Professor Beasley."

"Really? Why?"

"It's about Sara Grenthaler."

His expression changed from friendly to somber, but it was equally enthralling. "How do you know Sara?"

"Well, she's sort of my client. I mean, Grenthaler Media is. And she worked with me last summer at Winslow, Brown."

"So you've heard what happened to her." His voice was laced with concern.

I nodded. "In fact, I just came from UHS. I was talking to her roommate, Edie Michaels, and she explained about the letters Sara was getting. I told her I'd come talk to you. She's anxious that the police know about them, just in case there's a connection of any sort with the attack."

"Let's go up to my office," Jonathan suggested. "I can fill you in there." I willingly let him escort me up to the third floor and lead me down a corridor, nodding to various colleagues and staff along the way. He ushered me into his office and took my coat, hanging it next to his own on a peg on the back of the office door. I looked around while he cleared a stack of papers from one of his guest chairs. The walls were lined with bookshelves, and I scanned his collection. It was extensive and varied, ranging from the usual business texts to history and biography. I even saw the familiar double volume of *Norton's Anthology of English Literature,* its bindings worn and tattered.

"English 10," he said, following my gaze.

"I know. I've got the same set." I sat down in the now-empty chair, relieved to no longer have to trust my shaky knees, and he settled himself across from me at his desk.

"I was an Economics major, but I took that course senior year. I loved it. It made me wish I'd taken more English courses, but it was too late."

"It would be great to go back and take all of the courses that I missed. Well, except for the exams and papers."

"I know exactly what you mean," he replied with a rueful smile. "So, now that I think about it, it's all coming back to me. You know, my roommate had such a crush on you."

"He did?" I didn't remember his roommate. I'd had eyes only for Jonathan.

"It was almost pathetic. Clark Gibson. Do you remember him? He would spend every class staring at you and then make me rehash everything you said for the rest of the day. He was obsessed."

"Oh." I thought back and dredged up a hazy image of Clark Gibson. He had seemed to stare a lot, but I'd assumed he was staring at Luisa. Most men did. "Why did he never ask me out?"

"Well, you were always with your boyfriend. What was his name? The guy with the dark hair and little round glasses?"

"Who? Oh—you mean Jamie. He wasn't my boyfriend. He just lived in our dorm room. Because he hated his room-mates. You know how that is." Jamie would invariably sit on one side of me while Luisa sat on the other, each silently roll-ing their eyes at me when I passed them notes commenting on something Jonathan had said, or what he was wearing that day, or any of the other trivialities that are so important when you have a massive, hopeless crush on somebody who doesn't know you exist.

"You're kidding. I'll have to tell Clark. He'll kick himself, especially now that he's married and has three kids."

"And just think, they could have been mine." Jonathan chuckled. Little did he know how much time I'd spent dreaming of him and *our* three kids.

"So, the letters," I said, once again having to remind my-self why I was there.

"Yes, the letters," he repeated. He used a key to open a desk drawer and pulled out a stack of folded papers held together by a rubber band. "Take a look," he invited, handing the stack across the desk.

"What about fingerprints?" I asked.

"So many people have handled these—Sara, Edie, me—I doubt that there will be any useful prints. And I suspect that whoever wrote these was pretty careful. They could have been typed on any computer and printed on any standard laser printer."

I freed the folded pages from the rubber band and opened the one on top, scanning it quickly. Jonathan was right—it was entirely typewritten on regulation letter-size paper.

Darling Sara,
I saw you today, at a distance, your raven hair bent over your
studies, a pen grasped in your graceful hand, and my heart

*overflowed. I wanted to rush to your side and take you in
my arms.*
I see you and hear the words of the poet:
  "She walks in beauty like the night
  Of cloudless climes and starry skies"
*You are my night, you are my starry skies. But how can I con-
fess my forbidden love? I cannot. One day, perhaps, but not
today.*

I didn't blame whoever had written it for leaving it un-
signed—it was awful.

"Yeesh," I said. "Are they all like this?"

"What do you mean?"

"Nauseating?"

"You think it's nauseating?"

"Well…" I cast about, trying to find a more appropriate
word, but came up empty. "Yes. Nauseating. So gushy and
gross."

"Which one are you looking at?" he asked me.

I handed it to him, and he skimmed it. "Oh. I thought this
one was sweet. Romantic, with the Keats and everything."

"Are you sure it's not Byron?"

He looked at me for a moment, blankly, and then shrugged
and grinned. "I was just an econ major—what do I know? I
barely squeaked by in English 10."

"You could be right," I said. "It could be Keats." But I
was secretly tempted to get down his *Norton Anthology* and
prove it wasn't. That's what Ali MacGraw probably would
have done.

"Anyhow," he continued, "the Dean of Students asked me
to coordinate the investigation with the police, and I'm planning on showing these to them. I'm going to make sure they
leave no stone unturned. But I doubt that the notes are related to the attack."

"Why not?" I asked.

"They're love letters. Whoever wrote them clearly idolizes Sara."

"Yes, but he's also been totally invading her privacy. Edie said Sara found one on her bed."

"But they're not violent."

"They aren't on the face of it. But the fact that they exist, and that they keep showing up in personal places, is pretty scary. It's sort of like stalking, and stalking tends to end in violence." At least, it always did on Lifetime Television for Women, which was where I'd gathered what little information I had on the topic.

"I don't know much about stalking," he conceded. "And I don't want to downplay your concerns. That's why I'm going to make sure that the police take a look at them. It's just that after having read them all, I don't get the sense that whoever's writing them would want to hurt Sara. She's very attractive but also very aloof. It's not hard to imagine that somebody would fall in love with her but be too intimidated to actually ask her out. And there's this entire 'forbidden love' theme running through the letters. I don't know what it's about, but my guess is that whoever's writing these is smitten with her and doesn't know of any other way to express himself."

"What about Grant Crocker?"

"Grant Crocker?" Jonathan laughed. "I can't imagine that. Do you know Grant?"

"Sure. He used to work at my firm."

"I'd have a hard time picturing Grant writing these. He's not the most poetic guy. And I'm familiar with how he writes, from papers and exams. He sticks to pretty basic nouns and verbs. This stuff is a little more sophisticated."

Sophisticated was one word for it.

"Besides," Jonathan added, "the police seem to think that they may have an angle already."

"What angle's that?"

"Well, you probably haven't heard since you live in New York, but there's been a rash of murders in the area. The detective I spoke to thought there might be some connection. That Sara might have been the next victim, if the attacker hadn't been interrupted."

"You mean the guy who's been killing prostitutes?" I asked.

"How did you know about that?"

"A friend of mine's a doctor at a free clinic in South Boston, and one of the women who was killed was his patient."

"It might be the same guy. I guess there was something about the attack on Sara that jibed with what they know about him."

"Like what?"

"I don't know. They didn't tell me much, and I don't see how there could be a connection between a serial killer who's preying on prostitutes and what happened this morning in the boathouse. The important thing is that she wasn't seriously hurt. My guess is that it was probably just a random attack, and Sara happened to be in the wrong place at the wrong time. Either way, whoever did attack her is going to be in a lot of trouble when they catch him. I'll see to that," he said firmly.

"Good," I answered, somewhat reassured. And then my stomach gave an audible growl. I flushed. Again.

"Hungry?" Jonathan asked with a bemused smile.

"A bit. It's been a while since breakfast," I admitted.

"Well, I just picked up a sandwich at the student center. Want half?" I checked my watch. I still had an hour before I had to be back at the Charles.

"Are you sure?"

"It would be a pleasure." He stood and crossed to the door, retrieving a paper bag from his jacket pocket. "And I want to hear more about the last ten years of your life."

★ ★ ★

We had a little picnic there in Jonathan's office. He even had a small refrigerator in a corner from which he pulled two cold Diet Cokes. His calm assessment of the attack on Sara and his confidence that the attacker would be found and punished helped me to relax. We chatted easily as we ate. It was with reluctance that I realized it was time to go.

We exchanged phone numbers, and he promised to let me know if he heard any news about Sara and the investigation.

"Well," he said, helping me into my coat, "I'm sorry that we had to run into each other under these circumstances, but I'm glad that we ran into each other."

"Me, too," I said, suddenly feeling as awkward in his presence as I had at eighteen. Not that I'd actually ever stood this close to him when I was eighteen. "I guess I'll talk to you later."

"Sure thing," he said. And while I was figuring out whether or not it made sense to shake his hand, he bent down and gave me a kiss on the cheek.

I was out the door and a few steps down the hallway, feeling the familiar blush spreading across my face with renewed vigor, when he called after me.

"Hey, Rachel?"

I turned, hoping that my color wouldn't show in the fluorescent light of the corridor. He stood in the doorway to his office, his blue eyes bright.

"I hope it's not another ten years before I see you again."

I flashed him a smile and a wave and scurried off.

It wasn't until I was outside that I realized I hadn't thought of Peter once since I'd entered the building, much less mentioned him to Jonathan.

Eight

I had to tell someone about what had just happened. It's not every day that you run into the love of your life. Even though, I reminded myself, I'd only thought Jonathan was the love of my life when I was young and naive. Now I had Peter, the real love of my life, even if he had been acting a bit preoccupied of late and even if Jonathan's presence had been enough to erase all thoughts of him from my head for the better part of an hour. Still, I was bursting with the news.

I pulled out my phone as I hurried across the business school campus. My first thought was to try Emma, but if she was really starting a new series, she'd be too distracted to be of much use, so I dialed Jane's number instead. The familiar voice that answered was throaty, with faint traces of an exotic accent.

"Luisa?"

"Rachel? Is that you?"

"It is," I confirmed.

"How are you, darling? I can't wait to see you tomorrow."

"Me, too. But you'll never guess who I just had lunch with."

"Rachel, I took an overnight flight and I've gotten three hours of sleep in the last two days. You can't honestly expect me to guess."

"No need to be cranky. You give up?"

"Indeed. And I'm not cranky."

"Jonathan Beasley!"

"Who's Jonathan Beasley?"

"Who's Jonathan Beasley?" I repeated, amazed that she could have forgotten and forgetting myself that I had pretty much forgotten until I'd crashed into him. "Only the love of my life."

"Peter's the love of your life, darling. Nice try."

"I know he is. I'm talking about the love of my previous life."

"I thought that was Chris the Sociopath?"

"This predates Chris the Sociopath. Don't you remember? The guy from English 10?"

"No."

"The *Love Story* guy? You honestly don't remember him?"

"Hold on a sec." I heard her open a door and close it and then the sound of her lighting a cigarette and taking a drag. "Sorry, needed to step out onto the porch. I think Jane would have me arrested if I smoked in the house. Of course, she doesn't seem too worried about my dying from exposure."

"Come on, Luisa. Pay attention. Jonathan Beasley. Blondish hair, bluish eyes. Incredible smile. So beautiful. Just like Ryan O'Neal but smarter looking. And with a better voice. And maybe with some Robert Redford thrown in. A much younger Robert Redford. You must remember."

"Maybe I do. Dressed really preppie?"

"Uh-huh."

"And you'd sit there like a lump, ogling him and not doing anything about it? Just sort of pining away instead?"

"Uh-huh."

"Well, I hate to break it to you, but that pretty much describes a lot of your behavior in college. At least when it came to matters concerning the opposite sex." I heard her take another deep drag.

"Nice to talk to you, too."

"Okay, tell me, since you clearly want to. Where did you encounter Jonathan Beasley?"

I gave her a quick but comprehensive account of the events of the past twenty-four hours as I picked my way among the piles of slush and patches of ice on the bridge across the river.

"It sounds like you've had an action-packed visit so far," she commented. "I hadn't realized Cambridge had gotten so dangerous. I thought things had shaped up since we were in college. But someone attacked this woman—what is her name again, your client?"

"Sara. Sara Grenthaler."

"And they don't know who did it?"

"No." I filled her in on the various theories that had been floated so far. "But it was probably just a random thing. I can't imagine someone would really want to hurt her."

"I hope not. Anyhow, enough of this. I want to hear about Peter."

I hesitated. Seeing Jonathan Beasley had provided a welcome distraction from my earlier unease about Peter. And if I actually put my unease into words, talked about it out loud, would I make it true? But pretending everything was fine when it wasn't would invite the wrath of the Jinxing Gods. Not that I believed in them anymore. "He's been acting sort of weird," I hedged.

"What do you mean?"

"I don't know, really. I mean, he was fine last night, but he seems really stressed-out about work, and he's barely had time to speak to me today."

"He's probably just busy."

"I know. And I'm probably overreacting."

"But?"

"He has this new colleague."

"Let me guess. The colleague's a she, and you're jealous."

"She looks like Christy Turlington."

"Who's Christy Turlington?"

"The one who does all the perfume ads for Calvin Klein."

"Oh. That's not good."

"She called him twice between eleven last night and seven this morning."

"They are working together," Luisa pointed out. "And you know what start-ups are like. The pace is frantic."

"Two calls, Luisa. At times when people should be asleep. And I could hear her laughing in the background this morning when I called him. They were in her hotel room, together. He said they had work to do and rushed me off the phone."

"Darling, even if she does look like this Christy person, I think you may be imagining problems where there aren't any."

"I hope so," I answered, but the sense of foreboding was still there.

I reached the hotel and pushed through the revolving door. "Listen, Luisa, I need to get back to work. What do you have on tap for the rest of the day?"

"Jane and I had talked about a visit to Newbury Street to do a little shopping when she gets back from school." Jane taught math at a local private school, and this early in the semester it would be easy for her to skip out after classes ended.

"Give my regards to Armani. Is Hilary going, too?"

"No, she's off doing research. She's really excited about her book. And what about you? You're seeing Peter tonight?"

"Yes. Dinner."

"Good. You'll have a wonderful time and realize that you're making yourself crazy for no reason."

"I hope so."

"I know so. We'll see you tomorrow."

"See you tomorrow," I echoed and rang off.

I waited impatiently for the elevator, strategizing as to how I would explain playing hooky from recruiting that morning should Scott Epson ask. A young man came up beside me, wearing a dark overcoat over a dark suit.

He looked me over. "Interviews?" he asked.

I gave him a preoccupied smile. "Sort of."

"Nervous?"

I almost laughed. With a pleasant shock of surprise, I realized that he thought I was a student here to be interviewed, rather than to interview students. This was better than being carded at a bar. An interaction like this one was good for canceling out being called "ma'am" at least two or three times.

"Not really," I answered. The elevator arrived, and we got in.

"Floor?" he asked.

"Four."

"Me, too. Winslow, Brown?"

"Yes."

"They're really hard-core. They can get pretty much whoever they want. The competition's really intense this year."

"Yep," I agreed.

"And I've heard the interviewers are being really tough. No softballs." Now it was a struggle not to laugh. Not only did he think I was a student, he was trying to psyche me out.

"I think I can handle it." The elevator doors slid open, and we both turned down the corridor.

The door to the recruiting suite was ajar, and we entered together. Several students were milling about, waiting to be called for their interviews. "I think we're supposed to check in over there," my new friend told me, indicating the table where Cecelia sat.

"Thanks," I said.

Cece spotted me and waved me over. "Everything under control?" she asked.

"Sort of," I answered. "I'll fill you in later. How's everything been going here?"

"The usual." She turned to my companion and gave him a professional smile. "And you are?"

"Uh, Kevin. Kevin Sweeney." Kevin looked uncomfortable. I guess he'd figured out I wasn't another student.

"Well, Kevin, it looks like you've already met Rachel Benjamin. She's heading up recruiting this year. But you're a bit early—your interviewer's still out at lunch. He should be back in a few minutes. Please help yourself to a soda if you'd like." Cece pointed in the direction of the bar that had been set up in a corner of the room. She waited until he was out of earshot before continuing. "So, I've got good news and bad news for you. Which do you want first?"

"Any chance that the bad news will go away?"

"Nope."

"Okay. Let's get it over with."

"There's somebody here who wants to see you."

"Who?"

"Gabrielle LeFavre? She's been here since this morning. I've tried to get rid of her, but she insisted on talking to you."

"Drat."

"Yes."

"Where is she?"

"Waiting in the other room."

I managed not to grimace. "Okay. I'll go talk to her."

"Don't you want to hear the good news?"

"Oh, I forgot about that. What is it?"

"I've gotten you out of interviews for the afternoon. We

have enough people, and I thought you'd appreciate some free time."

"You are a goddess."

"I know, but it's still nice to hear people say it. Thanks."

I steeled myself for what was probably going to be an unpleasant discussion and crossed into the bedroom of the suite. Gabrielle was standing with her back to me, looking out the window. At least, I assumed it was she. From the back, it could have been anyone of any gender. She was tall, with short strawberry-blond hair and the requisite navy pantsuit. I wondered if she'd heard about Sara yet.

"Gabrielle?"

She gave a little start and turned around.

"Ms. Benjamin?"

"Rachel, please." From the front, she was most definitely not a man. Her hair was elaborately styled, and even the professionally cut suit couldn't hide her curves. And if you couldn't tell she was from the South from her accent, her frosted lip gloss and long nails, painted in a glossy bright pink, were a dead giveaway.

I shook her hand. "It's nice to meet you in person," I said. "Sara mentioned you to me."

"Thank you. Listen, Ms. Benjamin, I mean, Rachel, I don't know if you got the message I left for you—"

"I did," I interrupted as gently as I could. "And I'm really sorry, Gabrielle, but unfortunately there's just not much I can do. We have so many students coming through the process that we have to stick to the rules or things just get crazy. But I can probably arrange for the people who interviewed you to give you some coaching—that way you'll be even better prepared for your interviews with other firms."

"I don't want to work at another firm. Winslow, Brown is the best."

"There are a lot of great firms out there, and I'm sure you'll find a terrific job with one of them. And if you really feel so strongly about Winslow, Brown, you can always interview again in a couple of years when you have some more experience under your belt."

"But, you must need women. I mean, Winslow, Brown is so committed to diversity. That's what all of its brochures say."

I stifled a sigh. I was in no mood to tell her that this was neither about her gender nor about meeting quotas. There were plenty of women who'd made it through the first round of interviews—Gabrielle just wasn't one of them.

We went back and forth for several minutes—Gabrielle trying a variety of angles that I had to rebuff tactfully but firmly. She really didn't want to take no for an answer.

Finally I interrupted another impassioned argument. "Gabrielle, have you heard about Sara?"

"You mean about what happened to her at the boathouse?"

I nodded.

"Yes. But Edie said she's all right. That she wasn't really hurt."

"No, she'll be fine."

"She really shouldn't have been in the boathouse. It's dangerous so early in the morning, when it's still dark out."

That seemed like a strangely unsympathetic response from one of Sara's roommates, and my first thought was to just chalk it up to Gabrielle's current agitated state.

"Anyhow," she added, "that's one less woman vying for a job." This response, on the other hand, was nothing short of bizarre.

"What do you mean? Sara isn't even going through recruiting."

Gabrielle looked away, running a manicured hand through her hair. I noticed that one of her nails was broken. "All of these perfect girls around here, with everything handed to them on a silver platter," she muttered, almost as if she were speaking to herself. "Money, jobs, men. It makes me sick."

The business school could be a scarily competitive place, but Gabrielle's words took scary competitiveness to a whole new level. I remembered, belatedly, Sara's comments the previous evening about Gabrielle's crush on Grant Crocker, and her jealousy. I wondered if Sara was even aware of the extent to which she probably personified everything that Gabrielle resented.

Gabrielle seemed to recover herself and realize what she'd said was inappropriate. "Anyhow, about Winslow, Brown—"

She'd tried my patience enough. I cut her off. "Listen, Gabrielle. I'm afraid there's just not anything more to be done here. If I can give you advice about any of the other firms you're interviewing with, please don't hesitate to let me know."

She opened her mouth to say something else, but the expression on my face silenced her. Wordlessly, she gathered up her long hooded overcoat and scarf and left the room.

Nine

I made it up to my room without any more unpleasant run-ins with manic aspiring bankers, closing the door safely behind me and giving thanks that I wouldn't have to spend the rest of the afternoon interviewing more hypercompetitive stress cases. My conversation with Gabrielle had planted the seed of an idea in my head that I wasn't happy about. I wanted to believe that Sara had fallen prey to a random attack. But if that weren't the case, I'd just identified a person in Sara's immediate circle who seemed to wish her ill. It was hard to imagine that Gabrielle's jealousy and resentment could cause her to lash out violently, and I was hardly a mental health professional, but the woman I'd just met seemed less than sane. If the police determined that the prostitute killer wasn't responsible for the attack on Sara, they would do well to add the Psycho Roommate to the Creepy Violent Stalker on the list of suspects.

The room was clean and quiet, and I slipped off my shoes,

curling and uncurling my cramped toes in the plush pile of the carpet. I was grateful for the downtime; while the police tried to track down Sara's attacker, the least I could do was track down what, if anything, might be happening to Sara's company. My laptop was in my briefcase, and I took it out and set it on the desk. While it was booting up, I checked my Blackberry for messages. I hadn't heard the phone ring, but there was a voice mail from Edie Michaels. Sara was awake and doing well, but the doctors intended to keep her at UHS for a day or two more. I left a message back, letting her know that Professor Beasley had promised to share the letters with the police.

There were a bunch of work-related calls I had to return, but as soon as I finished I plugged the hotel's Ethernet cord into the computer and opened up my Web browser. I wanted to see what was going on with Grenthaler Media's stock.

I logged on to Bloomberg.com and typed in the Grenthaler stock symbol. Its price was up since I'd checked it a few days before. Then it had been at $250. It was now trading at $262, a five-percent bump while the market overall was flat, and it was up a full ten percent from a few weeks ago. I then turned my attention to the volume of trading. Of the two million shares held by the public, approximately one percent—or twenty thousand shares—traded hands on the average day. However, the average daily trading volume during the past two weeks was significantly higher—closer to fifty thousand a day.

Of course, some of that could be explained by Tom's death. Undoubtedly, investors were speculating as to who would be appointed as the new CEO and what it would mean for the company's future. But usually that sort of speculation wasn't good for a stock price. Tom had been well respected, and now the company's leadership was uncertain—if anything, that should send the stock down, not up. And it was odd that the increase in both the stock price and the trading volume had begun prior to Tom's death.

Perhaps Tom had been right to be concerned. It did look as if there was a player—or several—in the market steadily buying up shares. I checked out the list of headlines from the Associated Press and Reuters. There were reports from the previous week of Tom's death, and even an item about this morning's memorial service. I was glad to see that the wire services hadn't seemed to pick up the news about the attack on Sara. That was the last thing she—or the company— needed right now.

I closed out of Bloomberg and headed over to Yahoo!'s finance portal, typing in the Grenthaler stock symbol again and then clicking on the link to the message board. As a general rule, the message board was not the place for financial wisdom or disciplined technical analysis of a stock's performance. It was frequented by day traders, many of whom were lunatics and more likely to use a Ouija board to dictate their investment strategies than careful study of a company and its prospects. Still, I was curious as to what rumors might be flying about. The message board would be rumor central.

Here, too, there had been an unusual amount of activity. I scrolled through the postings. While in December there had been only a dozen or so posts each day, in the last couple of weeks it looked like there had been several each hour. I opened up some of the more recent ones at random, mostly incoherent rantings from people with screen names like VivaLasVegas and KermitLuvsGonzo about their esoteric investment philosophies, rife with misspellings and puerile insults for others on the board.

Then a message posted by one CuriousGeorge caught my eye: "Takeover in the works?" read the headline. I clicked it open.

Has anyone else noticed that there seems to be a lot of activity in this stock for no apparent reason? Is a buyout on the horizon? Hard to imagine since Grenthaler's privately controlled but maybe Barnett's shares will be up for sale? Anybody know anything on this?

Of course, this set of reasonable questions had been completely ignored by the likes of ExcaliburNYC and XBox-Roolz. I checked out CuriousGeorge's profile. Apparently he was a one-hundred-and-sixty-eight-year-old male living in Area 51 in Nevada. Needless to say, he hadn't included a photo in his profile.

While his profile may not have lent his posting much credibility, he raised a good point. Everything I'd seen made me wonder if he was right. Was a takeover in the works? It seemed unlikely, at best, given that only forty-nine percent of the company was publicly traded. Unless, of course, Barbara Barnett made her shares available.

I heard Sara's anxious voice in my head, her determination not to let control of the company get away from her. "I won't let that happen," I had promised her. And I had meant it.

With Sara laid up at UHS, it looked like it was up to me to figure out what was going on.

I called Jessica and asked her to dig up Grenthaler's company charter and e-mail it to me. Given that Grenthaler was privately controlled, Tom and I had never worried too much about setting up antitakeover clauses for the company. Of course, if a takeover was being launched against the company, it was too late to do anything about that now. But I at least needed to understand what we had to work with. I also asked her to run a Carson Group check for the names of institutions and individuals who had been major purchasers of the stock over the last few weeks. I then left a message for Brian Mulcahey at Grenthaler's Kendall Square headquarters, asking if he could meet me for breakfast the next day. Brian was Grenthaler's chief operating officer, and he was temporarily in charge until the board of directors appointed a new CEO.

Most importantly, however, I had to find out what Barbara Barnett planned to do with her ten percent of Grenthaler's stock. Without Barbara's shares, nobody could gain majority control of the company. I checked my watch. It was past three. Surely the reception after the memorial service would be long over by now. I needed to talk to Barbara and get a sense of her intentions.

I found the Barnetts' home phone number on Beacon Hill in my Blackberry, took a deep breath and dialed. A maid answered.

"May I speak to Mrs. Barnett, please?" I inquired.

"Mrs. Barnett is unavailable. Can I take a message?"

I thought for a moment. I wanted to make an appointment to see Barbara in person, but I could only begin to imagine how many people must have left messages of various sorts during the past few days. I doubted that she'd remember who I was in the sea of names and numbers. And I was sure that a good many of those names were from various investment houses, eager to help a new widow manage her wealth. Saying I was from Winslow, Brown wouldn't get her attention.

"Ma'am?" the maid prompted.

What was going on with me and the ma'am thing today? Had I suddenly become a senior citizen without even noticing?

"No message," I said. "Do you know when I can try to reach her?"

"I'm not sure. I believe she's at the gym."

Even grief couldn't get in the way of Barbara's strict workout schedule. "I'll try back," I said. "Thank you."

"Good day, ma'am." The maid hung up the phone. That was two ma'ams in one short phone call. A complex was beginning to take root.

Well, I knew one phone call I could make where I wasn't in danger of being on the wrong side of a ma'am. Edward and Helene Porter weren't in my Blackberry, but their number in Louisburg Square was listed. They were both members of Grenthaler's board of directors, and they might have some insight as to what Barbara was planning to do with her shares. Furthermore, if a takeover was, in fact, in the works, I could trust that they would be firmly aligned with Sara, and I wanted to prepare them for the remote possibility that we would need to mount a defense. Especially since I didn't want Sara worrying about it in her current position. Mrs. Porter answered the phone on the third ring.

"I don't know if you remember me, Mrs. Porter. This is Rachel Benjamin from Winslow, Brown. We met at a Grenthaler Media board meeting last year when I gave a presentation about the company's acquisition strategy."

"Certainly, dear. The redheaded girl." That was more like it. Of course, Helene Porter must have been pushing ninety, so a girl in her book was probably anyone not eligible for Social Security, but I'd take it.

"I'm glad you remember me."

"You were very memorable. Edward and I were both impressed by you."

"Well, thank you. And I'm sorry about what happened to Sara this morning."

"Yes, it was quite a shock for us. Fortunately, the doctor thinks she'll be as good as new in a couple of days. We just got back from the hospital, and she definitely seems to be recovering nicely. Now we just have to find out who did this to her."

"Absolutely," I said. "You must be very concerned."

"Well, she's only a child, and Cambridge's gotten so dangerous. We wish that she would live with us, but she insists on staying in the dorms."

"Still, it must be nice for her to have you so close by."

"I think we're more of a nuisance than anything else, but that's sweet of you to say."

"Mrs. Porter, if it's not too much trouble, I was hoping that I could pay you and your husband a visit. There's some company business I'd like to discuss, and I don't want to bother Sara right now."

"We would love to see you, dear. Perhaps you could come by tomorrow morning?"

I would have to get out of interviewing again, but Cecelia would cover for me. "That would be great," I agreed. We set a time and she gave me their address.

My Blackberry buzzed on the desk as we were saying goodbye. I checked it, wondering if Jessica had already managed to dig up the Grenthaler charter. But it was an e-mail from Peter.

Locked in a meeting right now, and it looks like it's going to go long. Really long, unfortunately. I think I'm going to have to take a rain check on tonight. I'll make it up to you, I promise. So so sorry. PF

Disappointment flooded through me. I'd been looking forward to a quiet romantic dinner for two, especially after the day I was having. I wanted to tell Peter about everything that had happened. More than that, I wanted to see him, to be reassured that all of my concerns about him and Abigail were in my head. That, as Luisa had said, I was creating problems where none existed.

I read the message again, trying to decipher any hidden meaning it might contain. And the more I read it, the more

I realized that I was feeling something other than disappointment and concern. I was annoyed, too. Unfairly, probably. But would it have been that much harder for Peter to call me? He knew I'd be upset, and e-mailing me to cancel seemed like a cop-out. Sure, he was trapped in a meeting, but he could have stepped out for a minute to make a quick call and talk to me in person, couldn't he?

I was composing a reply when the phone rang. I picked it up with happy relief. It hadn't taken Peter long to recognize the error of his ways.

But it wasn't Peter.

"Rachel? It's Jonathan Beasley."

I was in a vulnerable state from Peter's e-mail, but that wasn't enough to explain the effect Jonathan's voice had on me. Parts of my body tingled. Tingled! That shouldn't happen with anyone but Peter.

I feigned calmness. "Oh. Hi. Any news?"

"No, not really. I spoke to UHS a few minutes ago, and Sara's doing well. Nothing much from the police yet."

"Oh. Okay. Thanks for keeping me posted."

"I thought you'd want to be kept in the loop."

"I do. Thank you."

He paused. "Listen, you're probably booked, but—"

"Aagghh!"

"Rachel, what happened? Are you all right?"

I'd gotten up to retrieve a Diet Coke from the minibar and promptly stubbed my toe on the coffee-table leg. Now I was hopping around the room, waiting for the agony to recede.

"Uh-huh," I gasped, my teeth clenched against the pain. "Just bumped into something, that's all."

"You're sure you're all right?"

"I'm sure," I responded, struggling to keep my voice steady.

"Well, as I was saying, I thought maybe we could have dinner tonight."

I forgot about my toe. "Dinner? Tonight?"

"Sure. There's a little Indian place I know in Central Square. They do a mean vindaloo."

I'd been thinking that I'd call Jane and go over there, now that I had no plans, but I'd be seeing all my friends the next night. In fact, we'd be seeing each other all weekend. And I loved spicy food.

"I can do that," I said.

"Really?"

"Sounds good. Where should I meet you and when?"

He gave me directions. "Eight o'clock work for you?"

"Eight is fine," I affirmed.

"Great. Then I'll see you there. I'm looking forward to it."

I hung up the phone and limped into the bedroom. Housekeeping had been there, and the bed was now freshly made. Which reminded me that yet again I'd managed not to mention Peter to Jonathan.

I felt a brief twinge of guilt but quickly brushed it away. It was only dinner.

Ten

It was time for the recruiting roundup session. I shut down my laptop, put my suit jacket back on, stuffed my feet, complete with throbbing toe, into my shoes and grabbed my shoulder bag and coat.

Skipping the elevator, I took the service stairs to the floor below and headed down the corridor to the Winslow, Brown suite. I heard Scott Epson's nasal voice before I saw him.

"...can only benefit us," he was saying. Actually, he was bloviating, as he was wont to do. "Yes, it's unfortunate, but it does weaken their position." I turned the corner and nearly ran into him, which would have been a far less pleasant experience than smashing into, say Jonathan Beasley. Although I doubted Scott's concave chest would pack as much of a wallop.

"Hi, Scott," I said, stepping to the side to avoid a collision.

He gave a start of surprise then put his hand over the mouthpiece of his cell phone. "Oh. Hi, Rach. Just wrapping up an incredibly important call. I'll be right in."

"Sure," I said. He seemed strangely flustered, but I didn't give it much thought. It was Scott, after all.

I passed through the open door of the suite and selected a can of Diet Coke from the refreshments table. Several of my colleagues had already gathered, and most were busy on their assorted phone and e-mail devices. I said hello to Cecelia and made small talk with a guy from the Capital Markets department. Scott joined us a couple of minutes later, and when everyone was seated I called the meeting to order so that we could begin our tedious rehashing of the day's interviews.

Good bankers are usually clever rather than intellectual, quick rather than thoughtful. They get paid for getting deals done; the bigger the deals and the quicker they're closed the better. They tend to be the least self-reflective species on earth—self-centered and self-involved, yes, but hardly self-reflective.

I've thus never understood the questions that some of my colleagues asked of business school students, another species not known for their personal depth. When I interviewed students, I tried to understand whether a candidate was strong quantitatively, would work well with others and not embarrass us in front of clients, and had the drive and endurance required to handle the grueling pace of the job. Many of my fellow bankers, however, preferred to approach interviewing in a more Freudian way.

Scott, for example, loved to ask students about the biggest challenge they had faced and how they had overcome it. I never asked this question because the answer usually bored me—students were prepared for it, and they would usually give a canned response describing motivating an unwilling team or solving a thorny analytical problem. Scott, however, seemed disappointed with this sort of reply, but he would crow with enthusiasm over any candidate who used the question as an opportunity to discuss her parents' tempestuous divorce or when his dog was run over by a truck. "That really shows incredible character and sensitivity," he would say. That neither trait was particularly important in our line of work didn't matter much to Scott. Nor did he seem to realize that he was completely lacking in both.

My other pet peeve was the subtle undercurrent of sexism running through the discussion. It was rare that a male candidate was asked to do off-the-cuff bond math or grilled on his SAT scores to test his quantitative abilities. But female candidates were routinely asked to compute complex algorithms in their head or opine on options theory. The seven men and lone woman who'd performed that day's interviews weren't much different. I listened silently as a female student's quantitative skills were debated ad nauseam until I had to point out that she'd been an applied math major in college and earned top grades in her finance courses at the business school. I'd probably been only a low-grade feminist when I started at Winslow, Brown, but my experience there had turned me into a full-fledged radical. Compared to me, Gloria Steinem's politics were practically red-state.

We finally wrapped up at half past seven, and I was pleased with the results. Regardless of the various irrelevancies that Scott and like-minded participants kept harping on, we'd emerged with an accomplished and diverse slate of candidates to send to New York for the final round of interviews. I left a message for Stan Winslow to update him and took the elevator down to the lobby. The doorman put me into a cab, and I gave the driver the address for the restaurant in Central Square.

I felt pleasant anticipation as the taxi sped up Mass. Ave. I pulled my small cosmetics pouch from my shoulder bag to reapply lipstick and blush. My midwinter pallor needed all the help it could get.

Then I checked myself. What was I doing, putting on makeup for dinner with Jonathan? It was probably presumptuous of me to even think that he thought of this dinner as anything resembling a date. Furthermore, if he did think it was a date, I was ethically obligated not to primp and to at least drop a passing reference to my boyfriend. Yes, old crushes die hard, and it had been the crush to end all crushes, and Jonathan was even more gorgeous now than he'd been in college, but I was in a committed relationship. I was in love with Peter.

This line of thought was the cue for the mean-spirited little voice in my head to chime in. "Peter hasn't exactly been acting like he's in a committed relationship these past couple of days. Interrupting romantic evenings to take calls with Abigail, leaping out of bed at the crack of dawn, canceling dinner...."

"He's busy," I told the mean-spirited little voice.

"But what's more important, you or his work?" it answered. "Or maybe he'd just rather spend time with Abigail and is trying to let you down easy?"

That was especially mean-spirited, so I didn't justify it with a reply. Besides, the cab driver was looking at me oddly in the rearview mirror. I guessed he wasn't used to passengers who talked to themselves. In New York, he wouldn't have batted an eye.

I paid the fare and stepped onto the curb in front of the address Jonathan had given me. The restaurant was flanked by a newsstand, and I caught a glimpse of a headline as I walked past. Prostitute Found Strangled, it blared. Yuck. I wondered if it was the same woman who had been Matthew's patient, or yet another victim. It must be another victim, I surmised, if the paper was leading with the story.

Inside, I saw Jonathan already seated at a corner table, an open menu in front of him. He smiled and waved me over, standing to greet me. My heart did an involuntary flip. He really was beautiful. But, I reminded myself, I was going to mention Peter to him as soon as I found an appropriate opening.

"I'm starved and I'm thinking we should get some appetizers. Any interest in samosas?" Jonathan asked after leaning down to kiss my cheek, which caused the tingling from earlier that afternoon to begin anew.

"A lot of interest. That sounds perfect." A waiter hurried over to pull out my chair, but I was too busy tingling to see him coming and accidentally elbowed him as I was taking off my coat. He accepted my apologies with grace and got me into my seat without further incident.

Jonathan ordered samosas and two Kingfishers and we consulted over the menu. "How do you feel about spice?" I asked, trying neither to tingle nor nurse my elbow in any visible way. It seemed to have connected with a particularly bony part of the waiter.

"The hotter the better."

"Good answer." After some debate, we decided to share a vegetable biryani and a chicken vindaloo billed as "fiery." Jonathan gave the order to our waiter when he returned with our appetizers and drinks.

"I spoke to Clark Gibson this afternoon," Jonathan said, as I cut off a piece of the flaky potato-filled pastry and dipped it into coriander chutney.

"Clark Gibson? Oh, your old roommate."

"He sends his warm regards."

I laughed. "Like he remembers me."

"He remembers you all right. You made quite an impression. He always had a thing for redheads." There was an indefinable gleam in Jonathan's blue eyes as he spoke, and I felt my face turning the same color as my hair, the better to complement my tingling.

"That's embarrassing."

"Trust me. Nothing to be embarrassed about. So, tell me what you've been up to since English 10. You gave me the condensed version over lunch, but I want the details."

We filled each other in on the last decade between sips of beer and bites of vindaloo. I told him about my years at Winslow, Brown, and he told me about his path to professor-hood. I probably shouldn't have been surprised when Jonathan mentioned he was divorced. I knew he'd had a serious girlfriend in college—I'd spent a lot of time resenting her from afar. I even had my own private nickname for her: Perfect Girl. She was a willowy blonde with a sweet smile, and she was head of Phillips Brooks House, the organization that ran all of the community service programs on campus—pretty much the last thing you'd want for the guy you had a crush on.

But while Jonathan and Perfect Girl, whose real name, appropriately enough, was Angela, may have looked perfectly matched to the hopelessly pining freshman observer, the match wasn't made in heaven. They married shortly after they graduated but had divorced a couple of years ago.

"What happened?" I asked, a little too eagerly. Then I apologized. "I'm sorry. That's none of my business."

He shrugged. "No, it's okay. It's hard to explain, really. Ange earned her master's in social work after college, and she got pretty wrapped up in it. She was always off at a homeless shelter, or trying to rehabilitate addicts or get prostitutes off the street. And I was wrapped up in my work, too. We just sort of grew apart. Isn't that what they always say?"

"I think so. But I guess it still happens."

"So we split up. It was fairly amicable. She got the house in Cambridge, and I moved into a condo in Kendall Square."

Our conversation eventually turned to Sara and the police investigation. According to Jonathan, the police still seemed concerned that there was a link between the attack and the prostitute killer.

"He's been awfully busy, then," I pointed out. "I just saw a headline in the evening paper about another murder. Did you find out more about why they think there's a connection? There's a big difference between a student getting hit on the head and prostitutes being strangled."

"I know. I'm hoping to get more detail tomorrow."

"What's going on with the crime rate around here, anyhow?" I asked.

"Boston may not be New York, but it is a big city and it has all of the problems of any big city. There are a lot of lowlifes around getting into all sorts of trouble."

The word *lowlife* made me think of the Creepy Violent Stalker. "What did the police say about the letters she was getting?"

"The love letters? They're looking them over, but they didn't seem too excited."

"Really? They don't think there's a stalker angle to this?"

"I don't know." He shrugged again. "As I said before, the letters looked pretty harmless to me."

"But you never know."

"Of course not," he answered. "Still, there are a lot of other paths to explore."

"Besides the stalker?"

"I don't know if I'd call him a stalker. Probably just an anonymous admirer."

"I hope that's true. So, what's your theory?"

"Well, I don't have one, really, but I've been thinking. Much as Sara keeps a pretty low profile, she's high profile by definition. I mean she's smart, she's beautiful and she's an heiress. I could imagine that a lot of people would be jealous of her."

"What do you mean?" I asked, although his words instantly brought to mind my chat that afternoon with Gabrielle LeFavre.

"I'm not sure if I know. But let's say you're somebody who doesn't have all of the things that Sara has but has worked really hard to get to business school. You'd probably be pretty jealous." Gabrielle sure was, I thought.

"Sara's worked hard," I pointed out. "She definitely pulled more than her fair share of all-nighters when she interned at my firm last summer."

"Sure. And I've seen her in class, and she's always well prepared. But there are still people who would envy who she is and what she has. She's going to be CEO of a major company, sooner rather than later, and while we recognize that the path that's gotten her there hasn't necessarily been the smoothest, some people might not be so sympathetic. And HBS is an incredibly competitive and stressful place—people lose perspective."

Gabrielle definitely appeared to have lost perspective. That that sort of envy could trigger an attack seemed even more far-fetched now that I'd had two beers and a healthy portion of curry in me than it had that afternoon, but it was interesting to hear Jonathan put forth a similar theory. "So, you think Sara could be a symbol of some sort to an unhinged underdog type?"

"I know, it's crazy. But you know what it's like on campus."

"Yes. Especially during Hell Week."

"Anyhow, that's what I've been wondering about. It's probably stupid—I'm a professor, not a detective," he said with a self-deprecating smile. "So, what about you? Do you have any ideas?"

I washed down an especially fiery bite of vindaloo with a sip of beer. "Aside from the letter-writing stalker?"

"I doubt he's a stalker."

"No," I admitted, "I'm fresh out of ideas. Frankly, I'm more worried about Sara's company."

"Grenthaler Media?"

"Yes. There have been some weird things going on with the stock." I gave Jonathan a brief summary of the conversation I'd had with Sara on Wednesday night and the research I'd done that afternoon.

"I don't know what it's all about, and it's probably nothing," I concluded, "but I'm trying to gather some more information."

"I think you should tell the police what you just told me."

"Really? Why?"

"It just seems like a strange confluence of events. Somebody might be trying to take over the company of which Sara is the largest shareholder, and meanwhile she's been assaulted."

"You can't really think the two things are connected?"

"Probably not any more than the attack being connected with the serial killer. But you never know."

I thought about what he'd said. Had I been so busy trying to blame a Creepy Violent Stalker or a Psycho Roommate that I'd missed something important? It seemed to be taking far-fetched to a whole new level, but it couldn't hurt to make sure that the authorities charged with investigating the attack were aware of all the facts. Although, I was still hoping that my fears of a potential takeover attempt were unwarranted. I said as much to Jonathan.

"I'm sure you're right, but the police will probably appreciate being filled in. I'll arrange for you to talk to them tomorrow, if that works for you."

"That's fine," I agreed.

We lingered over dinner. Jonathan asked me a lot about myself, and he listened intently. At some point, his cell phone rang, but rather than taking the call he switched off his phone. I found this sort of undivided attention flattering, particularly when my putative boyfriend's attention had been so thoroughly divided of late. And the flattery had the logical effect of making me feel glowing and attractive, which also went nicely with the tingling. I hadn't realized how in need of an ego boost I was. Still, I resolved, I would tell Jonathan about Peter before the evening was over. I just had to find the right moment.

Jonathan insisted on paying for dinner and driving me back to the hotel. He'd parked on a side street near the restaurant, and he took my arm to help me pick my way through the slush and patches of ice on the sidewalk. He unlocked the passenger-side door of his old Saab, a car I'd always thought personified New England academia. He closed the door after me, and I watched him walk around to the driver's side. In his tweed jacket, with a crimson-and-white striped Harvard scarf wrapped around his neck, he was almost a cliché. But a very attractive one.

He took Mass. Ave. toward Harvard Square, neatly skirting the potholes that pocked the road. We spent the drive lamenting the demise of favorite old haunts. The Bow and Arrow, which had once been a fabulous dive bar complete with outdated pinball machines, was now a restaurant and Tommy's Lunch had metamorphosed into Tommy's House of Pizza. We laughed over the famous rumor about Ted Kennedy running into his professor while having a roast beef sandwich at Elsie's, another long-gone landmark. Unfortunately, Kennedy was supposed to be taking an exam in that professor's course when they ran into each other, and he had found someone to take the exam on his behalf. His professor was not amused. Or so the story went.

Jonathan pulled into the circle in front of the Charles and put the car into park. And I suddenly felt very, very awkward. Peter was probably upstairs, waiting for me, and I'd just had a very nice dinner with another, very handsome man. There was no escaping it. The time had come to tell Jonathan that there was a Peter in the picture. I couldn't wait anymore for just the right moment to assert itself—the evening had all but run out of moments.

I turned to Jonathan to come clean. But before I could get a word out, he'd reached over and rested one hand on the back of my head.

It looked like the last possible moment had arrived.

He hesitated for a second, as if he were trying to make up his mind about something, and I saw an opening.

"Jon—"

But before I could get the words out, he kissed me. On the lips. Or, it would have been on the lips if I hadn't turned my head. Instead, the kiss connected with my left jawbone. Even so, I was so utterly stunned by its impact that I could barely speak. While the earlier kiss on my cheek had resulted in tingling, this kiss had more intent behind it than a friendly greeting. Tingling didn't even begin to describe its effect. I didn't want to imagine what would have happened if the kiss had landed on its original target.

The hotel doorman chose that precise instant to open my door.

"Thank you for dinner," I managed to say.

Jonathan looked mildly surprised, as if he didn't know what to make of my nick-of-time head turn. "I'm glad you could come out tonight," he said. "I had a great time. Talk to you tomorrow?"

"Tomorrow," I replied.

The doorman shut the car door behind me, and Jonathan drove away.

Eleven

I walked into the hotel feeling as if I had a scarlet *A* tattooed on my forehead. I'd just kissed another man.

Well, that wasn't exactly true. I hadn't really participated in the kiss, although it had elevated my low-grade tingling to full-force vibrating. Still, I had been kissed, rather than actively kissing. And I'd managed to keep my lips uninvolved. It was really only a quasikiss. But Jonathan had meant to involve my lips. And if I'd mentioned Peter to Jonathan, I wouldn't have been kissed. So, on some level I was definitely a participant in the kissing.

Semantics will get you every time.

On the way up in the elevator, I wondered what I should say to Peter. This didn't really merit disclosure, did it? And the scarlet *A* wouldn't really show. But how would I feel if I knew he was out being kissed, even only quasikissed, by other women? Particularly during the same twenty-four-hour time frame during which we'd kissed, and done a lot more than kissed, each other.

I'd feel sick, probably. Betrayed and bereft. So I wouldn't want to know, would I? And Peter wouldn't want to know, either. The kiss had been Jonathan's idea, and my reaction had been purely chemical, nothing more. I'd clear things up with Jonathan when I spoke to him tomorrow. In the meantime, there was no reason to upset Peter.

With this twisted reasoning firmly under my belt, I was feeling sleazy but somewhat confident by the time I slipped my keycard into the door. I pushed it open and called out Peter's name.

There was no response. I consulted my watch—it was past ten. In fact, it was closer to eleven. And still no Peter. I took my Blackberry out of my bag, but there were no new voice mails or e-mails. Not a one. The scarlet *A* on my forehead was shining less brightly. Then I noticed that the message light was blinking on the desktop phone. So, Peter *had* called. The blinking light was a visual reproach, and I felt like a slut all over again.

I picked up the receiver and dialed into the hotel's voice mail. The message, however, was not from Peter. It was from Brian Mulcahey, Grenthaler's COO.

Rachel, Brian Mulcahey, here. I'm glad you called—there's something I want to run by you, as well. Give me a call back if you get a chance. Any time before midnight's fine. Thanks, and I'll look forward to hearing from you.

I jotted down the number and deleted the recording. Then I called Brian back, and we agreed to meet for breakfast the next day at the Four Seasons before I went to see the Porters.

I didn't fall asleep until well after two, alternately worrying about potential takeovers, my sluttish behavior and Peter's continued absence. The last worried me the most; what had been a hazy foreboding began crystallizing into dread as the minutes ticked by on the bedside clock. Was Peter dumping me, replacing me with Abigail? What other explanation could there be for staying out so late—with Abigail, no less—and not even calling? How could our relationship have fallen apart so quickly? Had I been too busy congratulating myself on how perfect everything was to recognize the signs of his waning affection? Had my cavalier dismissal of the Jinxing Gods spurred them into action?

I eventually fell asleep from sheer exhaustion, and I didn't even know what time Peter finally came in, but when the phone blared out in the morning with our wake-up call, he was there, snoring heavily.

Which meant he'd been drinking. Peter only snored when he had more than two drinks. He also slept right through the shrill noise of the phone. Another undeniable indicator that he'd been doing some serious imbibing the previous night. But I was just glad he was there. Surely that meant all of my worrying had been groundless?

I poked him and he grunted.

"Wake-up call," I announced cheerily.

He grunted again.

I poked him again.

He flipped over onto his stomach and pulled the duvet over his head.

I poked him through the duvet. "Good morning!"

"Go 'way."

I slipped out of bed and crossed to the windows, opening the drapes with a flourish. Then I returned to the bed and pulled back the duvet. "Rise and shine!"

"Argghh."

"Nice to see you, too, Sparky."

"What time is it?" he mumbled.

"Seven."

"Oh, no." He groaned and struggled to a sitting position. His hair looked like he was auditioning for a Flock of Seagulls tribute band.

"Oh, yes."

He let rip with a colorful string of expletives. "Oh, God. I'm late."

"But your hair looks really good."

"Do you have any Advil?"

"In the bathroom."

He lifted himself heavily from the bed. "Shower."

"Good." I moved to join him, eager to make up for doubting him, not to mention letting myself be quasikissed by Jonathan.

"No, Rachel. Me. Alone. I'm late."

"Oh. Okay. Fine."

The bathroom door shut behind him.

And all of my worries came flooding back.

Twenty minutes later Peter was out the door, already talking on his cell phone. I got a hurried and perfunctory kiss that missed my face completely and landed on my right ear. Jonathan's quasikiss had been nearly pornographic in comparison.

Twenty minutes after that, I was in a cab heading to the Four Seasons. I'd called Cecelia to check in, guilty that I was leaving her stranded again, but she professed to have everything under control. "Will you be all right for interviewers?" I asked.

"Sure. You and Scott are both skipping out, but I've got enough people to get by."

"Scott's not going to be there, either?" I asked, relieved that I wouldn't have to dodge his backhanded attempts to undermine me with Stan.

"No. Something about an 'incredibly' urgent client matter. Anyhow, go to your breakfast. I've got it all covered."

I definitely owed her, and not just flowers and a bottle of wine. A full day at Bliss Spa was in order, and only partly on the firm's tab.

I tried to look at the newspaper as the cab sped toward Back Bay, but reading in cars on an empty stomach made me feel sick, and the news did, too. There was an article on the front page about the prostitute killings—seven in the past six months if you included the two this week, and the seeming escalation in the number of murders was whipping the media into a frenzy. Definitely not the sort of thing to read about in a moving vehicle before I'd had any caffeine.

The cab pulled up in front of the Four Seasons, a modern redbrick edifice facing on the Public Garden. I settled with the driver and went inside, making my way through the lobby to the restaurant, Aujourd'hui. Mulcahey was already seated at a table by the window, a steaming cup of coffee before him.

He stood to greet me, shaking my hand and helping me with my chair. A waiter materialized to take our order, a bagel and orange juice for Mulcahey and an omelet and Diet Coke for me.

To date, I'd had few direct interactions with Mulcahey. As COO, his role was exactly what it sounded to be. He was the guy charged with running Grenthaler's day-to-day business. Most of my work with Grenthaler was either about acquisitions and divestitures or about financial planning—there'd never been much need for the two of us to work together. Still, I knew him by reputation as a good, strong manager. He kept everything running smoothly, and there was a lot to be said for that.

"So, Rachel," he began, running a hand through his close-cropped, curly gray hair before folding his arms in front of him on the table. "I'm glad you could make it this morning."

"I'm glad you could make it, too," I replied. "It sounds like we both have matters to discuss. What's on your mind?"

"Well, as you probably know, I've been acting as interim CEO since Tom passed away."

"Things must be pretty frenetic for you right now."

"It's a big job, and to be frank, I'm not the man for it. I'm happy to be the caretaker until we can find somebody better, but it's really not what I'm all about. I've always been more of a manager than a leader." Brian was in his early sixties, and he'd risen through the company ranks in a slow but steady way over the course of three decades. I admired that he had such a good handle on his own limitations, although I suspected he was underestimating himself. Still, since I was usually surrounded by people who were far more likely to overestimate themselves, his modesty was refreshing.

"What does the board think?" Grenthaler's board of directors would be charged with appointing the next CEO.

"We're having an emergency meeting tomorrow morning to discuss it." I nodded, wondering what was coming next.

"I think we both know who should probably be the next CEO."

"Sara?" I asked.

"Yes. She's still relatively young and inexperienced, but it's what her father wanted and it's what Tom wanted."

"What will the board think?"

"Probably that she's too young and inexperienced. That said, the board is weighted in her favor." Grenthaler's board included Mulcahey, Edward and Helene Porter, Barbara Barnett, and a handful of outsiders who had been handpicked by Samuel Grenthaler and Tom Barnett.

"There's probably a provisional solution," I pointed out. "Sara only has another semester left at school. You could stay on until she graduates, and for a year or two after, until she's really ready to take over."

"That's what I'm thinking. And I believe that most of the board would be amenable to that." He hesitated.

"But?" I prompted.

"There may be a faction on the board that won't be so amenable."

I had a feeling about where he was going. "Barbara Barnett?"

He nodded. "I think she's going to try to get Adam named to the position."

That hadn't occurred to me. I'd been more concerned about Barbara selling her shares than about her trying to get more involved with the company, and to bring Adam with her. I thought for a moment. "Look, Barbara has a significant stake in the company, but it's not much compared to what Sara has. I don't know how much influence she'd really be able to have over the decision."

"It doesn't seem like she could have much. But some of the external board members might be persuaded. Adam knows the company as well as anyone but Sara and me. And he's got a few more years of business experience than she does."

"Not really. He's always been in finance."

"We know it's not the same, but he's pretty impressive on paper."

I didn't say what I was thinking, which was that Adam sure wasn't impressive off paper, but I guessed Mulcahey was thinking the same thing.

Brian interrupted my thoughts. "Either way, Barbara does own ten percent of the company, and she may be able to swing some of the other directors around to her point of view. I'm worried that tomorrow's discussion could get fractious. I was hoping you could come to the meeting and sit in. I know it's a bit unorthodox, but you worked closely with Tom and the board on most of the big decisions we've made in the last few years. It would be great to get your input, not only tomorrow but over the next month or so as we get things sorted out."

"That's fine," I agreed, realizing that yet another opportunity for a leisurely room-service breakfast morning with Peter was going to pass us by. Which was just as well, since he would probably have to rush off to meet Abigail anyhow. At the same time I realized that there was a tiny little part of me that was thinking how convenient it might be to spend more time in Boston. I felt an imaginary pulse on my forehead, as if the scarlet *A* were back.

The waiter arrived with our food. "Now what was it you wanted to discuss?" Brian asked as I cut into my omelet.

"It almost seems less important now that you've told me about Barbara. But have you been following the stock recently?"

"Not really," he admitted. "That's not my area. And I've been so busy with everything else."

"There's been some strange movement. I can't imagine that it's much to worry about given that the majority of the company is privately held. But I'm trying to get in touch with Barbara to discuss what she intends to do with her shares. Yesterday didn't seem like the right time."

"No, probably not. But I'm glad that you've got your eye on it."

"I'm looking into it," I told him. "I'll be sure to keep you posted. And what you've said about Barbara is reassuring. Even if the CEO question ends up being a fight, if she does want Adam to have the job, it sounds like she intends to stay involved and to hold on to her shares."

Brian offered to drop me off on his way back to Grenthaler's headquarters in Kendall Square, but I still had time before meeting with the Porters, so I decided to walk. I could use the fresh air, and probably the exercise, too, although I generally tried to keep my exercise accidental or incidental. The path through the Public Garden looked particularly icy and slushy, so I stuck to the sidewalk on Arlington Street.

I glanced casually across the street as I passed the Ritz on the opposite side. And then I did a double take.

Three men were being ushered into a taxi, and from where I stood I thought I recognized them all.

My eyes were probably playing tricks on me, but the Caped Avenger's wardrobe was pretty distinctive. Not a lot of grown men wearing capes these days.

But what was he doing with Adam Barnett and Scott Epson?

Twelve

Curiosity and disbelief got the better of me, so I darted across Arlington Street, but I lost precious seconds trying to avoid being run over. By the time I reached the Ritz, the men I'd seen were gone, the taillights of their taxi flashing red as it made the turn onto Boylston.

The hundred yards or so I'd walked and then dashed had sated my need for exercise, so I let the doorman at the Ritz hail me a cab, and I gave the driver the Porters' address. I pulled out my Blackberry and called my office on the way. No, my assistant assured me, the Caped Avenger hadn't called. Maybe he was in Boston—it was possible, after all. But with Scott Epson? And Adam Barnett? It couldn't be. That would be just too weird. I really must be in need of glasses. It was simply the power of suggestion—they'd both been on my mind that morning. And dorky white men all tended to look alike, especially from a distance.

Ten minutes later I was climbing up the stone steps to the

front door of the Porters' brick town house in Louisburg Square, one of the more upscale parts of upscale Beacon Hill, a neighborhood that was home to John Kerry, Amos Hofstetter, and a number of characters in Henry James's novels. The walk in front of the house and the steps themselves looked as if they'd not only been swept but polished—the dirty slush and black ice that decorated Boston's streets in January had been exiled from this pristine spot.

I'd scheduled the appointment the previous day, when I was anxious about Barbara's intentions regarding her stock. My conversation with Brian had allayed that anxiety somewhat, but I still wanted to get the Porters' input. Even if Barbara's shares were safe, there was still the concern that an outsider would amass a sufficient stake to become a force to contend with in company matters. I wanted to prepare them for that, and it couldn't hurt to prepare them for Barbara potentially trying to secure the CEO position for her precious Adam, either.

A uniformed maid answered the door and took my coat before ushering me into a well-appointed room facing onto the square. A worn Persian rug in muted shades of blue and gray adorned the floor, and thick velvet drapes framed the oversize windows. The maid went to fetch the Porters, and I wandered over to the fireplace, where a wood fire was laid but not lit. A collection of silver-framed photographs graced the mantel, and I paused to study them. There was a charming picture of the Porters on their wedding day, which must have been at least sixty years ago, and several photos of their daughter, Anna, ranging from baby shots to her college graduation. The black-and-white prints gave way to color when Samuel Grenthaler made his appearance, his arm around Anna, and then there were pictures of Samuel and Anna with their daughter, and more recent ones of Sara alone.

I felt a pang of sympathy for the Porters. Anna had been

their only child, and it must have been devastating for them when she and Samuel died. I imagined them getting the news from the police in Vermont, the unfamiliar voice on the other end telling them about the Grenthalers' car skidding off the icy road. And then having to call and give Sara the news—not something that any grandparent should ever have to do.

I heard footsteps coming down the hallway and turned away from the photos. Helene and Edward Porter entered the room together, she leaning slightly on his arm. They were well into their eighties, but I knew from Grenthaler board meetings that they'd lost none of their mental acuity. Although increasingly frail, Helene's excellent posture and good grooming gave testament to her Brahmin roots. She was neatly dressed in a wool skirt and sweater set with a double rope of pearls at her throat, her white hair pulled back into a discreet chignon. She looked as if she were about to attend a meeting of the Daughters of the American Revolution, and she probably was. Edward had a more robust, almost florid look to him, with a significant paunch that even his well-tailored suit couldn't completely disguise. He'd been a senior partner at one of Boston's most prestigious law firms for decades, and he still maintained an office there. He also had a wide range of strange intellectual interests—I still remembered an oddly fascinating discourse he'd treated me to on mollusk breeding habits at a dinner following a Grenthaler board meeting.

They smiled when they saw me, but they looked tired, and I could tell that they were both tense. I didn't blame them. Sara was all they had left, and I couldn't even begin to imagine how distressing the past twenty-four hours had been for them. But they greeted me warmly, and Helene immediately began fussing over me. She seemed so disappointed when I declined her offer of coffee that I changed my mind. What I really wanted was a Diet Coke, but this definitely didn't seem like an appropriate place or time to ask for one. Helene pulled an old-fashioned tassel on the wall, and in moments the maid reappeared with a silver tray bearing an antique porcelain coffee service.

Edward steered me to an upholstered armchair and settled himself next to his wife on a brocade-covered sofa.

"Thank you for seeing me this morning," I began. "I hope I'm not inconveniencing you."

"Not at all, dear," said Helene. "We're going to the hospital to see Sara this morning, but visiting hours don't officially start until ten. We have plenty of time."

"I'm glad she's all right," I said.

"Yes," agreed Helene. "It's a relief."

"I just hope they find the miscreant who did it to her," said Edward. "I don't know what the world's coming to these days."

"Any news from the police?" I asked, although I'd gotten the update from Jonathan the previous evening.

Edward shrugged. "Not yet. And I'm worried they're not giving it their full attention. There's so much crime nowadays, what with the serial killers and drug dealers and lord only knows what else. I've made a few calls to some old friends, and I'm hoping they'll exert some pressure in the right places." I had every confidence that Edward was sufficiently well connected that no small amount of pressure would be exerted in all of the right places.

"I really wish Sara would stay here with us," said Helene. "It's so much nicer than those nasty dorms, and it wouldn't be hard to get back and forth from campus. I know she has good friends at school—that Edie Michaels is lovely—but I really don't care for some of those other people. You went there, too, didn't you, dear?"

"To the business school? Yes, but I graduated several years ago."

"Well, I must say, it does seem to attract a strange mix. That LeFavre woman, for example. She's a little too tightly wound for my tastes. And so pushy. Why, Sara brought them over for dinner one night, and she was practically shoving her résumé in Edward's face over the soup course."

"It wasn't as bad as that," protested Edward. "I think she was just hoping I might be able to introduce her to some people in the finance community. She seems very eager to get into your field, Rachel."

"I know," I said. "She interviewed with our firm."

"Well, she certainly doesn't have your polish, dear. And who was that boy we met last month, Edward? At that restaurant on Newbury Street?" Helene turned to me. "Edward thinks trying new places keeps us young, so he drags me to these hip places with loud music." The word *hip* sounded comical coming from her lips. "Anyhow, Sara was out on a date with a young man, and there was something strange about him. Very stiff and military." Grant Crocker, I guessed.

"He seemed like a very pleasant chap," Edward said. I loved that he could use the word *chap* without a trace of irony. And I wasn't surprised by his impression of Grant. Men always liked Grant more than women did.

Helene made a face. "Humph."

"What I'm worried about," interjected Edward, "are these letters Sara's been getting."

"You know about the letters?" I asked.

"Edie told us when we were at the hospital yesterday," said Helene. "Edward's very worked up about it."

"I'm not worked up. But our granddaughter was attacked, and meanwhile somebody's been sending her anonymous love letters. It smells fishy to me."

"I seem to remember a certain someone sending *me* love letters at one point in time."

"Yes, but I signed my name," her husband pointed out.

"Nobody who was in love with Sara would try to hurt her," said Helene. She clearly hadn't spent much time watching Lifetime Television for Women. "I can't believe that has anything to do with the attack."

"Well," I said, "I'm just glad that Sara's all right. I'm sure the police will figure it out."

"I certainly hope so," said Edward with a sigh.

"But you haven't come all this way to listen to us squabble," said Helene. "What is it you wanted to discuss, dear? Pass me Rachel's cup, Edward, so I can pour her some more coffee."

"I was talking to Sara on Wednesday night, and she was concerned about some unusual movement in Grenthaler's stock. And apparently Tom was also concerned before his death. I'm looking into it."

"Grenthaler can't be taken over if that's what you're thinking," said Edward. "Somebody would have to buy up all of the stock in the market plus acquire shares from Sara or from Barbara Barnett to get majority control."

"True. But the movement in the stock does suggest that someone's buying, and it would be good to know who and what his intentions are. One of the reasons I'm here is that I wanted to see if you had any sense of what Barbara Barnett might do with her shares."

Helene sniffed. "Who knows what that idiot might do."

"Helene!" said her husband, but he laughed. He clearly shared his wife's opinion.

"Well, she is an idiot, Edward. Miss Texas of all things. I have no idea what Tom saw in her." The way she said "Miss Texas" made Helene's feelings on the subject clear. "And that creepy boy of hers. He gives me the willies."

Edward laughed again. "Adam is a strange one," he acknowledged.

"She's such a stage mother—trying to maneuver that boy

into the spotlight at every opportunity. And talk about pushy!" continued Helene. "That woman! She's always trying to worm her way into things. She came right out and asked me to put her up for the Chilton Club. That's not how these things are done. And she just wouldn't fit in. This isn't New York, you know. All of that plastic surgery and the ridiculous clothes. She's very showy."

"Still," said Edward, "I don't think you have to worry about Barbara needing to sell her shares. She's very well situated. Tom left her quite comfortably off."

"That's good to know," I said. "Although, Brian Mulcahey's concerned, and I am, too, that if Barbara's not selling, she may actually seek to become more involved in the company, which brings with it its own set of problems." I related to them the highlights of my conversation with Mulcahey, which they reacted to with mild alarm, tempered by amusement.

Edward chortled. "Adam? As CEO? I think not!"

"You have no need to worry, dear," said Helene. "Barbara will meet with some stiff opposition if she tries to foist her son upon the company in such a way. Edward and I will be sure of that."

"I'm glad to hear it."

"We know everyone on that board, and they'll listen to reason," added Edward.

"I'm actually supposed to go to the board meeting tomorrow. Brian Mulcahey asked me to sit in."

"Excellent. It will be good to have another voice of reason in the room if Barbara does indeed intend to make such a preposterous proposal."

A grandfather clock wheezed into action from the depths of the house, striking the half hour. Helene jumped up. "I hadn't realized the time. Edward, we should leave now if we want to be at the hospital by ten. You know how hard it is to find parking."

They offered me a ride to Harvard Square, and I accepted it, climbing into the back of their ancient Mercedes sedan. Twenty minutes later I was back at the hotel.

Thirteen

My cell phone rang as I pushed through the revolving door into the hotel lobby. I managed to drop my bag and spill its contents as I was digging for the device, but I caught the call just before it could go into voice mail.

"Rachel Benjamin," I answered, cradling the phone between my ear and shoulder as I knelt to collect the items that had scattered on the rug.

"Rachel. It's Jonathan Beasley."

I'd somehow pushed all thoughts about Jonathan and the quasikiss incident aside for the past two hours, but the warm, deep timbre of his voice made the imaginary scarlet *A* begin pulsing on my forehead all over again. "Hi," I said lamely. The phone promptly slipped off my shoulder and fell to the floor. "Drat." I grabbed the phone back up, trying to politely wave away the bellman who'd come to my aid.

"You still there?" he was asking.

"Yes, sorry about that. Dropped the phone." Just in case

Jonathan hadn't already realized I was a total klutz. I felt my cheeks turning red, the better to match my scarlet *A*.

"Slippery little devils, aren't they."

"Absolutely."

"Anyhow, I wanted to thank you again for dinner last night. I had a great time."

"No, I should be thanking you. It was fun to catch up on the last decade." And sleazy of me to leave out salient facts. Like the one about my boyfriend. Assuming he was still my boyfriend instead of Abigail's.

"We'll have to do it again soon." I was struggling to answer that when he continued, "but I'm actually calling on business."

"Oh?" My refilled bag was back on my shoulder and, with the help of the persistent bellman, I'd returned to a standing position, brushing off the knees of my pantsuit with my free hand.

"I told the police what you told me about Grenthaler Media, and they would like to talk to you."

"Sure. I can't imagine that it will be of much help, but I'm happy to do it."

"Well, between the two of us, I think some pressure's being brought to bear from some important people, and the police want to be able to show they're covering every base." I wondered if the pressure was related to the calls Edward Porter had been making. I had the feeling he knew the home phone numbers of some very important people.

"Whatever I can do."

"They've set up temporary operations in a conference room down the hall from my office. Could you come by this afternoon?"

I did some mental calculations. "I think so. Maybe a little after four?" The interviewing was scheduled to finish at one, followed by a final roundup session. With any luck, we'd be done by three. I could run up to UHS to see Sara and then head over to the business school. If all went well, I'd be back in plenty of time to clean up e-mail and voice mails before the cocktail party Winslow, Brown was hosting that evening.

"That should be fine. I'll see you then."

I got to the elevator without dropping anything else and even pushed the correct button for where I was going. I reached the Winslow, Brown suite just in time for Cecelia to pair me up with another banker and send me off to actually do some interviews. I was glad to squeeze a few in— at least I wasn't completely neglecting my job.

We wrapped up the last set of interviews nearly on schedule, and my colleagues and I gathered in the suite for a buffet lunch and to complete the list of candidates to be asked to New York for the final round. The meeting went smoothly enough, probably because everybody was so impatient to be finished that they'd lost their appetite for debate. Scott Epson was unusually well-behaved, for once. Rather than nitpicking obscure line items on students' résumés, he was silent for the most part and even excused himself a couple of times to take calls that seemed to be genuinely important. I wanted to ask him if he'd been at the Ritz that morning, but I couldn't figure out how to do it without betraying that I'd been playing hooky from recruiting. Nor did I trust my eyesight sufficiently to think it really had been him with the Caped Avenger.

We finished before three, and Cecelia reminded us that we were expected to stick around for the cocktail party that evening. She met the chorus of groans with assurances that she'd have them all on the eight o'clock shuttle back to New York with plenty of time to spare. I thanked her yet again and hurried off to UHS, making a quick stop at a florist to pick up some flowers.

Sara looked much better this afternoon than she had the previous day. Her head was still wrapped up in white bandages, and there was a tube dripping clear liquid into her arm, but she was sitting up in bed and some color had returned to her face. Her friend Edie Michaels was with her, and they were in animated discussion when I arrived. Sara thanked me effusively for the flowers, which really didn't merit such gratitude, especially when a quick glance around the room showed me that she was already well stocked on the floral front.

"I'm sorry," I apologized. "I should have brought magazines or something."

"No, these are beautiful," she assured me as I settled into one of the guest chairs. "Besides, I have plenty of reading material. Edie brought me all of my class work for next week." She gestured to a pile on the bedside table and grimaced.

"Hey, you asked me to," protested Edie. She turned to me. "I told her that if there was ever an excuse to be unprepared for class, she had it, but she wouldn't listen. She's such a workaholic. It makes everyone else look bad."

I laughed, but the word *workaholic* reminded me of something. "Have either of you spoken to Gabrielle?"

Sara shook her head.

"Not since yesterday morning," said Edie. "I got her on her cell and told her what had happened to Sara. But we haven't heard from her since. We're not sure where she is. There's been no sign of her in the dorm. I don't think she came back last night."

"Really? I saw her yesterday afternoon." I explained about Gabrielle's visit to the recruiting suite the previous day, leaving out the details of our conversation.

"It's weird," said Sara. "I mean, for Gabrielle of all people, who's so gung ho on the recruiting thing, to just disappear during the middle of Hell Week."

"She's been so stressed-out," added Edie. "I'm hoping she didn't just completely lose it."

"Is she really that tightly wound?" I asked. That had been my impression, but Sara and Edie lived with her, and they knew her better.

Sara and Edie looked at each other for a moment. "She's fairly—" began Sara diplomatically.

"Neurotic," interjected Edie. "I mean, you went to HBS, Rachel. You know the type. She studies maniacally, networks frantically, and she's jealous of anyone who seems to be doing well. As if other people's successes detract from hers. She's just completely out for herself. Frankly, I'm sort of pissed that she hasn't at least called, much less come to see Sara. Although, she's so competitive with Sara that she probably wouldn't be much of a help right now. Sometimes I wonder if maybe she's a little unstable."

"She means well," said Sara. "She's just had a rough time of it." Edie shrugged in response.

Judging from their comments, neither of them were overly fond of their roommate, but neither seemed suspicious of her, either. I was probably overreacting. I'd seen Gabrielle at a particularly bad moment. But Gabrielle knew Sara's schedule. She had the opportunity. And yesterday, when I'd come into the room and Gabrielle had her back to me, I almost thought she was a man at first. The homeless man who'd witnessed the attack could have thought the same thing. And there'd been a hood on her long dark coat.

No, I was being stupid. There'd been plenty of high-strung, intensely competitive women in my business school class, but I was hard-pressed to imagine any of them actually physically attacking anyone else. Dreaming about it, yes. But actually doing it?

Edie interrupted my train of thought, looking at her watch

and jumping up. "I need to go," she said. "I've got a team meeting to get to." She turned to me. "Did they make you do all of these annoying group projects when you were in business school?"

I smiled. "You mean the ones that are supposed to teach teamwork?"

"Uh-huh. They're a total drag, and everyone always thinks he could do a better job on his own. Too many Type A personalities in one room."

"I hate to break it to you, but it's not that much better in the corporate world."

"That's depressing. Listen, Sara, I'll stop by later, okay?"

"There's no need, really," protested Sara. "You've done enough already."

"I'll come by, anyhow. I'll pick up some food and we can have a picnic dinner?"

"Well, I wouldn't object to Pinnochio's," suggested Sara hopefully, referring to the small storefront a couple of blocks from UHS that was widely considered to make the best pizza in the Square.

"They haven't turned it into a Starbucks yet?" I asked.

Edie laughed. "No, but I'm sure it's only a matter of time." She gathered up her coat and bag, gave Sara a hug and was out the door.

When I turned back to Sara, she was looking at me intently. "My grandparents told me about their conversation with you. Do you think Barbara's really going to try to get Adam named CEO?"

"I hope not. Although, it would be good news in a way. If Barbara's intent on getting Adam more involved with the company, she's unlikely to sell her shares. But it does look like tomorrow morning's board meeting is going to be a bit of a battle."

Sara laughed. "I know. My grandparents are already gear-ing up for combat. I think they're looking forward to it. Especially Gran."

Combat with Helene Porter was not something I'd want to face. Mrs. Porter may have had the entire frail, ladylike image down pat, but our conversation that morning had made it clear that you wouldn't want to get on her bad side.

"There might be some debate, but Barbara doesn't own enough stock to wield as much power as it would take to get Adam appointed CEO. I don't think you have anything to worry about on that front."

"Were you able to find out anything about the movements in the stock price?"

"Are you sure you want to be worrying about any of this right now?"

"Well, it's either worrying about this or worrying about why somebody wanted to hit me over the head with an oar."

"Not much of a choice, is it?"

She smiled, but the smile didn't reach her eyes.

"I looked into it," I said, giving her a quick debrief on the research I'd done the previous afternoon but leaving out my visit to the Yahoo! message board. "There are definitely signs that somebody's been buying up stock. Nobody's reached the five-percent mark as yet, or he would have had to file a statement with the Securities and Exchange Commission. I put in a request to get the names of the institutions and individuals who have been buying and selling. I should have it by the end of the day or first thing Monday."

"Good."

"And, as you well know, it would be hard for anybody to launch a real takeover without some assurance that they could obtain stock from you or Barbara. And we'll figure out if any outsiders are accumulating stock and what their intentions are."

"I'm looking forward to getting this resolved. I just wish

I could be at the board meeting tomorrow. The doctors are being ridiculous about my staying here."

"I'm sure they would rather be safe than sorry. You should relax. Rest. Focus on getting better."

"Right, like I can do that with everything that's going on," she replied, with a rare show of sarcasm that I interpreted as a sign of returning strength.

I sighed. "Give it a try. I'm keeping an eye on things, and so are your grandparents and Brian Mulcahey. We'll figure it out." I hoped I sounded more confident than I felt.

She was quiet for a moment. Then she turned to me, a gleam in her eye, and changed the subject. "Tell me about dinner with Professor Beasley. He's pretty cute, isn't he?"

"What?" I felt my cheeks burst into flames. I wondered if blushing burned calories. At the rate I was going, I'd be down a dress size in no time.

"I've had a lot of phone calls today. One was from Professor Beasley, and he told me he had dinner with you last night."

"Oh?" I said, trying to keep my voice neutral. The way my cheeks felt, the chances of pulling off a poker face were remote.

"I didn't realize you two knew each other from college."

"Neither did I," I admitted. "Not until I ran into him. When Edie sent me off to see Professor Beasley, he wasn't what I expected to find."

Sara smiled. "You were probably imagining the old guy from *The Paper Chase*."

"Wouldn't you? With a name like Professor Beasley?"

"Half the women on campus have a crush on him."

"That's not hard to imagine. They did in college, too."

"He seemed very curious about you."

"Really?" I asked before I could think better of it.

She nodded her confirmation. "Don't worry. I sang your praises."

I hesitated. "Did you mention anything about—"

"Your boyfriend? No. It didn't really seem like any of my business. However, if things with Peter go belly-up, I think you have someone else waiting in line."

"Good to know," I said, feeling flattered, skanky and anxious all at once. Sara couldn't be aware just how precarious things with Peter seemed to be right now. Belly-up was hardly out of the question.

Fourteen

Just as I was saying goodbye, Barbara Barnett breezed into Sara's hospital room. Her presence was like a splash of ice water—I felt the flush still in my cheeks subside immediately.

"Hello, hello!" she announced herself, with no small measure of theatricality. She was wearing what looked to be a mink coat and carrying a huge bouquet of hothouse flowers. The clutch of tulips I'd brought seemed to wilt in comparison.

Barbara leaned over and gave Sara a kiss on the cheek. "Sara, honey. I can't tell you how horrified I was to hear that you'd been hurt. How are you feeling?" The words came out at a rapid clip, but they were smoothed together by her Texas drawl.

"Much better," answered Sara, thanking her for the flowers. Barbara rushed about the room, moving a smaller vase aside to make space for her own bouquet on Sara's bedside table.

"Hello, Mrs. Barnett," I said, standing and holding out my hand. "I'm Rachel Benjamin, from Winslow, Brown. I think we've met before, at Grenthaler board meetings, and Tom brought me to dinner a couple of times afterward."

She flashed me her pageant-trained smile. "Of course. It's nice to see you again." She listened politely as I extended my condolences about Tom. "Why, thank you, honey. That's awfully sweet of you. But right now I'm just worried about Sara."

"There's nothing to worry about," Sara assured her. "I'm fine. Just a couple of stitches and a bit of a headache. It's not a big deal."

Barbara unbuttoned her coat, revealing a magenta suit that looked like it had been stolen from the wardrobe racks on the *Dynasty* set, and sat herself down in the guest chair that Edie had vacated. "Now where is that son of mine?" she asked. "He was finishing up a phone call, but he said he'd be right in."

"It's so nice of you to come by," Sara said. "I know this can't be an easy time for you."

"Don't be silly," replied Barbara. She turned to me. "This girl's like a daughter to me, Ms. Benjamin. Her daddy and my late husband were like this—" She held up two adjoining fingers to demonstrate just how close Tom and Samuel Grenthaler had been. "When her parents died, Tom and I felt an obligation to take care of their little girl. We were supposed to go with them that weekend to Vermont, you know. To the ski house. But my son came down with a touch of the flu and we had to cancel." It seemed like overkill that Tom and Barbara Barnett would cancel their weekend plans because Adam, who must have been well into his twenties at the time, had a tummy ache, but I guessed it was fortunate for their sakes that they had. She turned her attention back to Sara. "Now, have they found the person who did this to you? I really can't even begin to tell you how upset I am."

"No," said Sara. "But they're looking into it."

"I spoke to your grandparents, and they told me about

those nasty letters you've been getting. The authorities do know about them, don't they?" Barbara adjusted her skirt and reached up to smooth her already smooth, if big, blond coif.

"They do," Sara confirmed.

"Well, I sure can tell you, I've seen enough of those movies on Lifetime Television about stalkers gone mad. I hope they're taking these letters seriously." I was somewhat disheartened to learn that the only other person I'd encountered who'd been watching Lifetime Television for Women was Barbara Barnett.

"I'm sure they are."

"And what about this homeless man who says he saw everything? Are they sure he's telling the truth?"

"I know the guy," said Sara. "George wouldn't hurt a fly. He might talk it to death, but he wouldn't hurt it."

There was a muted commotion in the hallway outside the open door, and a moment later Adam Barnett came in. He was well over six feet, but I doubted he weighed much more than I did. With his beaky nose and mousy features, he looked like central casting's idea of Ichabod Crane. He was holding a cell phone in his hand, and we could hear a nurse's chastising words trailing after him. "No cell phones in the hospital. It's clearly posted. I don't want to have to tell you again."

Adam looked vaguely sheepish, or maybe that was just how he usually looked. He said a stiff hello to Sara and inquired after her health. I reintroduced myself to him and was rewarded with a blank look and a shake of his distastefully clammy palm. I wished again that I'd gotten more than a fleeting glimpse of the Caped Avenger's companions that morning, but from where I'd stood they could have been anyone. Besides, how would Adam and the Caped Avenger even know each other? He perched awkwardly on the windowsill next to his mother's chair, his hands shoved into his coat pockets.

"We were just talking about who could be responsible for this terrible attack," Barbara told him. "I think Sara's being stalked."

"Stalked?" asked Adam.

"Yes. Stalked. Some creep has been sending her anonymous letters. Honey, we need to do something about the security, here. Why, practically anyone can walk right in."

"As long as they're not using a cell phone," said Sara, catching my eye and clearly trying not to smile.

"Adam and his cell phone. It's work, work, work all the time for my boy," Barbara told me proudly. Now Sara rolled her eyes.

"We'll look into the security situation," Barbara continued. "Maybe we can arrange for a guard of some sort. I'll talk to your grandparents about it."

"Really, that's not necessary," protested Sara.

"You're right, honey. There's no need to worry your grandparents—they're already worried enough. Adam and I will take care of everything."

Barbara then launched into a long story about a TV movie she'd seen about a stalker. I quickly realized I'd seen the same movie and felt my eyes begin to glaze over. I wanted to excuse myself, but it occurred to me that if I waited her out, I might be able to get her alone and ask about her shares. I stole a glance at Adam as his mother rambled on, and he was staring fixedly at Sara. Probably still harboring a torch, or whatever guys like him did when they were suffering from unrequited passion.

Barbara finally wrapped up her spiel just as a nurse came in, insisting that it was time for Sara's medicine. Sara looked relieved. The color had receded somewhat from her face, and I had a feeling she could use a painkiller and a nap.

Barbara checked her watch. "Oh, my! I hadn't realized the hour. We really must get going." She said her goodbyes, but not before extracting Sara's promise that she would call if there was anything she needed. "And we'll see about the security. You have nothing to worry about, honey."

I said goodbye, too, telling Sara I'd check in later, and rode down to the ground floor with Barbara and Adam. "Adam, honey, will you get the car from the garage? It's so nasty out." Given that an extended family of fur-covered creatures had given their lives to ensure Barbara's warmth, her request seemed unnecessary, but Adam agreed dutifully, which was fine with me, as I now had my hoped-for moment alone with the chattering widow.

As gracefully as I could under the circumstances, I changed the topic from stalkers to stock by mentioning that I'd be at the Grenthaler board meeting the next day and asking if Barbara would be there, as well.

"Why, of course, honey. I do own ten percent of the company, now. I could hardly miss a board meeting. Now where did I put my gloves? I hope I didn't leave them upstairs. I'll have to go back and fetch them." She opened her handbag and began rummaging through its contents.

"I'm glad that you want to stay involved," I said.

"I sure do." She paused in her search for her gloves, meeting my gaze. "Grenthaler meant a lot to my husband, and my husband meant the world to me. The stock I inherited will keep his memory alive. For me and for my son."

"So, you intend to hold on to your shares?"

"More than hold on to them, honey. Those shares represent a family legacy, one that must live on."

I interpreted that as an indication that she wasn't interested in selling anytime soon, mitigating the threat of a full-fledged takeover. However, reading between the lines, it seemed like Brian Mulcahey's concerns about Barbara trying to secure her son the CEO slot were right on the money.

* ★ ★

I called Sara's room on the walk to the business school campus and reported what I'd learned. She sounded drowsy, and I had the feeling I'd awakened her, but I knew she would be reassured by my news.

After we hung up, I checked my Blackberry for messages. Again, there was nothing. Not a single voice or e-mail, and definitely nothing from Peter. I debated for a moment before dialing his number, but it went straight into voice mail anyway. I left a halfhearted reminder about dinner that night. Bitterly, I wondered what excuse he would make for canceling this time.

Then I called Jane's house. I needed to talk to someone about last night's quasikiss, the tenuous state of my union with Peter and my current emotional turmoil. Luisa answered the phone.

"Where is everyone?" I asked.

"Hilary's out doing more research, and Jane and Emma are grocery shopping."

"You didn't want to go with them?"

She laughed. "I'm probably the only person who'd be less helpful than you on that sort of outing."

"Thanks. I guess. So, Jonathan Beasley kissed me last night."

"*Love Story* guy?" she asked incredulously.

"Yes. We had dinner. And he kissed me. Well, he quasi-kissed me. He was aiming for my lips but I turned my head."

"Did you kiss him back?"

"No, of course not. I mean, I have a boyfriend, at least in theory. I totally spazzed."

"I'm confused. Where was Peter? Weren't you supposed to have dinner with Peter?"

"Yes. But he canceled. He didn't even call. He just sent an e-mail. And he was out half the night. With Abigail, I'm sure.

I think he's dumping me," I confided. This was the first time I'd said the words aloud, and they left an acrid taste on my tongue.

"What time are you getting here?" she asked. "We need to talk about this."

"By seven, I hope."

"Good." I was nearly at the door to Morgan Hall. "I've got to go, but I'll see you in a few hours. Oh—I nearly forgot to ask. How was your trip to Newbury Street yesterday? Any good purchases?"

Luisa hesitated on the other end of the phone. "It was all right. I'll tell you about it later."

I made my way up to Jonathan's office. His door was open, and he was seated behind his desk. I knocked on the doorframe, and he looked up and gave me a big smile. My heart did a traitorous flip-flop and the now-familiar tingling began afresh. He really was just absurdly cute.

"Hi," I said. "I'm here for my police interrogation."

"Great," he said. He stood up and helped me off with my coat. "They're finishing up with somebody else right now. I've got them parked in a conference room down the hall. It should only be a couple of minutes."

"Any news?"

"Well, I've found out why they think that there might be a link with the prostitute killer."

"What's that?"

"You're not going to believe this. Apparently they think that the guy who's been doing the murders has been using a scarf to strangle his victims."

"A scarf?"

"Not just any scarf." He closed his office door to hang my coat up next to his and gestured to the scarf that hung on one of the pegs. "This scarf."

"I don't get it. They think the killer's been using your scarf?"

He laughed. "Well, maybe not this one. But a Harvard scarf." I looked at the crimson-and-white-striped object in question. "And the witness to the attack on Sara said the guy was wearing one, too."

"But those are everywhere." Just in the past twenty-four hours I must have seen more than a dozen people wearing them. Jonathan himself, Gabrielle LeFavre, the annoying guy who tried to psyche me out in the elevator the previous day, Scott Epson, Grant Crocker—why even Adam Barnett had been wearing one, and he'd gone to M.I.T. Personally, I'd never understood the appeal of decking oneself out in Harvard paraphernalia, but I seemed to be in the minority on that topic.

Jonathan shrugged. "I don't disagree. But they seem to think that it might be too much of a coincidence that they have a strangler using one to strangle people while somebody's attacking a student wearing another."

"That sounds like a flimsy link to me," I said.

"I know. But they're also desperate to catch this sociopath who's been on a killing spree, and they're following up on any lead, no matter how tenuous. I'm just worried that it will take them off on the wrong tangent, and they won't catch the guy who attacked Sara. I mean, I want them to catch them both, but it seems like they're jumping to conclusions to think it's the same person."

"It seems that way," I agreed.

But I was getting distracted. We were still by the closed door, looking at the scarf hanging from its hook. And Jonathan was standing pretty close. He took a deep breath, and the way he paused reminded me of the way he'd paused the previous night. As if he were making up his mind about something. The last time he'd made a similar decision, it had been to try to kiss me. And I wasn't all that confident that I didn't want him to try again.

So I did what any normal person would do, and started talking about the weather. "Is there really supposed to be a blizzard this week—"

But it was hard to keep talking when his lips were descending toward mine.

Fifteen

Fortunately, or unfortunately, depending on one's perspective, there was a knock at the door. We sprang apart in an unconscious parody of guilty lovers caught in the act, even though there had been no act, and Jonathan opened the door. It was his assistant, letting him know that the police were ready to speak to Ms. Benjamin. I followed her down the corridor on slightly unsteady legs. I could feel Jonathan's eyes on my back, and I willed myself—successfully, for once—not to trip.

I was ushered into a small conference room with windows looking out on Baker Library. Two plain-clothed detectives stood to greet me. One introduced himself as Officer Stanley, a rather nondescript man in his twenties who seemed to be the more junior of the pair. The other was Detective O'Connell.

I did a double take when I saw him. It wasn't just the name, which was nearly identical to that of a certain Detective

O'Donnell I'd met the last time I'd had a police interview, when I'd had the good luck to find the murdered body of Emma's former fiancé. It was more that Detective O'Connell could have been Detective O'Donnell's twin. Six foot plus, thick dark hair with a smattering of gray-blue eyes that pierced, and chiseled features. He looked more like a GQ model than a police officer, despite the suit that was definitely not Zegna. Hilary had done her admirable best to make a play for O'Donnell, but he'd been immune to her considerable charms. I immediately started trying to figure out how I could arrange for her to meet O'Connell, happily noting the absence of a wedding ring on his finger. It would be a welcome distraction from trying to sort out my own love life.

They offered me a chair at the conference table, and when we were all seated they went through the formalities with which I'd familiarized myself during my last police interview. Actually, O'Connell went through the formalities. Officer Stanley didn't say a word after introducing himself but silently took notes as I told them my name, address and sundry other background details. Then I explained to them how I knew Sara.

"As you know," began O'Connell, "we're investigating the attack on Ms. Grenthaler yesterday morning, and Professor Beasley mentioned that you had dinner with her the night before."

"Yes. Sara and I are friends, but there was also some company business that she wanted to discuss." I briefly set out her concern about the movements in Grenthaler's stock price, and I also filled them in on what I'd learned yesterday. "If anything did happen to Sara, her grandparents would inherit her shares, and a takeover would require that either they or the Barnetts were willing to sell. Or, more accurately, Barbara Barnett. Tom Barnett passed away last week. To—" I hesitated, unsure how to word what I was going to say. "To incapacitate Sara wouldn't really accomplish much. So, I really doubt that there's a connection. Still, Jonath—Professor Beasley thought you should know."

"We appreciate that," said O'Connell, but he seemed vaguely disappointed. It occurred to me that Jonathan may have set his expectations for the importance of what I had to say a little high. "Can I ask you to keep us in the loop should there be any changes in the situation?" He passed me his card. I had the sense that he did so more out of habit than because he was interested.

"Sure," I agreed, tucking it into my shoulder bag. They seemed ready to conclude the interview, but I was too curious not to use this opportunity to find out what little I could. "Professor Beasley said that you thought there might be a tie between the attack on Sara and the person who's been murdering prostitutes."

"We're looking into it," acknowledged O'Connell. "We have reason to believe that the killer might be part of the Harvard community in some way. And the witness to the attack on Ms. Grenthaler said that her attacker had been wearing a Harvard scarf."

"But a million people must have those scarves," I pointed out, just as I had pointed out to Jonathan a half hour ago.

"True, but we don't have a lot to go on, either in the killings or in the attack on Ms. Grenthaler." He maintained the same courteous tone but his face betrayed a hint of either impatience or frustration.

"Have you found out anything about the person who's been writing the letters to Sara?"

He shook his head. "We're having the letters analyzed by a profiler. Taken at face value, they don't seem to be threatening, but given what's happened, they can't be ignored, either. Anyhow, thank you for your time. We appreciate your coming by today, and please call us if anything else comes to mind."

Now he definitely looked impatient. I'd been dismissed, professionally and politely, but dismissed nonetheless. I wasn't thinking quickly enough on my feet; the interview had concluded without me finding a way to introduce O'Connell to Hilary. If anything, I might have even annoyed him. And the only reason I had to call him was if something untoward happened with Grenthaler Media, which was the last thing I wanted.

I sighed as I left the conference room. I was the first person to recognize that the only reason I was thinking about Hilary's love life right now was to try to distract myself from the unpleasant fact that I'd come dangerously close to crossing the thin line between harmless flirtation and cheating. Although, did it count as cheating when you suspected you were being broken up with but just hadn't yet endured the actual break-up discussion? Regardless, I had to say something to Jonathan before things went any further.

Part of me was hoping to depart without seeing Jonathan again, to avoid having to come clean, at least for a while. But the eighteen-year-old part of me was rearing for another encounter. And that part won out, because I'd left my coat in his office. Either way, Jonathan seemed to have been waiting for me to emerge from my meeting with the police, because he rose to his feet as soon as I entered the room.

"Hey. How did it go?"

"Fine," I said. "But it's still hard to believe that there might be any relationship between what's going on at Grenthaler Media and this whole thing. They didn't seem to think so, either."

"Where are you off to now?" he asked.

"Back to the Charles. My firm's hosting a cocktail party for the candidates we're asking down to New York."

"I'll walk you over there," he volunteered. "I have a couple of errands to do in the Square. And I was going to stop by UHS to see Sara."

Inside my head, eighteen-year-old Rachel jumped up and down, while the more mature Rachel tried to figure out how she was going to set the record straight with Jonathan before she descended yet further into a quasiadulterous quagmire.

"Great," I said. It was unclear which Rachel was currently speaking for me.

He helped me into my coat and donned his own. I noticed that his shirt cuff was monogrammed—JEB. If we got married, I thought, and I changed my name, I wouldn't have to change any of my own monograms. Not that I'd ever been much of a monogrammer, per se. And Rachel Beasley sounded silly. Perhaps I could hyphenate? But Rachel Benjamin-Beasley sounded even sillier. I kept my mind focused on such thoughts, in order not to think about how nice and broad Jonathan's shoulders were under his coat, and how his lips might have felt if they'd actually connected with mine, and how I was going to use the ten-minute walk to the hotel to let him know about my phantom boyfriend.

The phone rang just as we were leaving Jonathan's office, and he apologized but excused himself to pick it up. I used the time to extract my Blackberry from my bag and check again for messages. With a mixture of relief and foreboding, I saw that there was an e-mail from Peter, which I took as an omen. He was making his presence felt, and there was no moral way I couldn't tell Jonathan about his presence.

But when I opened his message my resolve disappeared.

You're going to kill me, but we're still trying to get this client signed up. Abigail thinks we're going to need to do some serious wining and dining if we're going to ward off Smitty Hamilton, and I have to agree. It looks like I'm going to miss the big dinner at Jane's. I'll try to get there after we're done if it's not too late. I'll make it up to you—I promise!! PF

Humph. Not even a "love" or an "XO" at the end. And once again, he'd chickened out, choosing e-mail rather than a phone call. And could he really need to be spending so much time signing up this client? That's what he said he'd been doing the previous night, and if the snoring were any indication, he'd put in a pretty serious effort.

Maybe, said the mean little voice (which I was beginning to think might be in cahoots with my eighteen-year-old voice), he just wants to spend more time with Abigail. Maybe this client stuff is all about trying to let you down easy. Maybe he's doing the wussy-boy thing, by being so unavailable and busy that you're left with no choice but to break up with him simply out of pride. Leaving him free to do what he really wants. Leaving him free to be with Abigail.

I tried to silence the mean little voice, but it was hard, especially when Jonathan hung up the phone and gave me the sort of smile that was guaranteed to quiet all of the various insecurities the mean little voice seemed to represent. As if I were the most beautiful, fascinating creature he'd ever met. And as if he would never toss me over to spend time with the gazellelike Abigail.

"Sorry about that. Ready to go?"

"Sure."

Jonathan chatted on about the police investigation as the elevator descended to the ground floor. Outside of Morgan Hall, the late-afternoon air felt like it came directly from the North Pole. A scattering of lazy snowflakes drifted down, but the sky above was dark with the threat of more. A gust of wind hit us as we reached the river, nearly knocking me off my feet. Jonathan put his hand on my shoulder to steady me, and he kept it there as we crossed over the bridge.

Now, I thought, as we crossed the intersection at Memorial Drive. Now's the time to tell him. But Jonathan was telling a story about something that had happened in class that day, and it seemed rude to interrupt.

Now, I thought again, as we turned off JFK Street onto Eliot Street, and I could see the outline of the hotel ahead of us. But I was in the middle of a story about something similar that had happened to me when I was a student.

The next thing I knew, we had arrived at the small plaza in front of the side entrance to the hotel and I was feeling a level of awkwardness that eclipsed any sense of awkwardness I'd experienced previously. Which was a pretty high bar.

"So, here we are," I announced, still trying to figure out how I could casually mention Peter.

"Yes. Here we are," Jonathan agreed, shifting from one foot to the other.

"Listen, Jonathan—" I began, but he started speaking at the same time.

"So, I know it's another last-minute invitation, but any chance of dinner after your cocktail thing?"

"I can't," I explained, and what was left of my character was glad to be able to demur. I'd told him about my roommate reunion at dinner the previous night. "We have the kickoff to our reunion tonight."

"That sounds like fun," he said.

"It will be," I answered. I was looking forward to my friends' help in sorting out what had happened to my relationship with Peter and hearing what they thought I should do about Jonathan. Although, I wasn't sure I was going to be happy with what they told me.

I could have invited him to join us. Significant others were included in the reunion. But technically, I already had one S.O. And having Jonathan at dinner would make a discussion of my current S.O. issues impossible.

I knew I had to tell Jonathan about Peter. And I knew I should do it before things got any more tangled. I took a deep breath and was about to open my mouth to spill it.

But this time it wasn't Jonathan's lips that interrupted. It was an all too familiar nasal voice.

"Hi, Rach!" Scott Epson seemed to have materialized out of nowhere. "Ready for the big Winslow, Brown shindig?"

I'd never thought I'd be so happy to see Scott. I introduced him to Jonathan, and we engaged in some meaningless conversation as a threesome. Not only would I not be able to have a discussion with Jonathan about Peter, there was no chance that Jonathan would try to kiss me again, here, in front of my colleague, thus adding to my list of transgressions.

From somewhere the bells of a clock rang out, indicating that it was half past five. I told Jonathan I'd talk to him soon, gave him a quick peck on the cheek and followed Scott through the revolving doors into the hotel.

Sixteen

The party was due to start at six, so I dashed up to my room to change and get organized. The event called for business casual, rather than straight-out business attire, and with relief I exchanged my pantsuit for a less formal pair of trousers and a cashmere sweater, and my high heels for a pair of suede flats. I was in front of the mirror, making the usual vain attempt to tame my unruly hair, when I heard the hotel phone ringing.

I was hoping it was Peter, but it was Emma, which was just as well. "I tried you on your cell phone but it wouldn't go through," she said. "Luisa's been filling us in on everything that's been going on with your client and with Peter and with *Love Story* guy. It sounds like you have a lot to tell us."

"Yes," I admitted. "I think I'm becoming a skank."

"I doubt that."

"Don't be so sure."

"Well, we're all looking forward to talking it over. Everyone's here at Jane's, and we're already cooking. Will you be here soon?"

"I need to put in an hour at this Winslow, Brown event, but I hope to get there a little after seven."

"With Peter?"

"Peter who?" I asked, striving for a lighthearted tone.

"Peter 'Too Good to Be True' Forrest."

"No," I said, and sighed. "I'm beginning to think he is too good to be true. He's with Abigail, wooing a potential client. Or," I added dejectedly, "just wooing her."

"That seems unlikely."

"Who knows? He's been completely missing in action."

"I'm sure everything's fine. He's Peter, after all. Of course, you could always bring *Love Story* guy instead." Her voice had a teasing edge to it.

"Listen, no jokes about this. At least not yet. I actually thought about inviting him, but it just seemed like I'd be tangling the web even more. But I do have some good news. For Hilary, at least."

"Oh?"

"Remember our friend Detective O'Donnell?"

"Sure. The one Hilary tried to make a play for last summer."

"Well, his identical twin is alive and well and investigating the attack on Sara Grenthaler."

"You're kidding."

"Nope. And guess what his name is."

"What?"

"O'Connell."

Emma giggled. "I'll tell Hil. We'll have to figure out a reason to get her hauled down to the police station this weekend."

"Knowing Hilary, that shouldn't be too hard to pull off."

★ ★ ★

I was nearly out the door, some semblance of order restored to my hair, which hadn't been responding well to the various gusts of wind and snowflakes it had endured that day, when I noticed a pile of papers sitting on the fax machine's output tray. I grabbed them up and switched on the desk lamp.

Jessica had forwarded me the list of buyers and sellers in Grenthaler's stock. I scanned the list to see if I recognized any names. As far as I could tell, they seemed to be the usual collection of financial institutions and money management firms, but a few unfamiliar companies had popped up on the buy side several times over the past few weeks.

I checked the time. I still had a couple of minutes before I became officially late. I used my Blackberry to submit a request to Winslow, Brown's Research Services office, asking for profiles of the companies that seemed to be steadily buying. It would be good to know who was behind them.

The party was taking place at Noir, the lounge bar in the lobby of the Charles. The décor was strangely incongruous with the rest of the hotel: dark and minimalist, with odd red phallic-shaped lamps hanging over the bar. The decidedly un-hip garb of the aspiring Wall Streeters we'd invited was similarly incongruous. By a few minutes after six, the room was packed. Clearly, the various students who'd been invited hoped that their punctuality would be interpreted as a sign of their commitment to a career in investment banking.

I accepted a glass of white wine from a passing waiter, and dutifully began chatting to our guests. My objective was simple: to give everyone I spoke to the impression that Winslow, Brown was a wonderful place. At this stage of the recruiting process, we started shifting into "sell" mode, recognizing that a significant proportion of the students who were here tonight would receive offers not only from Winslow, Brown but from other firms with equally impressive reputations. I fielded questions about the work, the culture and the lifestyle one could expect at the firm as honestly but positively as I could. Of course, most of the students were still in interview mode, and many of their questions were thinly veiled attempts at schmoozing, something I've never had much of a stomach for. And none of them asked about the real reason they were interested in banking—the money. For some reason, talking about money as a motivation was a no-no, at least until after you had a job offer.

Scott Epson was in his element. Being schmoozed gave him the sense that he was everything he wanted to be: important, powerful, interesting. He seemed to be holding forth at length about something, so I headed in his direction to see if any of the students trapped by his monologue were in need of rescue.

He was waxing euphoric about his job and his own significance. "For instance," he was saying, "I'm working on this incredibly important deal right now, really complex. I've been in meetings or on the phone practically nonstop with some seriously high profile players. I can't tell you what's going on— it's all too confidential. But it's an incredible rush, knowing that what you're doing is going to be on the front page of the *Wall Street Journal.*" I tried not to snort. I doubted that anything Scott was working on would end up commanding more than an inch of column buried deep within the *Journal.* If he were, Stan Winslow or another senior partner would be all over it.

I inserted myself into the conversation, which gave two of the students the break they needed to quickly drain their drinks and excuse themselves for refills. The remaining one, a guy who looked like a younger version of Scott, seemed happy to listen on. I decided to leave them to it and turned away, nearly crashing into Grant Crocker.

I'd always had to acknowledge that Grant was good-looking, but tonight he definitely wasn't at his best. He had a real shiner around one eye, the skin tinged blackish-purple and clearly swollen, and both eyes were bloodshot. "What happened to you?" I blurted out, before I could think of a more polite way to begin a conversation.

"I walked into a door." Ah. The standard excuse of battered women everywhere.

"That must have hurt. It looks like you really did a number on yourself."

He shrugged. "Yeah, well, I got thirsty in the middle of the night, got up for a glass of water, and bang." He changed the subject. "It's a good turnout, isn't it? Winslow, Brown's a really hot ticket on campus this year."

"I hope so," I said. This was my first encounter with Grant since I'd heard about the letters, and I now had an excellent opportunity to try and figure out if he was behind them. If the police were wrong, and the attack wasn't linked to the serial killings, Grant remained my number-one candidate for Creepy Violent Stalker.

"So, you heard about what happened to Sara, right?" I asked.

"It's awful. I stopped by to see her just before the party but she was asleep."

I wondered if he'd run into Jonathan at UHS, but it seemed like too much work to explain to Grant how I knew Jonathan and why I was so aware of his movements. "The doctors think she's going to be all right."

He scowled and took a big swig from the beer bottle he was holding. No glasses for someone like Too Much Testosterone Guy. "I just hope they find the guy who attacked her. I wouldn't mind giving him a taste of his own medicine." He practically growled when he said this, and I noticed that he was holding his beer bottle with such a tight grip that his knuckles were white. While I could appreciate the sentiment,

I found the sight of so much barely controlled machismo a bit unnerving.

"The police seem like they're being very thorough."

"They'd better be," he said. "I know they've been talking to everyone on campus. But it's been a day and a half, already. They really need to cut to the chase. They can't just let things like that happen to people like Sara. She's too special."

I couldn't disagree with that.

But he took another deep swig of beer and went on, in an emotional way that seemed out of character with the Grant I remembered from when we'd worked together, and made me wonder how many drinks he'd had already. "She's so beautiful, and delicate, and she's all alone in the world. There's nobody to protect her. What kind of scumbag would take advantage of that?"

I didn't know what to say in response, but fortunately we were joined by another student. "Hey, man," he said to Grant.

"Dude, what's up?" responded Grant. They engaged in a complicated handshake that ended with a clinking of beer bottles.

"Where did you disappear to on Wednesday? We missed you at Pub Night."

"Had some things to take care of," Grant answered gruffly. He introduced me to his friend, telling me that they were workout partners, but I promptly forgot the friend's name. The party was swinging into full gear, with most of the students having done their best to make an impression on the various Winslow, Brown representatives and now chatting amongst themselves. I noticed that nearly all my colleagues had discreetly taken their leave, no doubt hoping to get to the airport in time for the eight o'clock shuttle back to New York.

I left Grant and his friend discussing the merits of different muscle-building supplements and found Cecelia giving instructions to the lounge manager to keep the bar open and the hors d'oeuvres circulating for another hour. "I'm going to take off," she told me. "I think we're all set here."

"Thanks so much for handling everything this week. It went great," I told her.

"Yes, it did go well, didn't it? But right now I'm just looking forward to getting home and taking a hot bath."

"I don't blame you. Have a good trip back." She slipped out the door with a smile and a wave, and I looked around the room. The noise level was rising, and the students were clearly slipping from professional to party mode. My duty had been done, and I could head for Jane's with a clear conscience. Well, except for the part of it that was worrying about being a two-timing sleaze in the process of being dumped by her alleged boyfriend.

I waited impatiently at the front door of the hotel for a taxi. There was a long line ahead of me. The doorman shrugged apologetically. "It's prime time on Friday night," he said. "I've called the dispatcher, but you might be better off catching a cab in the Square."

I took his advice and headed for the cab stand on Mass. Ave., in front of Holyoke Center and UHS. There was a line there as well, but it was far shorter, and it was moving quickly. I finally secured a taxi, and as it navigated the slow-moving traffic, I amused myself by counting Harvard scarves. I was up to six before we even turned onto Garden Street, next to the Cambridge Common, where I spotted the seventh, its wearer's hood pulled up against the cold.

There were fewer people on the street as we merged onto Concord Avenue, and no visible scarves to count. I took out my Blackberry to see if I'd missed any messages during the party, but there was nothing. I leaned back in my seat, feeling suddenly adrift. On a day like today, I'd usually be glad for a momentary respite to get my thoughts in order. Tonight, however, the last thing I wanted was to be alone with my thoughts. Nowhere my mind landed was a good place to be.

When the taxi slowed to a stop in front of Jane and Sean's house on Appleton Street, I stepped onto the sidewalk with no small measure of relief. A nice quiet night with my best friends, talking through everything that was going on in my life and hearing about what was going on in their lives, was just what I needed.

We'd eat and drink and talk, and I'd be back in my hotel room well before midnight, with all of my various messes sorted out. And maybe the Jinxing Gods would smile on me for once, and Peter would be there, too, banishing Jonathan Beasley from my mind and letting me know, in word and deed, that everything was all right.

So much for the best-laid plans.

Seventeen

Before I could even ring the bell, Jane's husband opened the door and enveloped me in a bear hug. Sean was a large man, bulky almost but in an athletic way. He and Jane had started dating our freshman year of college, and with the exception of a short "break" our sophomore year, they'd been together ever since. Whenever I worried that the possibility of a happy relationship between a man and a woman was a myth, thinking about Jane and Sean always reassured me. The two of them together was sufficiently inspiring to make you forgive the fact that they seemed to be dressing increasingly alike with each passing year.

"Hey, Rach, it's great to see you. Come on in." He helped me off with my coat, and I followed him into the foyer. The enticing scent of sautéing garlic and onions was in the air, and I felt a pang of hunger. "We're all in the kitchen. Jane decided on an Italian theme tonight, as you can probably smell."

"Wonderful," I said. Lunch seemed like it had been a very long time ago.

He led me down the hallway and into the kitchen. Hilary saw me first and gave a yelp of welcome, rushing to give me a hug that rivaled Sean's. She'd cut her platinum hair, and the new style flattered her, setting off her jade-green eyes and high cheekbones. "You're shrinking," she said, looking down at me from atop her high-heeled boots. That she was five feet eleven inches without the heels probably made most people seem short to her, and the flats I'd chosen rendered me even more diminutive than usual in comparison.

"I feel that way sometimes," I admitted. Then I turned to greet Luisa, who was her usual elegant self in a black sweater and slim trousers, a Pucci scarf knotted at her neck with the sort of casual ease that always eluded me. She kissed me on both cheeks and handed me off to Emma and Matthew, who embraced me in turn.

Jane waved from the stove. I decided not to comment on the fact that her blue blouse was almost identical to that worn by her husband but to stow it away for future use instead. "Hi, there. Somebody get Rachel a glass of champagne, already." Jane wasn't a big hugger.

"Yes, please."

The brightly lit kitchen was almost a parody of domestic warmth. Jane and Sean had knocked out the walls separating the kitchen, pantry and dining room, creating a large open space with an expansive center island for cooking, a big pine table for eating, and a cozy sitting area with overstuffed furniture and a fireplace complete with a busily crackling fire. Everyone had gathered around the island, where Jane was stirring something in an enormous pot. Her face had a rosy glow, and her dark brown bob shone beneath the warm halogen lights. There were plates of antipasti on the counter— cheese and olives and roasted peppers—circled by my friends' wineglasses, which were in varying states of emptiness, or fullness, depending on one's perspective. I hopped up onto the stool that Sean indicated and happily accepted the flute of sparkling wine Matthew handed me.

"Well, now that we're all here, I think it's time for a toast," suggested Emma. "We were waiting for you, Rach."

Sean and Jane looked at each other. He cleared his throat, and Jane's cheeks grew pink. "Actually," began Sean, "there's sort of an announcement that Jane and I would like to make."

I think we all knew what was coming, but we let them go ahead anyway. "I'm pregnant," said Jane.

"To Baby Hallard!" Hilary cried, holding her glass aloft. "Not that it's a surprise," she added.

Jane pinkened yet more. "How did you know?"

"It's been pretty obvious."

Jane looked down at her trim midriff. "What do you mean? I'm not showing yet," she protested, but she put a protective hand to her abdomen, and she couldn't hide the pleasure on her face.

"No, but you've been puking every morning since I've been here."

"Hilary," said Luisa. "I think it's good manners to at least act surprised. And not to mention the puking."

"I'm so glad," said Emma.

I wasn't surprised, either, but it was nice to have my suspicions confirmed. "Well, this definitely calls for a toast!"

Much clinking of glasses ensued, and we all drank to Baby Hallard. Even Jane clinked, breaking her own nonclinking rule. I noticed that her glass held seltzer rather than champagne.

Jane and Sean fielded the usual questions about due dates, gender and baby names: June, they didn't know yet, and they were open to suggestions but had a few ideas already.

"I have a ton of ideas about what not to name it," said Hilary.

"How surprising," Luisa said.

"No, seriously, the wrong name can ruin a person. I don't know what people are thinking these days. Honestly, you have to be on drugs to think that you're doing a good thing by naming a child Tacoma."

"We'll have to have a baby shower," suggested Emma with enthusiasm as Sean popped the cork on another bottle of champagne.

"But a good baby shower. With booze. And men," said Hilary. "Just don't expect me to babysit."

Luisa laughed. "Do you really think anyone would trust you to babysit?"

"I'm sure you'll all be begging to babysit and change diapers when the time comes," said Jane.

"You keep on hoping," said Hilary, but she smiled. "Anyhow, I'll probably be on tour with my book until the baby's well out of diapers."

I turned to her. "This sounds like it's going to be quite a book. And you haven't told me anything about it yet."

"Aren't you the lucky one," said Luisa.

"What's that supposed to mean?" Hilary was indignant.

"I think Luisa's just trying to say that maybe she's heard a lot about the book already," said Emma with her trademark diplomacy.

"Anyhow, Rach, it's going to be great. You know how much I travel, and most of my reading comes from airport bookstores. Well, I've noticed two things that really seem to sell: true-crime books and thrillers about serial killers. So I decided to write a true-crime book about a serial killer. And there is one, right here in Boston, who hasn't even been caught yet."

"This is the guy who's been strangling prostitutes?" I asked. She nodded.

"But what if they don't catch him?"

Not surprisingly, Hilary was reluctant to let reality stand in her way. "They'll have to catch him at some point soon. And in the meantime, I'll get most of the book written. Once they catch the guy, I can just slot in the stuff about who he is and how he ended up so twisted, and I'll be all set."

Given what I'd heard that afternoon from Detective O'Connell, it didn't seem like they were even close to apprehending a suspect. But at least now I knew how I was going to get him and Hilary together. "I just met with some of the detectives who are working on the case."

"What? You've got to introduce me. I've called the police station but nobody will talk to me."

I filled them in on my meeting that afternoon as we began carrying platters of food to the table. "Apparently, the police think it's someone related to the Harvard community in some way. He's been using a Harvard scarf to strangle his victims."

"Probably a Yalie," offered Sean.

Matthew gave an uncomfortable laugh. "Well, now I understand why the police spent so much time at the clinic yesterday. I have one of those scarves, and it was hanging on the coat rack in my office."

"The police came to see you?" asked Hilary.

"Yup. The most recent victim was a patient of mine, and she'd been in a few days before she died."

"This is great," enthused Hilary. "You both have to give me all of the details you have."

"I've told you pretty much all I've got," I said. "Except that one of the detectives I met seems to be just your type."

That really got her attention.

A couple of hours later we were lazily seated around the pine table, the remains of what had been a magnificent feast before us. Hilary had spent much of the first course discussing her research on serial killers. According to her, the prostitute murderer was following a classic pattern of escalation. "The time period between victims is getting shorter and shorter. Some people say that's because the killer starts losing control, and some people say it's because he wants to get caught."

"Well, I hope they catch him," said Matthew.

"Me, too. Otherwise, how will I ever finish the book?" Hilary replied.

"We all hope they find him and we're all looking forward to you finishing the book. Now can we talk about something else already?" interjected Luisa, sounding nearly peevish.

So we talked about Emma's latest gallery show and the new series she was starting, and Matthew's clinic and which room Jane and Sean would use for the nursery. Luisa was sufficiently beyond her breakup with Isobel to relate several amusing stories about the lesbian dating scene in Latin America. Between the champagne and the red wine we drank with dinner, the comfortable conversation among familiar faces, and the savory meal, I was feeling more relaxed than I had in days.

My friends didn't bring up Peter or Jonathan, but I knew they were just waiting. Sean and Matthew had probably been prepped to excuse themselves after dinner, leaving the former roommates alone to talk about touchy personal subjects.

"Who wants dessert?" asked Jane.

"I don't think I can handle dessert just yet," said Emma. "Why don't we get this stuff cleared up first?"

I was excused from the clearing up after I chipped a platter that had belonged to Jane's great-grandmother, and Luisa wanted a cigarette, so at her invitation I stepped out onto the back porch with her to keep her company.

The snow had really begun to fall, and the backyard was already blanketed in white. A pool of light spilled out from

the kitchen windows, and our shadows cast long dark silhou-
ettes on the otherwise unsullied expanse. Luisa lit her cigarette with an engraved lighter and took a luxurious drag.
"Much better," she said, with obvious relief.

"Much colder," I pointed out.

"That, too," she acknowledged. She took another drag.
"Rachel, there's something we need to tell you." She sounded
suddenly serious. "And I drew the shortest straw."

"What?" I asked, concerned. "Is everything all right?"

She glanced back toward the window. Inside, we could see
our friends busily tidying the kitchen. "I'm not quite sure
how to say this, so I'm just going to come right out with it.
When we went to Newbury Street yesterday, Jane and I saw
Peter."

"Oh?" That seemed harmless enough. The convention
center was only a block away, on Boylston Street.

"He was coming out of Cartier." My heart gave a little lift.
Maybe he'd been buying me a present, to make up for his
neglect this past couple of days? And at Cartier, to boot. That
could only be good. What a fool I'd been, doubting him.

"And?" I asked eagerly.

"And he was with a woman. Tall, with long dark hair."

My heart promptly sank. "Did she look like Christy Tur-
lingon, only even more gazellelike?"

Luisa nodded and took another drag. "We wanted to say
hello, and we called out to him. They were across the street,
and I don't think they heard us. So Jane and I followed them.
They went down Newbury and into Shreve, Crump &
Lowe." Another jewelry store. My heart was now lodged
somewhere between my knees and my ankles.

Abigail. The woman they'd seen could only have been
Abigail. Peter had been too busy to have dinner with me,
but he had plenty of time to hang out in jewelry stores with
Abigail.

I was shaking, and not just from the cold. "Did they look—" I wasn't sure how to frame the question. "Did they look like they were *together?*"

She shrugged. "It was hard to tell. They seemed to be talking and laughing up a storm." She hesitated. "And she had her hand on his arm. But the sidewalks were icy—he might have just been helping her."

I fought back a wave of nausea. I didn't know what to say.

"Rachel? Are you all right?"

"Not really," I admitted.

"Look, Rachel. It was probably nothing. Jane and I weren't even sure we should say anything, but we eventually agreed that we'd both want to know if we were in your shoes."

"No, you're right. It's better to know."

We were silent for a couple of minutes. Luisa finished her cigarette and stubbed it out in the ashtray that she'd carried with her.

"Let's go inside," Luisa suggested. "You could probably use another glass of wine."

Sean had taken Matthew to his basement workroom, where he was apparently building a cradle from scratch. The rest of us took our drinks and sat before the fire, and I spilled out everything that had been happening with Peter, and with Jonathan.

Hilary, of course, minced no words. "How dare Peter go jewelry shopping with any woman who's not you? Do you want me to talk to him for you, Rach? Give him a piece of my mind? I've had a lot of experience ditching people."

"That's kind of you to offer, Hil, but not right now."

Emma was less sanguine. "This doesn't sound like the Peter we know. He doesn't seem like the sort of guy who would cheat on you. And you said he was completely normal on Wednesday night. I don't see how so much could have changed in forty-eight hours."

"He could just be genuinely swamped with what he says he's swamped with. Maybe they were looking for a gift for you. Or for their potential client?" This was from Jane, the eternal optimist.

A gift for their client? "Like what?" asked Hilary impatiently. "A pair of earrings? I think you should cut your losses and move on, Rach. I remember this Beasley guy, and he was hot. The best cure for one guy is another guy."

"He is incredibly good-looking," I acknowledged. "And he's smart and nice and everything." I took a big swig of wine. "Oh, Christ. I don't know what to think, much less what to do."

As if on cue, I could hear my phone ringing in my purse. "Maybe it's him," I said.

But I wasn't sure which him I wanted it to be.

Eighteen

But it wasn't Peter, or even Jonathan. It was Edie Michaels.

Her words tumbled out in a breathless rush. Sara had gone into cardiac arrest. She was stable now, but the doctors at UHS had called in the police.

"The police?" I asked, confused.

"I know—I didn't get it either. But it's the same detectives who are investigating the attack at the boathouse. They must think that the seizure or episode or whatever you call it didn't happen naturally."

I'd had a couple glasses of wine and was having trouble computing her words. "You mean—they think someone *caused* this?"

"Uh-huh. Don't ask me how. But it's sort of terrifying. If the nurse hadn't come in when she did…" Edie's voice trailed off.

"Are you at UHS now?"

"Yes. Standard visiting hours have pretty much gone out

the window. And the police asked me to hang around so they could talk to me—they said that they're going to want to talk to everyone who visited Sara, and of course I was here this afternoon and then again earlier this evening. I'd brought Sara dinner, but she didn't have much of an appetite."

"I'll be there in fifteen minutes." I'd been there that day, so surely I was one of the people the police would want to talk to. It was good to have an excuse to find out in person what was going on.

"I'll be in Sara's room, if they let me. I don't want to leave her alone."

As soon as I ended the call the phone rang again. This time it was Jonathan Beasley. Edie had called him, too, and he was on his way to UHS. I told him I'd see him there.

I turned to my friends, who had been unabashedly eavesdropping on my conversation. "Somebody tried to kill Sara Grenthaler," I said.

"I thought that happened yesterday," said Luisa.

"No. I mean yes. But it happened again." I realized that on some level I'd been hoping that yesterday had been a random attack, regardless of police suspicions about serial killers and my own theories about stalkers and roommates. But it was becoming all too clear that whoever had attacked Sara the previous morning had intended to do far more than give her a headache. He'd meant to take her out, and tonight he'd come back to finish the job. Or she. And there was nothing random about it.

I told them what Edie had told me. "I'm going to go to UHS and see what I can learn."

"Did you decide to do that before or after you found out that Jonathan was going to be there?"

I didn't justify Hilary's question with a response.

Jane stood up. "I'll drive you. I'm probably the only per-

son here who's safe to be behind the wheel." We'd all graciously pitched in during the evening to drink Jane's share
of wine, a team effort designed to ensure that Baby Hallard
remained unpickled.

Hilary jumped up. "I'll come, too."

"Why?" I asked.

"You could probably use some moral support. Besides, nobody I've called at the police station will talk to me. This
could be the best chance I'll have to meet your detective.
Maybe I can talk to him about my book. And you said he
was just my type."

I knew from experience that it was useless to argue with
her. And I had wanted her to meet O'Connell. Maybe this
wasn't the ideal situation for a setup, but it would do.

"I'll get Matthew," said Emma, already heading for the
door to the basement and Sean's workroom. "He can ask the
doctor what happened and then translate for us. Plus, I want
to see this Beasley guy. I never took English 10."

Luisa looked up from where she was now sitting alone.
"So, my choice is either to go to UHS with all of you or to
stay here, in which case you'll probably expect that I'll use
that time to finish the dishes?"

Jane nodded.

Luisa cast one glance at her perfectly manicured nails and
another at the dishes, pots and pans that still littered the kitchen
counter. With a shrug she went upstairs to get her coat.

We piled into Jane's car, which was new since I'd last visited
her. Even under the circumstances, we had to mock her. "This
was the real reason I knew you were pregnant," said Hilary. "I
mean, why else would anyone have a Volvo station wagon?"

"It could be worse—they could have gotten a minivan,"
Emma said. She was perched on Matthew's lap in the front
passenger seat.

"We looked at minivans," said Sean, from where he was wedged in the rearmost seat.

"I thought we agreed not to tell anyone that," said Jane in an even tone. The snow was coming down hard, and the windshield wipers beat a steady rhythm as she steered carefully along the slick roads.

"That we looked at minivans? They're very practical."

Hilary gave a moan of what seemed to be genuine pain. "Don't you know that it's a slippery slope? First the Volvo station wagon. Then in a couple of years it *will* be a minivan with a built-in DVD playing a nonstop loop of *Finding Nemo*. Next thing you know, you wake up one morning and you're a middle-aged Republican with sensible hair."

"I think you may have skipped some stuff between *Finding Nemo* and middle age," Matthew pointed out.

"And Jane already has sensible hair," added Luisa.

Miraculously, there was an empty parking space on Mount Auburn Street directly in front of UHS. In the ground-floor lobby, we decided that only a couple of us would go up, since the seven of us at once would likely cause somebody administrative to protest, even if visiting hour regulations had gone by the wayside. Over Hilary's protests, I chose Matthew to accompany me. Besides scaring people to death, I had no idea how somebody could cause somebody else to go into cardiac arrest, but Matthew was the most likely candidate to help me find out. And if we did have any trouble getting in, he was probably the best qualified to run interference at the nurses' station. When Matthew went into his professional doctor mode the Shaggy resemblance completely disappeared.

We emerged from the elevator and stepped into the fifth-floor lobby less than thirty seconds later. Because she'd pulled similar stunts on more occasions than I could count in the past, I shouldn't have been surprised to find Hilary chatting up the nurse at the front desk. How she'd managed to beat us up there was a complete mystery to me, but I had a feeling it would stay that way.

I waved to the nurse as if I knew exactly what I was doing and where I was going and hurried off with Matthew. We'd only walked a few yards when we ran into Detective O'Connell rounding the corner of the hallway. He'd lost the suit jacket since I'd seen him that afternoon, as had Officer Stanley, who was trailing in his wake. O'Connell paused when he saw us, looking up with a tired expression.

"Detective O'Connell. Hi. Rachel Benjamin. Remember me? We met this afternoon?"

"What are you doing here, Ms. Benjamin?" His voice, as before, was polite but wary. He must be having a very long day. Officer Stanley stood silently by, which, judging by his silence when I'd met him before, must have been his role.

"Sara's friend, Edie, called me. She seemed pretty worried, and she mentioned that you would probably want to talk to the people who visited Sara today. And I wanted to check in on Sara and see if I could help out in any way. I've brought a friend of mine, Dr. Matthew Weir."

O'Connell turned to take in Matthew. "Why does that name ring a bell?"

"A couple of your colleagues came to visit me yesterday. I run a free clinic in Roxbury, and one of the murdered prostitutes was a patient of mine. Rachel's an old friend, and we were having dinner tonight when she got Edie's call. I was hoping to have a word with the doctor who's treating Ms. Grenthaler."

He nodded. Then he looked over Matthew's shoulder. "And you are?"

I followed his gaze. Hilary, despite the three-inch spike heels of her boots, had silently crept up behind Matthew. She gave O'Connell a radiant smile, the one that usually reduced men to slavering beasts. "Hilary Banks."

"And what are you doing here?" O'Connell was not one for slavering, apparently, but his tone was courteous enough.

"I was at the dinner, too. But I've been hoping to meet you. I'm writing a book on the prostitute killer, and I've heard that you're just the man I should talk to." Hilary said "man" the way some people said "chocolate" or "caviar." I guessed that she'd found my assessment of O'Connell accurate.

"You've left messages for me, haven't you? At the station?" Hilary nodded.

"I thought the name was familiar." A vein pulsed in O'Connell's temple that hadn't been pulsing before, and I wasn't sure if that was a good sign or a bad sign for Hilary. He turned back to me. "Just for the record, Ms. Benjamin, can you tell me about your whereabouts this evening, before you were at dinner with your friends?"

I quickly sketched out where I'd been since I'd met with him on the business school campus. "Then Edie Michaels called, and I came right down here. Can you tell me anything about what happened?"

"Was it suspicious?" asked Hilary. "Do you think it was foul play?"

O'Connell sighed. "The doctors are concerned that something abnormal occurred and we're looking into it."

"And you think it may be related to the prostitute killings? That's why you're working both cases?" O'Connell raised an eyebrow but didn't answer Hilary's questions.

"Was she given a stimulant or amphetamine of some sort?" asked Matthew. "There aren't many other reasons why an otherwise healthy twenty-five-year-old woman would suddenly go into cardiac arrest. It sounds like her head injury wasn't serious and that she was in stable condition."

O'Connell sighed again, but there was something about

Matthew. People instinctively trusted him, and they told him things they might not tell others. "We think somebody might have put something in Ms. Grenthaler's IV bag. It's being checked out, and they're also doing blood tests to see if there's anything unusual in her bloodstream."

"You mean, somebody just walked right in and tampered with her IV?" I asked.

"How did the three of you get in?" replied O'Connell.

"Good point." UHS wasn't exactly Fort Knox. "But surely there must be security cameras at the entrances to the building?"

"We're looking into it," he said. "But in weather like this, when everyone's bundled up, they tend not to be too useful. At least, unless the perp thinks to look straight up and smile for the camera. And there are a bunch of kids in here with the usual midwinter flu, so the place has been especially busy."

I'd thought Barbara Barnett had been overreacting when she'd mentioned arranging for private security, but her suggestion now appeared a lot more reasonable. I made a mental note to call her—she'd said she'd take care of it, but the task must have fallen to the bottom of her to-do list. And then I had another thought. "A guy named Grant Crocker was here this afternoon. Did you know that?"

"Yes, we are aware of that. Meanwhile, so were several other people, including yourself, Ms. Benjamin. Listen," continued O'Connell. "Ms. Grenthaler's fine now, and she's resting comfortably. I appreciate your coming by—it saved me a phone call. But the best thing for you to do right now is to go on home. Ms. Michaels is with her, I've posted an officer at her door and I'll have one there until we resolve all this, and I'm about to give the people at the nurses' station and the folks downstairs a pretty stern lecture about keeping a better eye on who's coming and going." He was slowly but firmly ushering us back through the lobby and toward the elevators.

"Can I have your card? In case I think of anything? That's what they always do on *Law & Order,*" said Hilary.

"What would you think of?" asked O'Connell, distractedly punching the call button for the elevator.

"Leads. Clues. Stuff like that. And I'd like to interview you for my book. You're going to be one of the main characters, after all."

"I'm going to be one of the main characters?" His voice was flat with exhaustion, but I thought I detected an undercurrent of amusement mixed in with his usual politely veiled impatience.

"Yes. I'm a journalist, so I've written a lot, but this is my first book. And I'm really looking forward to working with you." Hilary's radiant smile flashed again, but O'Connell's poker face betrayed no discernable impact.

"To working *with* me?" O'Connell repeated her words. This time the amusement was tangible.

"Sure."

An elevator announced its arrival with a beep, and the doors parted. A sea of people spilled out, and I recognized them all. Edward and Helene Porter rushed immediately to the nurses' station, with Barbara Barnett following on their heels. Behind them were Grant Crocker and Jonathan Beasley.

Jonathan gave me a wave and bent down to kiss me on the cheek. Over his shoulder, I saw Hilary and Matthew exchange a look. I was definitely going to be hearing about this later. "I need to talk to Detective O'Connell," said Jonathan. "Are you going to be around for a while?"

"Um. Just a bit." I'd been about to leave, but now I wanted to find out why Grant Crocker had shown up. He still had my vote as most likely to be a Creepy Stalker, and Violent, too.

"Well, I'll call you later, then, if I miss you on the way out."

He caught O'Connell's eye, and the two of them disappeared around the corner, with Officer Stanley mutely bringing up the rear.

I signaled to Hilary and Matthew that I needed a minute and intercepted Grant Crocker. He was heading toward Sara's room, but he stopped when I put a hand on his elbow. His black eye looked even worse in the harsh fluorescent light. "What are you doing here?" I asked, managing to keep the hostility I was feeling out of my voice.

"I ran into Professor Beasley in the Square. He was on his way here and told me what happened." I looked at him carefully, eager to discern anything that would indeed betray him to be the Creepy Violent Stalker, but all I saw was a guy with a serious shiner and what appeared to be serious concern on his face. Although, the ability to dissemble effectively was likely a prerequisite for a Creepy Violent Stalker. "Anyhow, will you excuse me? I want to make sure Sara's all right."

I didn't want to excuse him, but I didn't have a valid reason to stop him. I doubted he'd be able to get past the policeman outside Sara's door, anyhow, and if he did, Edie was in there with Sara. If he were the Creepy Violent Stalker, it would be hard to try to kill her again tonight.

The Porters were busily conferring with someone who looked like a doctor (he was wearing a white coat), and Matthew had surreptitiously joined them. Barbara Barnett was standing off to one side, peering at the small screen of her cell phone. Despite their oddly limited mobility (Botox-induced, perhaps), her features had managed to twist themselves into an expression of impatience. She looked up when I approached and gave me a forced smile.

"This is very upsetting," she said. "Edward and Helene were actually at my house this evening, paying a condolence call, when we heard what happened. I've been trying to track

Adam down. I asked him to help with security, and he said he'd be able to line someone up for tonight, but we clearly need to get somebody on duty right now."

"I think it's been taken care of," I explained, and told her about the police officer outside Sara's door. I said goodbye, and she joined the Porters as they headed for Sara's room. I met Hilary and Matthew back at the elevator. "I think we're done here," I said.

"Are you sure?" asked Hilary.

"Not really, but I don't know what else I can do." I pressed the call button for the elevator, and this time the doors immediately slid open. The three of us got in, and Matthew pushed the button for the ground floor. The doors had almost slid shut when we heard a voice call, "Wait!"

Matthew fumbled for the door-open button, getting to it at the last possible moment. O'Connell and Officer Stanley rushed into the elevator.

"What's going on?" I asked.

"I can't say," said O'Connell in the sort of tone that shut off further inquiry, even for Hilary. We were silent as the elevator made its laborious descent, and he was off like a shot as soon as the doors opened, his partner running silently after him.

Nineteen

O'Connell managed to give Hilary the slip on the way out of UHS, largely because the rest of us were physically restraining her. We offered up a nightcap at Shay's, one of our favorite college haunts, as a consolation prize.

"Cheer up," said Jane. "It will give you an opportunity to hit on undergrads."

"True," agreed Hilary. "But what if he was rushing off because they've found something out about the prostitute killer? Or maybe another body? It would be amazing to see a fresh crime scene. I mean, I trust in my journalistic abilities to paint a vivid scene for the reader, but it would be a lot easier if I were actually there."

"Yes, but we don't know if there even is a crime scene, much less where it is," Emma said. "So come along to Shay's and have a drink."

She agreed, but she wasn't happy about it. "Rachel was right. O'Connell is just my type."

"You have a type? Just one?" asked Luisa skeptically.

It was now close to eleven on a Friday night, and not surprisingly the place was packed. In warmer months, we would have opted for the front terrace facing JFK Street, but since the snow was still coming down and the wind chill must have been a few hundred degrees below freezing, we pushed our way inside. While Hilary and Luisa negotiated with undergrads for their tables and Jane went to the ladies' room, the rest of us threaded our way through the crowd to fetch drinks at the bar. As Sean struggled to catch the bartender's attention, I turned to Matthew. "What exactly did the doctor say?" I had to yell to make myself heard over the cacophony of music and voices.

"Pretty much what I'd thought. Some sort of stimulant or amphetamine injected into the IV bag."

"Is that the sort of thing that's readily available?" asked Emma.

"Sure," he answered. "Not necessarily at the drugstore, but without too much effort, especially online. For example, there are pills and powders that you can get from dozens of Web sites that contain ephedra. A bunch of people had heart attacks when they were taking it, and it's been banned by the FDA, but it's still not hard to come by."

"What's it for?" I asked.

"And if it's so dangerous, why would anyone take it?" added Emma.

"A lot of people use it for weight loss. And athletes take it, too. For weight loss, and to do more—run faster, hit harder—that sort of thing."

"You know," I said, remembering, "I think my boss, Stan Winslow, was on something like that last year. He was even more manic than usual but he lost ten pounds. But not without driving everyone crazy in the meantime."

"It amazes me what people will do to lose weight," said Matthew.

"That's easy for you to say. Not everybody has to worry about ordering extra desserts to maintain zero percent body fat," said Emma.

"Hey, we all have our problems."

"Matthew," I asked, "is ephedra the sort of thing that body builders would take?"

"Sure."

"Excuse me for a minute. I need to make a call."

Inside was too noisy, so I stepped out onto the front terrace, bracing myself against the bitter chill of the wind. Between the streetlights and the light spilling out from the bar, I could make out the phone number on the card O'Connell had given me earlier that day. I punched in the digits once, but my fingers were stiff from the cold, and the phone slipped from my grasp and clattered on the ice-covered flagstones. I cursed and stooped to retrieve it. Only after I'd turned it off and then on did I get a signal, and I dialed the number again. I'd hoped to get a receptionist or an answering service that could connect me directly to the detective, but instead I got his office voice mail. I left a detailed message, letting him know that he might want to look into the supplements Grant Crocker took as part of his weight-training regimen.

I returned to the Charles shortly after one in the morning, exhausted and uneasy after a tumultuous day. My friends and I had managed to secure a corner table at Shay's, and we'd talked for a long while about who could be behind the attack on Sara Grenthaler and my suspicions of Grant Crocker, which led to a long and animated discussion of Detective O'Connell, which led in turn to a long and animated discussion of Jonathan Beasley. His good looks were uniformly acknowledged, even by Matthew. We skirted around the topic of Peter, and for that I was grateful.

I checked for messages on my way up to the room, but there was still nothing. It was just as well—I didn't have the heart to listen to whatever additional excuses and lame apologies Peter might have come up with for his continued absence.

The suite was quiet. A single lamp glowed dimly in a corner of the living room, and a thin trail of light came from the bedroom, likely left on by the housekeeping staff when they'd come to turn down the bed. I hung up my coat and kicked off my shoes. The new attack on Sara and everything that had ensued had given me an excuse to put off thinking about Peter and Abigail on their jewelry-store crawl for a couple of hours, but the still room and its feeling of emptiness now seemed like an overly obvious metaphor for how I was feeling inside.

So, I did what I usually did in such situations and stole a page from Scarlett O'Hara. Tomorrow, I said to myself. I'll think about it tomorrow. I went into the bedroom, steeling myself for the empty bed and the breakup it foreshadowed.

But Peter was there. Not awake, but not snoring. He lay sprawled on his stomach, a pillow cradled in his arms, his shoulders brown against the white of the duvet.

I probably should have awakened him and had it out, there and then. But I lacked the energy. And part of me wanted one more night as Peter's girlfriend. I'd liked it, liked how he made me feel, and I didn't relish the prospect of giving it up, even though I recognized I had to, because either he was going to dump me for Abigail or I was going to dump him before he could dump me.

I sank down onto my side of the bed, and he stirred a bit but didn't wake up. He just kept breathing, evenly and deeply. There was a note on my pillow, a folded piece of paper. I opened it up and read it by the light of the lamp on the nightstand.

I suck for having missed tonight. It's just that we're so close to getting the deal signed up—I'm hoping we'll have it in the bag by end of day tomorrow. I know I keep saying this, but I'll make it up to you. Really. XXX, P

At least it wasn't an e-mail. And, if I hadn't known about his shopping trip with Abigail it might have done the trick. And if I hadn't been quasikissing Jonathan Beasley, I would have felt just dandy. In fact, I would probably have tried to coax Peter awake. But it was all too clear that the only reason he was even here was to grab a few hours' sleep and a change of clothes.

Instead, I undressed, put on an oversize T-shirt, and slipped into bed.

Tired as I was, I did the requisite tossing and turning. There was just too much going on, and none of it good, to possibly sleep. I tried to focus on mentally preparing for the board meeting at Grenthaler Media, but this made me think of the commitment I'd made to Sara, to protect her interests, which inevitably led me back to the attacks. My bet was definitely on Grant Crocker as the perpetrator, and I tried to piece together not only how he had done everything but why. Lessons learned from Lifetime Television for Women could only provide so much insight. Male psychology had never been my area of expertise, I commented to myself. Which, of course, brought me back to Peter, and Abigail, and Jonathan. All in all, I'd had more peaceful nights. I finally drifted off around four but woke up briefly at six, conscious of Peter's arms around me, warm and familiar. I drifted off again, with a renewed sense of well-being, but when I reawakened at eight he was gone and so was the well-being.

The drapes were open, revealing that the snow hadn't let up. If anything, it was coming down harder than the previous evening. The thick white flakes swirled outside the window, almost completely obscuring the view to the river. Below me, the park was completely blanketed in white.

I showered and then padded into the living room for my first Diet Coke of the day. Peter had left another note, this one stuck to the door of the minibar. He'd written it in a hurry, judging by his scrawl, but it seemed to say that he was on his way back to the conference and would something indecipherable me later. I called UHS as I popped my soda open. Sara was sleeping but in stable condition, I learned, and yes, there was a police officer stationed outside her door.

I wanted to crawl back into bed, and I definitely looked like I should, but I'd promised too many people that I'd be at the Grenthaler Media emergency board meeting that morning. I surveyed the clothes hanging in the closet with distaste. On a day like today, nobody should have to put on anything but sweatpants or, at the very best, jeans. But here I was, struggling into stockings and the same black suit I'd worn to the memorial service on Thursday and trying to corral my hair into a passable imitation of professional calm.

I was scowling by the time I got into a cab. My mood was rapidly descending from less-than-chipper to downright ornery. Even worse, the driver wanted to chat. About politics.

It was a very long fifteen minutes.

Samuel Grenthaler had launched his company from a poky apartment in Somerville. Now its headquarters occupied a redbrick complex that sprawled over the better part of a full city block in Kendall Square, a neighborhood better known for biotech and software start-ups and shiny new condos. Even on a Saturday, the lobby was bustling. Several Grenthaler magazines were published from this building, and for their employees weekends happened after an issue was "put to bed," which could be any day of the week.

The receptionist had my name on a list, and he gave me a pass and buzzed me through the glass-paneled doors that led to the elevators. The security here was much better than it was at UHS. The meeting was on the second floor, so I opted for the stairs rather than wait for the elevator, deciding I could now cross out "exercise" on the day's to-do list. I reached the boardroom a few minutes early, but there was nobody there as yet, so I ducked into the ladies' room. The ten-foot dash between the cab and the building's entrance had exposed me to a massive gust of snow and wind, and I had the feeling that it hadn't done much for my hastily fashioned chignon. Sure enough, the mirror above the sink reflected somebody who looked like me but had a red mop on her head instead of hair. I undid the clasp and began fiddling with the wayward strands.

The door opened and Barbara Barnett strode in. I was wearing what I'd always thought of as my "Power Suit," a severe black Armani. Barbara seemed to be wearing her own version, an alarmingly bright royal blue outfit that looked like the product of a *Falcon Crest* costume designer channeling her counterpart on *Dallas*. But I had to give Barbara credit. The miniskirt might not be the outfit of choice for the sorts of meetings I was used to attending, but she still had the legs to carry it off.

She gave me a big smile, and we made ladies' room small talk, mostly about Sara's condition and the security at UHS. Watching her touch up her already perfect makeup was fascinating to me, given that the contents of my own makeup bag yielded little but a tube of drugstore mascara and a Bonne Bell strawberry-flavored Lip Smacker. "I bet Abigail uses grown-up makeup," said that mean little voice in my head. I mentally shushed the mean little voice while simultaneously managing to secure my hair back in a knot that looked almost intentional.

It seemed only polite to wait for Barbara, so I watched while she finished outlining her lips with one brush and then used another brush and two different pots of lip gloss to fill in between the lines. "You have such beautiful skin, honey. It must be nice not to need all of this war paint," she said to me, putting away the tools she'd just used and taking out a small pillbox.

"I probably do need it," I replied. "I just lack the hand-eye coordination required to put it on."

She laughed. "It does take practice. But a young, fresh-faced gal like you—you don't need as much help as I do. And how do you keep your cute little figure?" She looked me up and down with an evaluative eye before opening the pillbox and selecting a yellow tablet, which she swallowed dry. She put the pillbox back in her bag.

I'd never really thought of my figure as "cute." Mostly just scrawny. And klutzy. When what I'd always longed for was willowy and graceful. "I miss a lot of meals," I said. It made for an easier answer than trying to argue with her assessment. And it was the truth. Too many evenings found me scavenging for food among the vending machines in the pantry at Winslow, Brown, hungry but unwilling to prolong my hours at work by taking the time to order in a proper dinner.

"Well, you're a lucky one," she replied as we left the ladies' room.

I didn't feel particularly lucky that morning. But I thanked her, assured her of her own enviable svelteness and followed her into the boardroom.

A half hour later I was feeling even less lucky.

Brian Mulcahey called the meeting to order. Tom had not only been CEO, he'd been chairman of the board, and Sara, who served as vice chair, was out of commission for today's meeting, so running the agenda fell to Brian. The other board members seated around the table included Barbara, Edward and Helene Porter, and four "outsiders," including the senior partner at one of Boston's more prestigious law firms, the CEO of a local insurance company, the CEO of a local industrial concern and a retired professor from M.I.T. The crackdown on corporate governance in the post-Enron era had called for more outsider presence on the boards of public companies, but since Grenthaler was privately controlled it had felt little pressure to reshuffle its board's composition, and it was still more than half "insiders."

Mulcahey began by offering his condolences to Barbara, which were echoed by those of us gathered around the table and met with the widow's gracious thanks. Then he cleared his throat. "As Tom's death was so sudden, and so unexpected, we find ourselves without a formal succession plan. Now, I have a proposal that I wanted to put before the board—"

I wasn't surprised when Barbara interrupted with a bright smile. "Actually, Brian, I have a proposal that I think the board needs to hear first."

But I was surprised when she pushed back her chair, stood and crossed to the door. When she was confident that she had the full attention of everyone in the room, she threw it open.

And in walked Adam Barnett, Scott Epson and the Caped Avenger.

Twenty

This can't be good, was my first thought.

This is really bad, was my second thought.

But at least I knew I didn't need glasses. I *had* seen the three of them leaving the Ritz the previous morning; my eyes hadn't been playing tricks on me. Still, I had a feeling that soon I would wish that they had been.

"Barbara, what is this all about?" asked Brian Mulcahey.

"Adam will tell you," said Barbara, her voice bursting with maternal pride.

Helene Porter emitted a delicate sound that wasn't a snort but conveyed similar feelings, albeit in a far more genteel way.

Barbara nodded at her son. "Go ahead, honey."

"Good morning," said Adam. His voice sounded more confident than I'd ever heard it before, and he seemed less überdorky than usual. But that might just be because he was standing next to Scott Epson. Scott, meanwhile, was wearing his favorite tie, pink silk with green alligators. The Caped

Avenger, standing next to Scott, caught my eye and gave me a wave and a look that managed to combine a raised eyebrow, a wink and a leer all at once.

Adam continued, "My mother, as one of Grenthaler Media's major shareholders and board members, invited us here to make this announcement in person. Allow me to introduce my partner, Whitaker Jamieson, and our advisor, Scott Epson of Winslow, Brown. Mr. Jamieson and I have established a private corporation that has acquired four-point-nine percent of Grenthaler Media's shares in the open market. We have also negotiated an agreement with my mother to acquire the ten percent of the company that she owns."

I stole a glance at Barbara. Her lips were moving silently as her son spoke, and I had little doubt that she'd helped Adam prepare his speech.

Adam went on. "Before the close of business yesterday we filed with the Securities and Exchange Commission a notice of our intent to make a tender offer for the remaining publicly held shares. We submitted a press release to the wire services announcing the tender offer just this morning."

Barbara couldn't hold back any longer. "Isn't it exciting!" she cried. "Adam's going to take over the company!"

And I was going to murder Stan Winslow. Now I knew why the Caped Avenger had been so quiet of late. Somehow he and Barbara Barnett had found each other, and now he was financing the takeover attempt. Given how less than impressive I'd found Adam to date, I had no illusions that Barbara wasn't the driving force behind it all. Meanwhile, Stan had steered Whitaker to Scott to handle the deal, probably just as much to intensify any competition between us as to avoid navigating any conflict of interest on my part, given my professional obligations to Grenthaler's current management.

I was also amazed that Barbara had been able to put this

together so quickly. I remembered Scott blithering on about his new deal on the shuttle Wednesday evening, talking about the client's unrealistic expectations as to how soon they'd be able to get things done. It had been barely a week since Tom had died. Did Barbara have this all plotted out before his death? Was she just waiting for her husband to die to put her plans in motion? Tom had rebuffed his wife's attempts to get Adam more involved in company affairs. But without the shares she'd inherited from Tom, Barbara, Adam and their team didn't have a leg to stand on—and Tom would never have sold his stake or allied himself in any way against Sara.

Meanwhile, I'd completely misinterpreted Barbara's stated intention to stay involved in the company. The most I'd worried about was her trying to use her stake to have Adam appointed CEO, and that the activity in the company's stock simply meant that an unrelated third party was accumulating shares. The dots had been there, begging to be connected, but I hadn't put them together.

"What about Sara?" asked Helene Porter. "It's her company," she protested.

Edward took her through the math, quickly and in a subdued voice. Unless Sara found an extra hundred million dollars, and likely more given that the takeover would drive up the stock price, she wouldn't be able to acquire the shares she needed to secure majority ownership. The race had begun, and meanwhile Sara was essentially out of commission.

With a chill, I remembered what I'd overheard Scott saying on Thursday night—"Yes, it's unfortunate, but this can only benefit us." Had he been talking about Sara? Had Barbara Barnett been on the other end of the phone? That Sara was lying in a bed at UHS, and that she'd been attacked twice in the previous two days, suddenly seemed a little too coincidental for my tastes, Creepy Violent Stalkers notwithstanding. I'd dismissed the possibility of any link between the attacks on Sara and anything that might be going on at the company, fixating instead on Grant Crocker when I wasn't speculating about Gabrielle LeFavre, the Psycho Roommate. But had Barbara been behind them in some way? She seemed too flaky, but the timing of events was too convenient for comfort given how much easier Sara's absence made her run at the company.

I looked from Barbara to Adam Barnett. She was beaming at her son, clearly overjoyed by what she perceived as his righteous ascendance to power, and he was surveying the room as if he owned it.

Which he shortly would, unless I did something about it. And did something soon.

The reasoned discussion of succession plans that Brian Mulcahey had envisioned devolved into turmoil. The Porters and Mulcahey were horrified, although they didn't seem to have noticed how fortunate the timing of Sara's injuries was for Barbara and her team's threatened coup d'état. Helene let rip with a few choice words for Barbara, which under other circumstances I'd have been storing up for future use. She had a unique ability to deliver the most devastating of insults without resorting to vulgarity or even raising her voice. Perhaps because of this skill, Barbara Barnett didn't even realize that she was being insulted.

While Helene was decorously savaging Barbara, I was conferring with Mulcahey and Edward Porter.

"I hadn't realized exactly how necessary your presence would be, Rachel," said Brian. "This financial stuff just isn't my thing. Can you tell us what our options are?"

I still hadn't seen the company charter, but I doubted it would be much help, given that we'd never felt the need to incorporate antitakeover clauses. As things were, there were really only four options that I could think of, and probably not even that many. I briefly summarized them for my listeners.

The first was to find a way for Sara to acquire an additional ten percent of the company, which would involve raising a lot of money, fast. While the Porters were well off, I doubted that their assets would come close to the kind of ready cash we needed, and it was unlikely they'd be able to easily raise such a large sum among their circle of friends. The second was to find a "white knight"—someone friendly to Sara who could purchase that ten percent. Given the time frame, I wasn't optimistic about option two, either. The third option, however, was even more unlikely: the odds of convincing Barbara not to sell her shares to her son's consortium were slim given that she'd probably set the entire thing up. But were these odds any slimmer than those for option four? Was it possible to convince Whitaker Jamieson, a man who I well knew to have mogul aspirations, to withdraw his support? Overall, it wasn't the most encouraging of situations.

I scanned the room from the corner in which I was huddled with Mulcahey and Porter. Adam, Scott and the Caped Avenger were busily schmoozing the four "outside" directors. I had little hope that they would vote against a takeover when the time came. Their fiduciary responsibility was to the shareholders—all of the shareholders. And that meant maximizing the value of the stock. Whoever could pay the most would win.

Helene had finished lambasting Barbara, not that Barbara had seemed to notice. She moved to join her son, flashing her pageant smile at the group on the opposite side of the room.

Helene turned to where I stood with her husband and Mulcahey. "We can't let this happen," she said. "This company should be Sara's. We can't just let these people take it away from her." The composure that usually made it difficult to guess her age had fled, replaced by alarm, and she looked every one of her years.

"I won't let it happen," I promised her, despite the bleakness of the options I'd just sketched out.

Of course, I'd promised her granddaughter the same thing a few days ago, and that hadn't done much good.

Mulcahey managed to restore enough order to adjourn this emergency board meeting and call another one for Monday morning. I had forty-eight hours to figure out our defense. And while I wasn't sanguine about any of the four options I'd outlined earlier, I intended to make it clear to the Barnetts that this deal was far from assured.

People were filing out of the room, and I missed Barbara but hurried to intercept Adam before he could leave. Fortunately, Scott Epson had monopolized the Caped Avenger for the time being, so I was able to get Adam alone.

"Look," I said, speaking with a confidence that I didn't feel and wishing that I was a foot taller. Adam was hardly an imposing presence, but it would be nice not to have to crane my head up to look him in the eye. "We're going to fight this every inch of the way."

He shrugged, casually, but I sensed that he was nervous. "I don't see what you can do. We've got my mother's shares and the financing for the rest locked up. Unless you can find someone to outbid us, you're screwed. And Whit has pretty deep pockets, and he's excited about being part of this deal. This is what my mother wants, and she usually gets what she wants."

"We're not just going to roll over. Tom Barnett's body is barely even cold—"

"Actually, Dad's body was cremated. 'Barely even cold' probably isn't the right phrase."

The way Adam said this, with an utter lack of effect, made

me wonder if he had Asperger's syndrome, but I pressed on, speaking over his words.

"—and the majority shareholder has been incapacitated due to a series of suspicious attacks. Let's just put it this way, I think the police are going to want to know about what's going on here."

Adam shrugged again, but he swallowed. "Be my guest. But I would think twice before getting on my mother's bad side."

Twenty-One

Adam left the boardroom and headed down the hallway, leaving me alone in the conference room.

The ornery mood I'd been in when I'd arrived at the meeting had devolved yet further. I was way past ornery. Cantankerous was a distant memory. I'd reached belligerent, and it wasn't pretty.

My cell phone rang, a jarring angry noise, perfectly in keeping with my mood. I dug it out of my bag. "What?" I barked.

"Hi, Rachel. Stan Winslow, here."

I took a deep breath and counted backward from ten.

"Rachel? You still there, old gal?"

My voice, when I found it, managed to convey just the tone of sunny warmth I was aiming for, even when speaking through gritted teeth. "Hello, Stan. How are you? Are you having a nice weekend?"

"Just wanted to check in with you. I guess you've found

out about what my old friend Whitaker Jamieson's been up to. I hope you don't mind my putting Scott on this, but I knew you'd probably have a conflict." He chuckled. Actually, it sounded more like a cackle.

"It makes perfect sense," I answered in the same sunny tone while inwardly I began chanting one of my most oft-used mantras. *Must not yell at boss. Must not yell at boss.*

"I'm sure you'll both do a great job," Stan continued. "You know, this is the sort of situation that really separates the partner material from the, er, from the—well, from the non-partner material." This was Stan's idea of an inspirational pep talk. I wondered if he was planning a similar conversation with Scott Epson. Or if he'd already had one.

"I hope so," I agreed.

"Well, good luck. Keep me posted."

"I'll do that. And thanks for your advice, Stan." Not that he'd given me any, but he liked to feel needed.

"No problem, old gal." He hung up, and I threw the phone across the room with a muffled shriek.

It turned out that the Blackberry didn't really appreciate being thrown across the room. It had hit the wall with a loud thwack, but the wall didn't look so hard, and the carpet it landed on was relatively plush. Still, it made a whiny noise when I picked it up, and I had to turn it off and then on again before the annoying sound stopped.

I stowed the device back in my purse and headed upstairs to the executive offices, repeating another oft-used mantra to myself. *Bonus. Bonus. Bonus.*

But it was January, and I'd just received my bonus for the previous calendar year. It would be eleven and a half months before I received my next bonus. As incentive pay went, it would be a significant chunk of change, but its motivational powers had a direct correlation with its proximity.

I amended the mantra. *Rachel Benjamin, Partner, Winslow, Brown. Rachel Benjamin, Partner, Winslow, Brown.* But who knew when that would happen?

I stopped in at Brian Mulcahey's office to offer some re-assuring words and to scramble up Grenthaler's head of corporate communications. She didn't seem too happy to hear from her boss on a Saturday, but we gave her the instructions she needed to start working on press releases and she promised to get on it. By the time I got outside I was fresh out of mantras, which was just as well, because I required all of my concentration to figure out my next move. I'd lost track of the Porters, so I'd missed out on that potential source of transit. And even if any members of the Barnett contingent had lingered, I could hardly beg a ride from them.

I probably should have called a cab from the lobby, but the freezing air was strangely bracing, so I started walking, thinking I'd find a cab soon enough. I'd forgotten my gloves and scarf, of course, so I turned up the collar of my coat and shoved my hands deep into my pockets, pausing to get my bearings. I was only a few blocks from Mass. Ave., Cambridge's main drag. I'd promised to meet my old roommates at Copley Place in Boston for brunch and shopping, although given everything that was going on, I was probably going to have to skip the shopping part. Sustenance, however, was very much in order.

I trudged along, trying to figure out my plan of attack while keeping my eyes peeled for a cab. I'd only worked on one takeover defense before, in my first year at Winslow, Brown, and that had been on a much larger scale—one corporate behemoth seeking to swallow another that was nearly as large in a deal valued at more than twenty billion dollars. A team of six from Winslow, Brown had been dispatched to thwart the takeover. We solicited competing bids that drove up the price significantly, although ultimately our client was indeed taken over. Its shareholders, however, were pleased enough with the higher value paid for their shares, and everyone went home happy, including the bankers from Winslow, Brown, who had collected several million in fees for a few weeks' work.

In comparison, this potential takeover was a blip on the radar screen of high finance. And I doubted that Stan would authorize a team of any size from the firm to help me out. I was on my own.

The obvious course was to divide and conquer in some way. As far as I could tell, the weakest link was probably the Caped Avenger. A quick call to the weekend staff in my office yielded his number from my Rolodex, and, swallowing my pride, I left him a message asking him to call me as soon as possible.

That done, I considered the other links in the chain. Appealing to Scott Epson wasn't going to work, even if I could stomach it. He undoubtedly saw this deal as a way to solidify his position with Stan while also making me look bad—definitely a win/win in his book. Adam Barnett had seemed perfectly happy to let his mother secure him his key to the executive washroom, and Barbara clearly saw the takeover as the fulfillment of her most cherished fantasies for her son. Everything about her screamed stage mother—it was highly unlikely that she was going to do anything that would pull Adam out of the spotlight.

Which made me wonder whether or not I should discuss my suspicions with Detective O'Connell. Surely he'd want to know about the most recent developments? Although, perhaps I was overreacting, jumping to conclusions. The last time I'd done something like that, Peter had been arrested for a murder he didn't commit. Adam had appeared calm when I mentioned my suspicions, but perhaps his nervous swallow was a tell, an indication that he, too, had his concerns about what his mother might have been up to. Still, it wasn't like I had proof of any sort. And only last night I'd called O'Connell to point my finger at Grant Crocker. But the level of coincidence here seemed too much to ignore. O'Connell could laugh at me if he wanted, but it was probably better to tell him than not to tell him.

I consulted the call history on my Blackberry for his number, but the device seemed to have decided to punish me for its mistreatment by eating its phone log. Fortunately, I still had O'Connell's card in my wallet. But no sooner had I retrieved the card than an enormous gust of wind ripped it from my hand.

I let loose with a vulgarity of which Helene Porter most certainly would not have approved, and ran after the card as it skittered along the icy sidewalk. It was nearly in my grasp, and I leaped to catch it, promptly losing my balance and pitching headfirst into the filthy snowbank that lined the street.

"Need some help?" said a voice beside me, proffering a hand in a shearling glove. The voice was familiar, and somehow I wasn't surprised when, after wiping the dirty slush from my face, I found myself looking up into Jonathan Beasley's blue, blue eyes.

"You're—you're ubiquitous," I sputtered.

He laughed and pulled me up to a standing position. "Among other things. Are you all right, though? That was a nasty spill you just took."

My coat was covered with blackened snow, and I was pretty confident I'd ripped my stockings and that my hair had returned to mop mode. A quick inventory, however, let me know that I didn't seem to have injured myself.

"I'm fine," I said. "But what are you doing here?"

"I was about to ask you the same thing," he replied. He pointed over his shoulder. "My condo's right over there." We were outside a generic but pleasant-looking brick building. "But what brings you to my neighborhood?"

"A board meeting for Grenthaler Media." It occurred to me that running into Jonathan just now was fortuitous. I could bounce my suspicions about Barbara Barnett off him before potentially embarrassing myself with the police.

"Oh, that's right. Their headquarters are around the corner. Listen, do you need a ride somewhere? I was about to head to the Square. There are a couple of things I need to do in my office. My car's right over there. I was loading it up when I saw you."

I followed his outstretched arm with my gaze. His Saab was parked across the street.

I hesitated. "I don't want to inconvenience you. I'm actually going in the opposite direction. I'm meeting some friends at Copley Place. But it would be great if you could drop me somewhere where I'm more likely to find a cab."

"No problem. I'd be happy even to drive you over to Copley, if you'd like. It won't take long." He took my elbow and began guiding me toward the car.

"No, that's all right. But I am glad I ran into you. I'd love to get your opinion on something."

"Sure. Anything." He looked down at me and grinned, and my heart did the proverbial flip accompanied by the familiar tingle. No man who wasn't a movie star or a male model had the right to look this good, especially when I looked as bad as I probably did. "Here, why don't you get in out of the cold while I finish putting my gear in the trunk." He unlocked the passenger-side door for me and swung it open. I slid in and he shut it after me.

I watched while he went around the back of the car and opened the trunk. Then I watched through the driver's-side window as he came around the other side. His crimson-and-white-striped scarf had come loose, and he knotted it around his neck firmly before stooping to pick up a large duffel bag that he'd left on the curb. The duffel was clearly an antique— it bore the logo of the Harvard Men's Ice Hockey Team, and was probably left over from when Jonathan played Varsity and used the oversize bag to carry his pads, stick, helmet and skates. It looked unwieldy, too; he hefted it awkwardly.

It wasn't even eleven in the morning yet, but it had already been a long day. And I'd recently had a faceful of dirty snow, so maybe my vision was clouded.

But I could have sworn that I saw a woman's foot poking out from one end of the duffel.

Twenty-Two

My fairy godmother, who had been egregiously negligent of late, made a cameo appearance in the guise of the empty cab that was pulling up the street. I was out of Jonathan's car like a shot, yelling a hasty goodbye and promising to talk to him later while throwing myself in front of the taxi. It skidded to a stop, and I raced around to the side, opening the door and slamming it shut behind me. "Copley Place," I said, "and step on it." The driver obliged, and I turned to look out the back window. Jonathan was standing by his car, clearly stunned. I gave him a fake smile and a wave and reached over to lock the doors on either side of me.

My head was spinning. I felt like Linda Blair in *The Exorcist,* minus the satanic possession and spewing green slime parts. Jonathan Beasley—*Love Story* guy himself—was a serial killer?

My head slowed its spinning long enough to begin ticking off pieces of evidence. First, nobody that good-looking could be normal. Second, he had one of those stupid scarves that the police had linked with the crimes. Third, now that I thought about it, he did seem to have a complex of some sort when it came to Boston's underclass. I remembered the off-putting way he'd spoken of how his ex-wife had become caught up in their problems, and the resentment that seemed to tinge his words. Maybe that was what motivated him?

But the clincher pretty much made all these pieces of evidence superfluous—because the clincher was that Jonathan Beasley was carrying bodies around in duffel bags and loading them into trunks.

And, even worse, he'd quasikissed me.

Blechh.

And not just once.

Double blechh.

I found a piece of Kleenex in my coat pocket and used it to scrub at my cheeks and lips until the tissue disintegrated into pieces of lint that I had to pick out of my mouth. We were crossing the river on the Mass. Ave. Bridge by then, and the driver was eyeing me in the rearview mirror with a concerned expression.

"Everything okay back there?" he asked.

"Sure," I said with dignity, forming the words as clearly as I could around a mouth full of tissue fragments. I seemed to be making quite an impression on the Boston area's fleet of taxi drivers.

Copley Place had sprouted several new appendages since I was last there, including a couple of new hotels, a new office building that bore more than a passing resemblance to R2-D2, and a maze of shopping arcades. I'd passed the same Ann Taylor three times before I realized that I was repeatedly missing the turnoff that would take me to the pedestrian walkway to Copley Place proper and the restaurant we'd designated as our meeting place.

I scurried along the passageway, ignoring the stores I passed and zigzagging through the crowds of Saturday shoppers in search of post-holiday bargains. By the time I'd reached my destination I felt as if I'd run a marathon.

My friends were seated calmly around a table on the floor of the mall outside the restaurant, chatting and sipping coffee and orange juice. "Hil, do you have Detective O'Connell's card?"

She smiled. "Well, good morning to you, too. There's something white on your lip."

I tried not to snarl. "Do you have it?" I repeated.

"Do you want me to help you get it off?"

"Get what off?"

"The white thing."

"No, I want to know if you have O'Connell's card."

"Of course I do."

I knew that I could count on Hilary for something. "Give it to me. Now."

"Will you give it back?" she started to ask, but then she got a better look at the expression on my face and handed the card over without saying anything else.

I found a relatively quiet corner and dialed O'Connell's number, swiping at the bits and pieces of tissue that were stuck to my lips. I may have been ambivalent about calling him to report my suspicions regarding Barbara Barnett, but I was pretty comfortable calling to tell him that I knew who his serial killer was. I decided in advance that I would leave out the part about the serial killer having kissed me.

My fairy godmother had returned to the cave where she seemed to be hiding out of late. It took three tries for my call to go through, and when it finally did O'Connell wasn't there and whoever answered his phone refused to page him, which seemed irresponsible, at best. I left a message, stressing repeatedly the urgency of the matter.

That done, I returned to my friends' table and handed the card back to Hilary. Then I deposited my frazzled self in the empty chair, gripped the edge of the table with my hands, and began beating my head against it at a slow but steady pace.

"Something wrong, Rachel?" asked Luisa dryly.

"Everything's wrong," I answered plaintively.

"Stop that," said Emma, grabbing hold of the knot of hair at the back of my head. "You'll end up doing serious damage."

"Do you think anyone will be able to tell the difference?" asked Hilary.

"Rachel, why don't you sit up straight and tell us what's going on." Jane had her matronly voice of reason on, the one that she usually reserved for recalcitrant students.

"Poor Baby Hallard," I said.

"What do you mean?" Now Jane sounded offended.

"Eighteen-plus years of being lectured to by your matronly voice of reason."

She laughed. "Just imagine how Sean feels. But seriously, Rach, what has you all worked up?"

"Where should I start?" I asked dejectedly.

"At the beginning," said Emma. "And look, we got you a Diet Coke." She waved the can before me, and I perked up.

"Wow," said Hilary. "If only Pavlov could have seen Rachel and Diet Coke. He wouldn't have needed to keep tormenting those poor dogs."

Under the careful questioning of my friends, I recounted that morning's adventures, starting with the takeover the Barnetts had launched and my suspicions about the attacks on Sara being a little too convenient.

"Let me get this straight," said Luisa, ever the skeptic. "You think that Barbara Barnett tried to kill Sara? All so that she could help her son take over a not very big company when they already have plenty of money?"

"From everything you've said before Adam sounds like such a weenie," said Hilary. "Are you sure he has it in him?"

"Adam's just the puppet," I said. "Barbara's the puppet master."

"I just can't believe that she would be chatting you up about makeup and diet tips in the ladies' room if she were behind the attacks on Sara," added Jane.

"Oh my God. I am a complete idiot," I blurted out.

"Don't be so hard on yourself, Rachel. Everybody jumps to conclusions sometimes," said Emma. "It's perfectly understandable that your thoughts got a bit convoluted."

"No, it's not that at all. If anything, I just realized how unconvoluted my thoughts are."

"We're listening," prompted Jane.

"Ephedra. Or some other sort of diet pill. I bet that's what Barbara was taking in the ladies' room this morning. And it's the exact sort of thing Matthew was talking about last night. If you gave a big dose of that to someone you could kill her. Hell, a big dose put Sara into cardiac arrest. Barbara Barnett has a stash of ephedra, and she used it to try to kill Sara."

Hilary snorted. Unfortunately, she'd been drinking orange juice at the same time, so some of it dribbled out of her nose. Jane grimaced and handed her a napkin. "You're saying that Barbara Barnett tried to kill Sara with *diet pills?*"

"I don't know. But maybe. I mean, she was at the hospital yesterday afternoon, too. And when we left she was saying that she'd left her gloves in Sara's room. Maybe she sneaked back in and put something in Sara's IV while she was asleep. It's possible. Anyhow, the takeover and Barbara trying to kill Sara are only part of the problem. I haven't even told you the worst part yet."

"You mean the part about your boyfriend cheating on you?" asked Hilary.

"No, the other worst part. The part about *Love Story* guy being the prostitute killer." I filled them in on my encounter with Jonathan Beasley and his hoisting bodies into the trunk of his car with a telltale Harvard scarf knotted around his neck, the same one he'd used to strangle various Boston area "lowlifes."

This time Luisa snorted orange juice out her nose. "You've got to be kidding. You really think Jonathan Beasley—the Ryan O'Neal to your Ali MacGraw—is a serial killer?" I knew I should never have told her about the Ryan O'Neal/Ali MacGraw thing.

"Why not? I mean, Ted Bundy was supposed to be totally charming."

"Rachel's right," said Hilary. "Ted Bundy was a hottie."

"I can't believe you just called Ted Bundy a 'hottie,'" said Jane.

"I can't believe you just used the word 'hottie,'" said Luisa.

"I didn't even get a chance to see him," said Emma sadly.

"Ted Bundy?"

"No, you idiot. *Love Story* guy."

"He's very cute," said Hilary.

"In a Ken doll sort of way," added Luisa.

"But Rachel likes that sort of thing," interjected Jane.

"Could you all shut up already?" My voice, which had been plaintive before, now sounded downright whiny. "I need your help, here. On any other day, I could handle it. But not when everything with Peter is going up in flames. Or down in flames. Whichever."

Emma patted my hand solicitously and flagged the waitress for another Diet Coke.

"Which part is worse?" asked Hilary. "That Peter's cheating on you or that your other love interest is a serial killer?"

"Is that a helpful comment, Hilary?" asked Luisa.

"You'll feel better once you can tell the police everything," Emma reassured me. "I mean, it's one thing for you to have to worry about the takeover and whatever's going on with Peter, but they should be dealing with all of the other stuff."

How could I tell her that all of the other stuff was almost a welcome distraction from the takeover and whatever was going on with Peter?

"Oh, no," said Jane.

"Oh, no what?" I asked.

"Don't look now." In unison, we all turned to look in the direction she'd told us not to look.

We were sitting near the base of an escalator leading down from the shops on the upper floors. So when I saw the woman on the escalator carrying the trademark blue Tiffany's bag, laughing up at something her companion had said, it didn't immediately register. After all, there was a Tiffany's up there, among other stores.

Then I noticed that the woman holding the Tiffany's bag looked familiar.

With a sinking feeling, I realized that not only did I know her, the man standing next to her, the one making her laugh, was someone I knew very well. In fact, we'd shared a bed the previous night.

It was Peter, with Abigail. And they looked as if their shopping expedition had been an unqualified success.

Twenty-Three

They moved as if in slow motion, she standing one step below him on the escalator. I watched as she turned back toward him, to better catch his words. The movement made her long dark hair swing, a silken curtain flowing from one shoulder to the other, and as she tilted her face up the light glossed the fine curves of her high cheek-bones, delicate nose and oval forehead. I could see Peter's familiar profile, bending down to make himself heard, gazing into her expressive dark eyes with the affectionate look I knew so well and speaking with the lips I knew even better.

"Is that Abigail? If so, she really does look like Christy Turlington," said Hilary.

Jane, Luisa and Emma shushed her in unison, and I was pretty confident that Jane added a sharp elbow to Hilary's ribs.

"I mean, she looks like how Christy Turlington would look if Christy Turlington were a hussy. You're much prettier, Rach." But I could barely hear her over the laughter of the Jinxing Gods.

Peter and Abigail stepped off the escalator and paused, still deep in animated conversation. He put his hand on her arm, as if to emphasize a point. Then Abigail kissed him on an indeterminate spot somewhere between the cheek and the lips—it was hard to tell from where we were sitting since the back of her head blocked his face. Being tall and gazellelike, she didn't need to stand on tiptoe to kiss him, the way I did. Then Peter headed off in the direction of the convention center at a rapid clip.

"That's it," said Hilary. "He can't treat Rachel like this. I'm going after him. He needs to get his head on straight." She was half out of her seat, but Jane and Luisa each took an arm and managed to restrain her.

Abigail, meanwhile, had started toward the Starbucks adjacent to where we sat.

I don't know what possessed me. If I'd been thinking clearly, I would have hid under the table until she'd passed. But so much had happened already that morning that I seemed to have entered an altered state of consciousness. Unbidden, *Twilight Zone* Rachel called out Abigail's name, loudly and in a welcoming tone.

Abigail stopped and looked around, trying to identify where the voice had come from. I stood and waved, a forced smile plastered on my face, until her eyes focused on our table. I didn't think I imagined the way her expression changed, morphing from pleasant calm to flustered embarrassment, but by the time she reached us she seemed calm again, although slightly pinkish in the cheeks. And she clutched the Tiffany's bag in one hand, trying to shield it with her body, as if I would snatch it from her and run off with it.

"Rachel!" she cried. "What a surprise. What brings you

here?" She leaned her willowy self down and gave me an awkward one-armed hug, careful to keep her body between me and the Tiffany's bag.

"Slut," I heard Hilary mutter under her breath.

When in doubt, be gracious. These were words I tried to live by, usually unsuccessfully. And I wished I felt more doubt about what I'd just seen. Still, I dredged up enough graciousness to introduce Abigail around.

"It's so nice to meet you all," she said, her smile revealing even, pearly white teeth and a fetching dimple in her right cheek. "Peter mentioned you have your annual reunion with your college roommates this weekend. It sounds like a great tradition—I should do something like that with my friends from college."

Hilary muttered something else, but Emma's coughing fit covered up her words.

"It is a great tradition," I agreed. And then, scraping the bottom of my graciousness pool, I managed in a voice that sounded genuinely nice, "It's just too bad that Peter's been too busy with work to join us. How's the sales effort going?"

"Slowly," she answered. "The negotiations have been pretty intense."

"Not too intense to get some shopping done," Jane pointed out, in a tone that could only be described as arch. I turned to her, surprised. Arch was a tone I'd never heard before from Jane. Perhaps pregnancy was sharpening her tongue.

The pink in Abigail's cheeks seemed to deepen into red, but it could have been a trick of the light. She shifted the Tiffany's bag from one hand to the other. "Um, yeah. Actually, it's, um, a gift for the, um, the client. If we get them signed up as a customer. We got them some, um, some—"

"Pens?" supplied Emma helpfully. Only if you knew Emma as well as I did would you pick up on the sarcasm in her tone. And sarcasm from Emma was even more rare than archness from Jane.

"Yes. Pens. As a gift."

"How considerate," said Emma.

"Well, I'm glad I ran into you, Rachel, and it was great to meet you all, but I need to get going. I'd just stopped to get some coffee before heading back to the convention center." Abigail indicated the Starbucks. "We have yet another meeting with the potential client, and I don't think I can handle it without a big dose of caffeine. I haven't had a decent night's sleep since I got here."

This time I heard what Hilary said, but Abigail was busy saying goodbye to everyone, and she didn't seem to notice.

"Knock 'em dead," I said as she rushed off.

Hilary turned to me. "Knock 'em dead?"

"What was I supposed to say?"

"You could try 'Keep your hands off my boyfriend, you skank,' for starters. Are you sure you don't want me to go after her? I'd be delighted to tell her for you."

"Hilary," began Luisa, "I think we may be on the wrong track—"

The ring of my cell phone was a welcome interruption from their spatting. I checked the caller ID, relieved to see that it was neither Peter, with more lame excuses, nor Jonathan Beasley, my favorite serial killer. "Hello?"

"Ms. Benjamin. This is Detective O'Connell. I'm returning your call. You said it was urgent?"

My friends were concerned enough about my delicate mental condition to insist on coming with me to the police station for moral support. In fact, Hilary volunteered to accompany me before the phrase "moral support" had even been uttered.

Ten minutes later we'd retrieved Jane's Volvo from the garage where she'd parked. I sat up front with Jane, trying to ignore Hilary's monologue about the various things she would do to Peter, and to Abigail, if she were in my shoes. I knew that this was Hilary's way of being supportive, but mostly I was just wishing I weren't anywhere near my shoes. My phone rang again, as if it could sense when I needed a break from Hilary. This time it was the Caped Avenger.

"Rachel, darling. Whitaker Jamieson here."

"Hello, Whit." He liked to be called Whit. He felt it lent him a raffish air that went nicely with his cape.

"Wasn't this morning fabulous? Such a rush. And this deal's going to be such fabulous fun! I only wish you could have been part of our side of it, but Stan Winslow said you'd have a conflict of interest or something absurd like that. I tried to get around him, but he foisted me off on this Epson fellow. I must say, my dear, that boy's nowhere as much fun as you are. He never wants to go anywhere fabulous for dinner. And he definitely lacks your charms." The way the Caped Avenger said "charms" made me wish I didn't have any, but it was probably a good thing I did. Or at least that he thought I did. Otherwise, he would never have agreed to meet me in an hour to discuss his "fabulous" deal. ("The bar at the Ritz, darling. It's so fabulous.")

I must have passed the Cambridge police station in Central Square on more occasions than I could count, but I'd never been inside. It turned out that I hadn't been missing much.

Jane found a metered spot across the street from the entrance, so she parked and we all went inside together. Hilary didn't bother to hide her disappointment when O'Connell sent a uniformed officer to bring me, and only me, up to see him. Telling my friends I shouldn't be long, I followed the policeman up a flight of stairs and down a hallway.

O'Connell's office defied all stereotypes. I was expecting

chaos, overflowing ashtrays and coffee mugs with dregs of whisky remaining from the bottle any seasoned detective must keep stowed in a drawer. Instead, O'Connell's desk was spotless except for a couple of neatly labeled file folders and a liter bottle of Poland Spring water that didn't look like it was even spiked.

The man himself looked nearly as spotless as his office—he'd clearly managed a shower and a change, even if the haggard set of his features suggested that he hadn't managed to sleep since I'd last seen him. He rose when I came in and ushered me into his visitor's chair with a grave courtesy before resuming his seat behind his desk. He rested his elbows on its surface and templed his fingers together, balancing his chin on their tips. "What can I do for you, Ms. Benjamin?"

"I'm sorry to bother you—I know how busy you must be—but this is important. I'm actually here about two of your cases."

"*Two* of my cases? Now this is a blue-ribbon day." Sarcasm seemed to be in the air today; if it had infected Jane and Emma, I held out little hope that a hardened police detective would be immune.

"I think I know who the prostitute killer is. And I also think that I may know who's behind the attacks on Sara Grenthaler."

"Yes, you mentioned that in your previous message. Grant Crocker."

"I know, but I may have been wrong about that." I related the events of this morning's board meeting to O'Connell. "I think Barbara Barnett might have tried to smooth the way by making sure the primary opponent to a takeover was out of commission. The witness said he wasn't sure if he saw a man or a woman, and Barbara's tall. And really fit for a woman her age."

"So let me get this straight," said O'Connell after hearing

me out. "Barbara Barnett attacked Sara Grenthaler in the boathouse in order to prevent her putting up a fight for control of the company."

"I think so. She probably knew about Sara's rowing schedule. And she probably has one of those scarves. It seems like everyone has them."

"And then, when the first attempt didn't work, she put ephedra in Ms. Grenthaler's IV bag?"

"She was at the hospital yesterday afternoon," I pointed out. "We left at the same time, but she mentioned that she had left her gloves in Sara's room. Sara had just taken a painkiller when we left, so she was probably asleep, and Barbara managed to get drugs into her IV. And then maybe it took a while for the drugs to work their way into her system and have any effect. I'm pretty sure that Barbara's on some sort of diet pill. I saw her taking something this morning, and she's obsessed with weight loss."

Why was it that what had seemed to make perfect sense in my head sounded so flimsy when I laid it out for someone else? I had the same feeling I'd always had as a child when I'd been sent to see the school nurse. I could have been puking my guts out, but she still made me feel like I was faking. I shook my head to clear that memory but now that I was actually telling my story to a trained professional, it did sound pretty absurd.

"Look," I went on, "I know it sounds implausible. But having Sara out of it while her son's making a run for her company makes it all a lot easier. Barbara had motive, means and opportunity." I'd read my share of Agatha Christie novels, after all.

"It's an interesting idea, and I'll look into it. Now, let's move on to the other case. Who's the perp in that one?"

I was having a bad day, and this time there was no smile to take the edge off his tone. I stood up. "I am not, I repeat, not, a hysterical female. I wouldn't be here if I thought I was wasting your time."

He ran a hand through his hair. "Please. Ms. Benjamin. Sit down. I don't mean to make light of your hypotheses."

I didn't sit down. "Listen, buddy." I had no idea where the "buddy" came from. "I'm not here for my health. You may be fine and dandy with Jonathan Beasley running around killing prostitutes willy-nilly, but I think some of the area's concerned citizens might be a little upset about it." I had even less an idea as to where I'd come up with "fine and dandy" and "willy-nilly."

Now his lips were pressed together, as if it were the only way he could contain his laughter. After a long pause, he seemed to trust himself to open his mouth. "You think that Professor Beasley is the prostitute killer."

"Yes, I do," I said in my most confident and authoritative voice. And I used the same voice to tell him about watching Jonathan load a body into the trunk of his Saab, as well as my theory about his potential motivations.

"You really saw a foot poking out of the duffel?" O'Connell asked me.

"Yes. Caucasian. With red toenails." I gave an involuntary shudder.

"Caucasian?" he repeated, arching an eyebrow.

"I watch *Law & Order*. Isn't that the term I'm supposed to use?"

"And the bag seemed heavy?"

"Beasley's a pretty strong guy, but he was having trouble lifting it, like it was unwieldy."

"Okay. I'll check into it."

"Really?"

"Really."

"And the thing about Barbara Barnett? You'll check into that, too?"

"I'll check into that, too," he affirmed. "And in the meantime, we've still got a guard at the door of Ms. Grenthaler's hospital room and UHS has beefed up their security protocol."

He seemed to be taking me seriously, but I hadn't forgotten his barely suppressed laughter. "I'll be going then," I said in my most haughty voice and headed for the door.

He called after me. "Listen, Ms. Benjamin. Rachel. Wait."

"What?" I asked, spinning around to face him. There was nothing smug or supercilious about the expression on his face. If anything, he looked embarrassed.

"I—I owe you an apology. I didn't mean to be rude. And I hope I didn't give you the wrong impression. I do appreciate all of this information. It's just that I'm really, really tired. We found another body last night. I've been up for two days straight, and I'm sort of on edge."

This, of course, made me feel guilty. "Oh. That must be hard."

"It is. And we have hardly any leads, and you wouldn't believe the phone calls I'm getting. When they're not nutcases confessing to crimes they didn't commit, they're city officials threatening to have my job."

"Oh," I said again.

"And here you are, trying to do the right thing, and I was being a jerk."

"No. You weren't." Well, he had been a little bit of a jerk, but it was hard to blame him. Even I had found my story to be outlandish. "I'm sorry, too. I didn't mean to yell at you."

"I probably deserved it."

"I probably was a little hysterical. I've had a bad couple of days, too."

"Either way, I owe you one."

We looked at each other, mutually sheepish. Then I had an idea.

"I know how you can make it up to me."

★ ★ ★

His phone rang, and he apologized to me before picking it up. "Sorry, they wouldn't have put it through if it weren't important." I didn't point out that I had said my call was urgent and that they hadn't put it through. "O'Connell, here." There was a pause while he listened to whomever was on the other end. "Uh-huh…uh-huh."

My cell phone rang, so I picked it up.

"Rachel? It's Edie. Edie Michaels."

"What's wrong?" I asked.

"I'm here with Sara, in her room at UHS. And we found another letter."

"In her room?"

"Yes. It was in the folds of a magazine I brought her. Only somebody must have put it there after I gave it to her. I bought the magazine at Out of Town News yesterday evening before I picked up the pizza, and then I came directly here. I'm sorry to bother you, but Professor Beasley didn't answer his phone, and I called the police and they said Detective O'Connell was in a meeting."

"I know, he's actually meeting with me, but he's on a call right now." I looked over at O'Connell, and he was still occupied with his phone. Then I heard the beep that indicated I had another call coming through. "Edie, can you hold on?"

"Okay."

I fumbled with the handset for a moment before finding the flash button. "Hello?"

"Hi. It's me." It took me a second to realize it was Peter.

"I'm on another call," I said abruptly. "I'll call you back."

I pressed the flash button again and returned to Edie.

"Listen, Edie, I'll tell O'Connell about the letter, but it's probably nothing to worry about." If Barbara Barnett was behind the attacks on Sara, it looked like her Stalker was only Creepy and not Violent. "Can you hang out with Sara for a bit longer?" I checked my watch. I was due to meet the Caped Avenger in a half hour, but then I would go to UHS. I wanted to check on the security for myself, and I also needed to update Sara on everything that was going on with the company. I wanted to make sure she wasn't alone in the meantime, just in case Barbara Barnett decided to pay a visit.

"Sure."

O'Connell and I finished our calls at the same time. I told him about the new stalking letter as he escorted me back to the reception area. His brow furrowed. "I'm not happy about that."

"Not happy about what?" asked Hilary brightly, rising to greet us.

O'Connell looked at me, and I nodded at him. He turned to her, and his smile was only slightly stiff. "I need some coffee," he said. "I've got to make a couple of phone calls first, but if you can wait until I'm done, maybe you could come with me and we could do that interview you mentioned?"

Twenty-Four

We left Hilary with O'Connell and returned to the car. Jane offered to drop me off at the Ritz. I no longer seemed to be on the verge of a nervous breakdown, so my friends had decided they could trust leaving me to my own devices and resume their planned shopping expedition. They were heading back to Copley Place and the Ritz was conveniently on the way.

"Call us after you're done," said Jane. "If this meeting doesn't take too long, you can catch up with us."

"A little retail therapy might be nice," added Emma.

"I'd love to, but I'm going to UHS after this," I said.

"Maybe we can pick some things up for you," suggested Luisa.

I shook my head. "No, that's all right. But thank you." Luisa's family practically owned a small South American country, and even with my lavish year-end bonus, I doubted that our respective ideas of "picking some things up" would have much in common. Luisa's would likely have a few more zeros at the end of it than mine, and I had no desire to take out a second mortgage on my apartment.

Jane pulled up in front of the familiar hotel on Arlington Street. There was a newer Ritz, across the Public Garden and Boston Common, but I'd known without asking that the Caped Avenger would automatically choose the more traditional option, the one that was a Boston institution. Besides, I'd seen him here the previous day.

The doorman helped me out of the Volvo, and I waved my friends off. The urge to abandon my responsibilities and go with them was strong; the yearning was practically physical it was so intense. But I was on a mission. Probably a fruitless one, but a mission nonetheless. I squared my shoulders and let the doorman lead me into the lobby.

It was only two o'clock, but the Caped Avenger had said to meet him in the bar, so that's where I went. It was an elegant but welcoming room, and it looked much as one would think the bar at the Ritz in Boston should look—lots of dark paneling and heavy upholstered furniture and the general air of rigorous good taste that had made Ralph Lauren sublimely rich. While the bar was a popular meeting place for power drinks, it also served light meals, and a handful of people were seated at the various tables scattered around the room, the remains of their decorous lunches in front of them. It was a nice spot for a leisurely Saturday meal, particularly when the weather outside was as unpleasant as it was today.

"Rachel, darling!" Everyone in the room turned to the corner from which the flamboyant greeting came, and I was sure that nobody was disappointed by what they saw. It would have been hard not to notice the Caped Avenger before, sitting by the window in his idiosyncratic attire, but when he got to his feet, swept his cape over his shoulders, and beckoned me toward him with a dramatic wave of his (fortunately empty) martini glass, you'd have to be blind to miss him. Heads swung first to him, and then to me, obviously curious as to what sort of person would be meeting the bizarre septuagenarian who seemed to be dressed in his Halloween costume several months after Halloween.

I felt my cheeks burning as I threaded my way through the crowded room to his table. The Caped Avenger gripped me by my shoulders and gave me a Continental triple kiss: one cheek, other cheek, first cheek. While it was never easy to gauge the Caped Avenger's level of sobriety from his behavior, I had the sense that the empty glass he flourished had not contained his first drink of the day. If I knew the Caped Avenger, and unfortunately I did, he'd probably come straight here from the board meeting.

"Hi, Whit."

"Sit down, my dear, sit down! No, not over there, you silly gorgeous goose. Here, next to me. The banquette's far more comfortable."

I smiled (when in doubt, be gracious) but ignored his suggestion and sank into a chair instead, carefully ensuring that the low mahogany table was between us. The Caped Avenger snapped his fingers, and a waiter appeared instantaneously.

"This young lady needs a cocktail, my good man. And I would adore another vodka martini."

"Ketel One?"

"I'm thinking Belvedere this time. And very dry. Just *kiss* the glass with vermouth."

"Very good, sir. And what can I get you, miss?" I took an appreciative note of the "miss." I liked this waiter already. Maybe the twenty years I'd aged in the past two days hadn't yet taken its toll on my appearance.

Without warning, my stomach growled. A barely touched bread basket beckoned from a nearby table, and I realized I was starving when I had to repress the urge to make a grab for it.

I'd had no breakfast, I remembered, nor had I eaten anything at brunch. "May I have a cheeseburger and a Diet Coke?"

"Certainly, miss." The waiter's expression remained professionally detached, as if my uncouth order was perfectly appropriate for our high-brow surroundings.

"And does that come with fries?"

"Yes, miss, it does."

"Could I get extra fries?"

"Certainly, miss."

"And a lot of ketchup? Extra ketchup?"

"Of course, miss."

I sat back in my chair, relieved as the waiter hurried off with our order.

The Caped Avenger beamed, albeit lasciviously. "There's nothing more attractive than a woman with a healthy appetite. You need some more meat on your bones." This comment made me doubly glad I wasn't sitting next to him. Similar comments in the past had been accompanied by a good pinch to demonstrate just how much meat I lacked, although Whitaker usually chose one of my meatier body parts to pinch.

"So, Whit," I began. "I was surprised to see you this morning."

"Isn't it exciting? Such a fabulous deal! Although, I have to admit, I was surprised to see you there, as well. I hadn't realized you were involved with the company. Stan had simply said that you'd have a conflict of interest and insisted that I work with that Scott person. Really, that young man has no sense of humor. And he certainly lacks your fashion sense, darling."

I couldn't disagree with that.

"So, tell me, Whit. How did you get involved with the deal?"

"Oh, you know how it is. I have my ear to the ground,

darling. And I'm known in certain circles as the man to see when you want to get a deal done." I couldn't imagine what circles those might be, and I wasn't sure I wanted to. "Besides, I've known Adam since he was just a tyke. His mother was an old flame of mine and we stayed in touch, even after she remarried. Not that she can hold a candle to you, darling."

Barbara Barnett and the Caped Avenger? Now that was a match made in heaven. Or somewhere. It was nice to have one mystery solved, at least. And I supposed that I should be flattered that Whitaker felt that a former Miss Texas couldn't hold a candle to me.

"So," continued Whitaker, "when I was asked to help put this deal together, I could tell my superior experience and know-how would come in handy." Whitaker's deep pockets were handier than his experience and know-how, but I knew that there was nothing to gain by saying that out loud.

"When did you get involved?" I asked.

"I'm sorry?"

"Did Barbara call? Or Adam? And when?" Was it before or after Tom Barnett's death was what I wanted to know. I was still curious as to how long Barbara had been hatching her plot.

"Oh, last week sometime. Or maybe the week before? Time flies, darling, it just flies away. On wings." He demonstrated the movement of time by fluttering his arms, nearly knocking over the fresh martini our waiter had delivered.

I tried, in vain, to get the Caped Avenger to give me more detail. I didn't think he was holding out on me; rather, he simply didn't remember, and the measure of undiluted vodka that he'd downed in two gulps wasn't helping.

My cheeseburger arrived, and I doused it liberally with ketchup before inhaling it. Whitaker, meanwhile, inhaled a couple more martinis. While the drinks didn't help him to remember much about when, specifically, he had been brought into the deal, it did loosen his tongue about Adam.

"Frankly," he told me, smoothing his cravat (yes, he wore a cravat) with a wizened hand, "I think if it weren't for my involvement young Adam would be in over his head. He's a bright enough boy, but he really lacks the experience to carry this off. And I do get the sense that he had an ax to grind with his stepfather."

"Tom wasn't enthusiastic about Adam being involved in the company," I explained.

"Well, I'm sure he would have approved if he'd known that I'd be on board, guiding young Adam with a sure hand. You know, in a senior statesman sort of role." I admired his ability to say "senior statesman" without slurring his words. By my count, he had at least four martinis under his belt.

"Did Barbara or Adam say anything about Sara Grenthaler?" I asked. "She does own more than forty percent of the company, and her father was the founder. Tom always intended for her to take over from him when she was ready."

"Oh, Barbara mentioned that she has a big stake. But she gave me the sense that the girl was a bit of a dilettante. One of those spoiled trust-fund types. Gracious—I've seen enough of them, darling. In fact, I almost was one myself." The unspoken comparison was there, implicit in his words: he, too, could have been mistaken for a spoiled trust-fund type—that is, before he became a takeover artist and media mogul in his eighth decade of life. "Anyhow, Barbara assured me that she wouldn't be a problem."

Once again, Whitaker was vague on the timing of Barbara's comments about Sara. But I sensed my opening and went for it. "So, Whit, are you financing the entire bid single-handedly?"

"Why, yes, yes, I am," he answered proudly.

"That's a pretty big chunk of change to lock up in one deal."

"Well, yes, it is. And I'm sure my advisors will all act like nervous Nellies and counsel me against it. You know how they are about putting all of one's eggs in the same basket.

But how often does a fabulous opportunity like this come along?" He signaled for yet another martini. I was still on my second Diet Coke, although I'd made short work of the burger and fries.

"Not often," I agreed. "But, you could be part of the majority ownership consortium without using up all of your eggs."

This point seemed to reach its mark, although I was starting to feel buzzed just watching the Caped Avenger down his most recent martini.

"What do you mean?" he asked. The Caped Avenger was too rich to have missed out on the cheap gene that seemed to accompany so many great fortunes. He'd bragged to me on several occasions about having his capes made by a Hong Kong tailor for a mere fraction of what he'd have to pay in New York or London. And I'd just suggested to him that he could get something he wanted for less than he thought he'd have to pay for it. Whitaker Jamieson might not be the sort of white knight found in fairy tales, but if I could convince him to withdraw his support and partner with Sara instead to finance her acquisition of an additional ten percent stake, the company would be safe from a potential takeover, even if the Barnetts did manage to scramble up another source of backing.

The Caped Avenger was intrigued, or at least he seemed to be intrigued through his vodka-induced haze. He assured me he'd give it some thought. And then he blinked. But his eyes stayed shut. A moment later, he was snoring gently, seated upright on the banquette.

I picked up the tab, including a generous tip. The bar had cleared out, and the waiter said he'd keep an eye on Whitaker. I took one last look at him before I left. I hoped that somewhere in his drunken snooze he was thinking about my pitch and debating its merits. He probably hadn't noticed that I'd essentially thrown myself on his mercy, but that was pretty much what I'd done. If he didn't switch sides, my side's goose was well on its way to being cooked.

The doorman flagged down a cab for me, and I asked the driver to take me to Harvard Square. My wallet was stuffed with cab receipts already, and I hadn't even been in Boston for seventy-two hours. My trip was turning out far differently than I'd imagined, I thought, remembering how contentedly I'd anticipated the weekend when I'd been on the shuttle up from New York. Instead of romantic room-service meals, I'd been in one taxi after another going from one frustrating encounter to another. And here I was, off to have yet another unpleasant discussion. It was all my fault, really. I should have known better than to anticipate a trip with such pleasure. It was a guaranteed way to screw up even the most carefully laid plans. At least I'd ensured that the police were investigating the Barnetts and tracking down Jonathan Beasley.

Still, I wasn't looking forward to updating Sara about the takeover attempt, but I'd told the Porters and Brian Mulcahey I'd take care of it—in fact, I'd insisted on it. I was determined not to let her panic, and even though I was panicking, I felt that I stood a better chance of reassuring her on this front than they did. Sara had enough to worry about, just getting well. A thwack on the head and cardiac arrest in less than two days couldn't be good for a person.

Although, at the rate I was going, enforced bed rest didn't sound so bad.

Twenty-Five

I used the downtime in the cab to make a phone call. I knew it was probably futile, but I owed it to Sara to explore every option, and that included Barbara Barnett. Just because I suspected she was a frustrated murderer didn't preclude my making an attempt, however vain, to try to talk her out of launching a takeover and into respecting the wishes of her late husband instead. And it wasn't like she had any reason to try to kill me.

Barbara answered the phone herself, which surprised me. She didn't seem like the type to give the maid weekends off. She greeted me warmly, as if there were no sides in this struggle but we were instead one big happy family. I'd barely identified myself before I was treated to a breathless spiel about how exciting it all was and wasn't Adam impressive this morning? I made noncommittal noises until her words finally slowed to a trickle, at which point I asked if it would be possible to get together and talk.

"Why, I'd love to, honey, but I'm just booked today," she drawled. "I've got a hair appointment and then the yoga instructor comes by and then I'm due at a drinks party." One would never have guessed that her husband had died only eight days ago. She seemed to be taking the term "Merry Widow" to heart. As if reading my thoughts, she continued on. "You know, Tom's death has been so hard on me. I miss him every minute of the day, but I've been trying to keep myself busy. And all of this excitement with the company has really given me a new lease on life. It's so wonderful to have something to look forward to, honey."

"I bet," I said, trying to keep the sarcasm out of my voice. Tom would be rolling over in his grave if he knew what was happening. Although, if he'd been cremated then I guessed he didn't have a grave. And, so soon after lunch, I didn't want to imagine how his ashes might be reacting. "How about tomorrow morning?" I suggested. After all, it wasn't like I'd be spending the time snuggling in bed with Peter, assuming he was even there. And I'd make sure that plenty of people knew where I was going, just in case Barbara did decide that there was a reason she wanted me dead.

She agreed that tomorrow morning would be fine before launching into a reprisal of her favorite song, titled "My Son the Tycoon." Its various verses and repeated chorus kept me on the phone until the cab reached Harvard Square.

The elevator ride to the fifth-floor infirmary was beginning to give me a feeling of déjà vu, and the nurse at reception gave me a familiar wave, as if we were old friends. This really wasn't turning into the weekend I'd planned.

O'Connell was as good as his word, and there was a uniformed police officer posted outside Sara's door. He had a clipboard with a list of names. Fortunately, mine was on it, but he insisted on seeing a photo ID. I showed him my New

York State driver's license, and he carefully checked my face against the thumbnail-size picture, ultimately deciding that there was enough of a resemblance to risk sending me into the room. "Thank you, ma'am," he said, handing back my license.

This "ma'am" really hurt, given that it took into account both my looks and my date of birth, which was plainly marked on my license. On any other day, I might have taken him aside and let him know that recklessly ma'am-ing people was not a recipe for success. In fact, if anything it was likely to slow one's pace of advancement through life. But today I had too much else on my agenda to show the guy the error of his ways. Instead, I gave the door a gentle knock and let myself in.

"Hi, Rachel." Sara was sitting up in bed, and, all things considered, she looked well. Still, there were more tubes and wires attached to her than there had been the day before. I guessed that the hospital was monitoring her condition carefully after the events of the previous evening.

Edie was there, too, as promised. It was fortunate that she wasn't going through recruiting, because she'd definitely been putting in the hours here by Sara's side. "You just missed Professor Beasley," she told me.

Sara gave me a look that was almost conspiratorial. "If I'd known you'd be here so soon, we would have tried to make him stay longer."

I felt myself blanch at the suggestion.

"Did he say where he was going?" I asked. If he did, I could call O'Connell so he could track him down.

"No," said Edie. "He just said he had an appointment. He left right after we showed him the letter. He didn't seem too worried about it."

Probably because he was too busy thinking about where he was going to find his next prostitute or other Boston-area

"lowlife" to strangle and dump. Or perhaps he was still figuring out where to dispose of the body he had stashed in
the trunk of his car. I didn't want to be the one to tell Sara
and Edie that their revered professor was a serial killer, and
if Beasley had come and gone without incident, there was
probably no compelling need to do so. Besides, it would be
breaking from pattern for him to try and kill a student. According to Hilary, who, sad to say, was the closest thing to an
expert I had, serial killers tended to stick to a pattern, choosing the same type of victim for each repeated crime.

"He brought me a book and those flowers," Sara said,
pointing out a colorful arrangement. "I don't know when he
thinks I'm going to be reading poetry, though. I'm already
days behind on my class work."

"Speaking of which, any word from Gabrielle?" I asked.

Edie shook her head. "Nope. She's still MIA. We were actually just talking to Professor Beasley about it."

"It's very weird," commented Sara.

"Has she ever disappeared like this before?"

"No," said Edie. "Never. And she's not one to step aside
when anything of significance is going on. Usually she likes
to be in the middle of any action."

"Odd," I said. But now that I thought I knew who was
behind the attacks on Sara, I couldn't work up much interest in her Psycho Roommate. Nor was I terribly interested
in the Creepy Stalker, but I asked anyhow. "So, tell me about
the most recent letter."

"It's not a big deal," said Sara.

"It is too a big deal," protested her friend. "See that copy
of *US?*" She pointed to the popular weekly on the bedside
table. I nodded. "I bought it at Out of Town News yesterday afternoon before stopping by. Sara and I were actually
looking at it together while I was here. If there'd been a let-

ter in it then we would have seen it. But the letter would have had to have been in it when I bought it, which would be hard to pull off, or I would have had to put it in myself."

"I knew it," joked Sara. "You're the one. Why didn't you just tell me how you felt?" she asked with mock seriousness. She handed me the letter.

It was a good thing that I'd had the cab ride to digest my cheeseburger. This newest installment definitely scored high on the upchuck meter.

My love —
My fury knows no bounds. What degenerate would dare to bring you harm? Never fear, my darling. I am doing everything possible to ensure you remain safe, as befits your rarified beauty.

"Yuck," I said.

"I know. It's pretty awful," Sara agreed. "But at least it's short."

"Nice way to find the silver lining," I said.

She gave a modest shrug. "I try."

"So," I summarized, "somebody slipped the letter into the magazine between when you two were reading it yesterday afternoon and this morning. Who's been here between then and now?"

Sara grimaced. "I've been over that already with the police. Although, they're more worried about whatever was put in my IV last night than the letter. But the list is pretty short, assuming somebody didn't sneak in while I was asleep, which is entirely possible. Just Edie, you, Professor Beasley, my grandparents, Barbara and Adam Barnett, and Grant Crocker."

She reeled the names off casually. I didn't have the heart to tell her that by my count there were as many as two evildoers and one Creepy Stalker on that list alone. The good news, I guessed, was that they'd all been flagged as such to the police.

The nurse came in to give Sara some painkillers while we were talking, and Edie headed out shortly thereafter, leaving me alone with Sara. I couldn't procrastinate any longer, but the nurse's timing had been superb. I'd been worried about Sara's reaction to the news about the takeover, but having her sedated in advance was helpful.

"I've got something to tell you," I said, "and before I do I want you to promise that you won't worry." I should have known that was a bad way to start. Her shoulders seemed to rise up a couple of inches, assuming a stressed-out position around her ears. I hoped that the medicine wouldn't take long to begin working its magic.

"What is it?" she asked, her voice grave with foreboding.

In as few words as possible, I laid out what had transpired at that morning's board meeting.

She was quiet for a moment, thinking over what I'd told her. "I didn't know Barbara had it in her," she said eventually. "I mean, I always knew she wanted Adam in on the company, and it was pretty clear that neither Tom nor I were going to let it happen. But she's found another way. And I'm sure she's ecstatic, isn't she?"

"Pretty much," I agreed. Ecstatic was a fairly accurate way to describe Barbara's reaction.

"More importantly, what do we do now?" She'd swung her legs out from under the covers and seemed to be getting ready to leave. She began examining the ways in which the various tubes and wires were attached to her, figuring out how to detach them.

"Oh, no, you don't," I told her. "You're not going anywhere. You're not going to help anyone by leaving here before you're ready." And with the guard posted by her door and Barbara Barnett still at liberty, this seemed to be the safest possible place for Sara right now.

"I'm ready," she said. "Besides, I can't just sit here while this is going on." But she had to stifle a yawn while she said it.

"Yes, you can. First of all, you're on medication and will probably be asleep in a few minutes. And second, I'm doing everything there is to be done." I sketched out for her my assessment of our options, and then I related my discussion with the Caped Avenger, as well as my planned meeting with Barbara the next day.

"This guy, Whitaker Jamieson—do you really think he'll change his mind?" she asked me.

"It's a strong possibility," I said. I hadn't included the part about the Caped Avenger downing a quart of vodka and passing out on the banquette at the Ritz in my narrative. It didn't seem like it would instill much confidence. Still, I held out a faint desperate hope that if I nagged him enough he would withdraw his support from the Barnetts. Or, even more faintly and more desperately, that Barbara would be arrested for attacking Sara and the entire takeover attempt would fall apart. It would be hard to implement a takeover from jail.

"Even if he does, do I want him as such a significant stakeholder in the company?"

"Let's cross that bridge when we get there," I advised. "I've known him for a while, and he fundamentally means well. I think he can be controlled. And he's currently our best bet on the white-knight front."

"That's not very reassuring," she said, her eyelids drooping with fatigue.

I couldn't disagree. "Look, even if he doesn't withdraw his support, we can file lawsuit after lawsuit to hold this thing up. I just don't want it to have to come to that. Businesses get run into the ground while people are fighting over them. There may also be the option to work out something amicable with Barbara."

Sara was unable to keep her eyes open anymore, but she gave a soft laugh. "Good luck with that. She's a freak. And she'd do anything for Adam."

"Listen," I said. "Try not to worry. I'm doing everything possible. It will all work out. I promise." I hoped my words didn't sound as hollow as they felt.

She dragged her eyes open; I could sense the effort it took.

"Do you think…do you think she had something to do with this?" she asked.

"I don't know," I admitted as her eyes closed again.

I don't know if she heard me or if she'd already drifted off into unconsciousness. But I gave the security guard a lecture on the way out, urging him to take extra care, particularly where anyone named Barnett was concerned.

Twenty-Six

A few minutes later I was standing in front of the Au Bon Pain at Holyoke Center with absolutely no idea as to where I was going to go next. The snow was still coming down steadily, and across Harvard Yard I could hear the bells of Memorial Church ringing the hour. Four o'clock, and there were no new messages on my Blackberry. I wasn't due back at Jane's until eight for cocktails and dinner, and it was probably too late to catch even the tail end of my friends' shopping expedition.

A steady stream of students and tourists passed me by as I stood in the snow and consulted my mental to-do list.

First on the list was to thwart the takeover of Grenthaler Media. I'd pleaded my case with the Caped Avenger, and I had plans to see Barbara Barnett the next day. Grenthaler's director of communications was putting out the appropriate press release. There was nothing much else I could do about it on a Saturday afternoon except fret. And I was definitely fretting. I was elevating fretting to an art form.

Second on the list, and, I hoped part of thwarting the take-over, was to prove that Barbara Barnett was guilty of attacking Grenthaler Media's primary shareholder and prevent any further attacks. Here, too, I wasn't sure what else I could be doing. Barbara seemed unlikely to suddenly confess. The police knew all about my suspicions, and O'Connell seemed to be on the case. Whether my earlier hissy fit had helped or hindered the effort was unclear, although at least it had served to extract an interview for Hilary. And the security guard seemed sufficiently competent, except for his tendency to ma'am people without cause. Again, all that was left to do was fret, but I was confident that I could fret about Sara and the takeover simultaneously. If fretting were a marketable skill, I would have been a billionaire by now. With my own reality TV show.

The third item on the list was my love life. I didn't know why I even kept it on there. It had reverted to its usual state of bleak and ugly disorder. Perhaps I should just accept my fate and acknowledge once and for all that the Jinxing Gods saw me as nothing more than a plaything, a human target in their never-ending game of Whack-a-Mole. I might as well just give it up and take myself out of the game for good. Then I'd have more time to fret over things that actually had the potential to turn around.

I'd been rejected before; in fact, I'd been rejected in more ways than I could count. The episode of *Sex and the City* in which Carrie's boyfriend broke up with her by Post-it had left me unmoved. I could top that Post-it blindfolded and with both hands tied behind my back. Watching Peter and Abigail practically make out in the middle of Copley Place left that Post-it in the dust. Especially when you took into account just having discovered that Peter's backup was a serial killer. That Post-it crumbled into insignificance when compared to my actual life.

Or lack thereof.

That's it, I decided. Right there, at that moment, standing in the middle of Harvard Square as the snowflakes danced around me, my choice came with startling swiftness and complete clarity.

I was giving it up.

I would resign myself to being perpetually single, buying my own jewelry, zipping the backs of my own dresses and never having a date to a wedding ever again, much less ever being a principal in a wedding. I knew that there were advantages to being single: the much clichéd but definitely valuable perk of full control of the remote, for example, not to mention no more apologizing for having nothing but Diet Coke and condiments in one's refrigerator. But now I was going to embrace my singledom. Just think, I told myself with growing excitement, of the money and time to be saved on grooming alone. And all of the eccentricities I could cultivate, strange eating habits and odd wardrobe choices, now that I had abandoned any concern for attracting members of the opposite sex. I'd be free of the Jinxing Gods at last.

Of course, there were children to consider. I wasn't sure if I wanted them, but this course did tend to rule them out, at least without the involvement of a sperm bank or adoption agency. And I probably lacked the appetite for single motherhood. Still, I had a couple of nieces I could spoil rotten. They would look up to me in an Auntie Mame sort of way, and potentially write fond memoirs one day, especially if I gave them particularly lavish gifts. I could afford it, since I wouldn't need to save up for orthodontia, piano lessons or college tuition for my own offspring. And I could spoil the children of my friends, as well.

I'd come to a crossroads and I'd chosen my course. I now felt invigorated—refreshed even. I decided to begin with the spoiling immediately. Baby Hallard wasn't due for nearly six months, but surely it wasn't too early to start showering him or her with presents? The Harvard Coop was across the way, and it seemed to me that Baby Hallard was desperately in need of a cotton onesie with Harvard Class of 202X emblazoned across the front. It was the sort of obnoxious garment that I'd never dress my own child in, but now that I'd decided I'd never have my own child, that was no longer a problem.

Harvard Square had changed dramatically since I'd first encountered it as an undergrad. It was hard not to walk through it without saying silent eulogies to landmarks long gone. Favorite boutiques, the infamous Tasty diner where many a night had culminated in early morning indulgences in greasy, fried food, even shops I'd never entered—I felt nostalgia for them all now that the vast majority of them had been transformed into Starbucks or painted over with a similar brush. I couldn't believe how many Starbucks there were, all congregated into an area a few blocks square. It wasn't that I hadn't been heavily caffeinated throughout my college years, but my caffeine had come from more individualized venues, with the sort of character—or, conversely, the simple lack of charm and pretension—that couldn't be easily franchised in malls across America.

The Coop itself hadn't missed out on the Starbucks-ination of the Square, but I eventually found my way to the annex where they sold novelty apparel. Nor had I been hoping in vain that I would find baby clothing with Harvard stamped all over it. There were a number of onesies to choose from in crimson on white, white on crimson, crimson-and-white striped, and even pink and blue, which seemed like it should be against the rules.

I made relatively quick work of selecting a couple of items for which Baby Hallard would doubtless be eternally grateful and waited patiently while the clerk wrapped my purchases in crimson-and-white tissue paper. I had a feeling I was going to enjoy the role of mad, frivolous auntie.

It turned out that neither my life-changing decision nor my shopping expedition had taken very long, so I decided to spend some time browsing through the books section before returning to the hotel to change for the evening's activities. What had once been a maze of haphazardly shelved texts had also been transformed by a decorator who must have trained at Barnes & Noble. In fact, I realized belatedly, it now officially was a Barnes & Noble. I happily passed up the self-improvement section since I'd decided to let myself go to complete and utter seed. I probably needed some new and eccentric interests to go with my embrace of a Miss Havisham lifestyle. Perhaps I could take up rug hooking. Or spelunking.

However, none of the books in the Hobbies section seemed to call out to me, although I did toy briefly with a coffee table tome on papier-mâché. But it weighed as much as a few lead ingots, and the mere thought of hauling it back to New York left me exhausted. It was time for a fresh infusion of Diet Coke. I abandoned the book and went off in search of caffeine.

True to the Barnes & Noble décor, there was a café on the second-floor balcony, and since I no longer cared about things like cellulite I purchased both the brownie and the Rice Krispies Treat instead of wasting precious time choosing between them. I found an empty table and sat down to enjoy my version of afternoon tea. I quickly settled in to a nice rhythm: a bite of brownie, then a sip of soda, followed by a bite of Rice Krispies Treat, and then another sip of soda. Heaven. I hadn't felt this good in days.

My table offered an excellent view of the first floor below

me, and I gazed down at the shoppers in a state of chocolate/sugar/caffeine-drenched euphoria, amusing myself by counting Harvard scarves. I was up to sixteen when I noticed that one of the scarves was draped around a familiar pair of broad shoulders browsing the shelves. Its owner's blond head was bent down to examine an open text, and there was something familiar about the blond head, as well.

It was Jonathan Beasley, studly professor by day, crazed killer by night.

My reaction was a bit slow. On the one hand, his sinister presence should have jolted me into a state of high alert. On the other hand, I was having such a nice time with my soda and empty calories that I didn't want to interrupt it by panicking. It would be such a waste of truly delicious junk food.

Then he looked up in my direction. Our eyes nearly met, but I quickly pulled the bag with Baby Hallard's onesies onto the table and ducked my head behind it. When I peeked back around the edge of the bag a moment later, Jonathan was flipping through another book.

I still didn't panic. Rationally, I didn't really think Jonathan would try to kill me or anyone else in the middle of the Coop. But a crazed serial killer was, by definition, crazed, and it didn't seem to make sense to take any unnecessary risks. With a sense of calm resignation, I gave a last, wistful look at my brownie and my Rice Krispies Treat. Well over half was left of each. But I had to find a safe spot to call O'Connell and tell him where he could apprehend his suspect. Giving up on love didn't mean neglecting my civic responsibility to help fight crime.

With a sigh, I collected my things and followed signs to the stairwell, staying as far away from the balcony railing as possible in order to keep myself out of Jonathan's line of sight. The safest thing to do was find a ladies' room and call from there, and I was pretty sure there was one on the third floor, which had the added benefit of being where they kept books about science, which didn't seem to be one of Jonathan's areas of primary interest. I headed up the flight of stairs, my legs powered by the amounts of caffeine and sugar I'd managed to ingest before being so inconveniently interrupted. The ladies' room was deserted, and I locked myself in a stall and reached for my cell phone. I was getting so used to being perpetually freaked out that my hands were perfectly steady. I was in great shape to perform surgery or operate heavy machinery if the opportunity should arise.

Of course, all I wanted to do was make a simple phone call, but I should have known better than to think anything that I tried to accomplish that day would be easy. I stared at the screen of my cell phone in frustration as it searched fruitlessly for a signal. Nothing. I turned it off and then on again, but instead of the little bars indicating signal strength the space showed a lonely X. And the phone persisted in making the same whiny noise it had been making earlier in the day.

So much for the relative safety of the ladies' room. I obviously needed to find a quiet spot closer to a window, but I'd stay up here with the science books. Holding the Blackberry in front of me like a dowsing rod, I kept my eye on the screen as I wandered through the rows of bookshelves, all stuffed with texts on various 'ologies, waiting for some little bars to appear.

I probably shouldn't have been so confident that everyone's favorite psycho killer wasn't scientifically inclined. I had to skirt more than a few nerdy-looking types who'd plopped themselves down on the floor to better examine books about spiders and quasars, but I wasn't expecting to turn a corner and nearly collide into Jonathan Beasley. He was leaning against the shelves with his back to me, a book propped open in his hands.

Whatever he was reading must have been gripping, because my gasp of horror didn't register. I hightailed it back around the corner from which I came and made a beeline for the stairs. Except that I'd been so focused on my cell phone screen I'd completely lost track of where the stairs were. And I'd never been gifted on the navigational front. This deficiency, combined with being somewhat challenged in the height department, left me at a bit of a loss. I was essentially trapped in a maze of bookshelves I couldn't see over, without a clue as to the direction in which my escape route lay. Which would have been all right if there weren't a serial killer a few feet away who was likely only temporarily distracted by whatever he was reading.

I scampered up one row of shelves and down another, turning to the left and then the right, hoping eventually to locate a perimeter of some sort that I could follow. Instead I just found science nerds, using their breaks from the research lab or computer center to hang out in the bookstore and create a human obstacle course. When I judged that I was at least a few rows away from Jonathan, I stopped to ask one if he knew where the stairs were only to find that he didn't speak English. The second guy I asked favored me with a look so blank that it left me wondering if I spoke English.

The calm resignation I'd felt a few minutes earlier was gone, morphing into a far less calm sense of panic. I quickened my pace as I threaded my way through the seemingly endless rows of shelves. Relief flooded through me when I finally spied a red exit sign on a distant wall.

I leaped over the sprawling limbs of a couple more science nerds, my eyes focused on the exit sign and salvation. I cleared the last row of books and headed for the door.

Out of the corner of my eye I saw a flash of crimson-and-white wool. Then an arm encircled my neck, nearly throwing me off my feet as it drew me into its grip.

Twenty-Seven

I screamed.

And no pathetic girly shriek, either. A bloodcurdling siren of sound that would have done any horror-movie starlet proud. I half expected to hear windows shattering.

The arm unloosed itself from my neck. My eyes flew upward to its owner's face and landed on Jonathan Beasley's blue, blue gaze.

"Don't worry," he said, his voice low and threatening. "I'm not going to kill you."

Then he cracked up.

A slew of science nerds had come running, and they were all staring at us, clearly trying to decide whether to come to my aid.

I'd been scared before. Now I was pissed, too. As if my day hadn't been bad enough. Now a serial killer was laughing at me, uproariously and in public, if you could describe an audience comprised of half the population of the molecular chemistry department as public. "You think it's funny?" I demanded, hands on my hips.

He was laughing too hard to speak. In fact, he was laughing so hard that he had to lean against the nearest shelf of books for support. Taking their lead from him, the assorted science nerds also erupted into laughter.

I turned on my heel and started heading for the exit sign again, but this time Jonathan caught me by the elbow. "No, Rachel, wait—" he managed to get out before another wave of hilarity got the better of him.

"Let me go."

"Look," he said, struggling to get himself under control. "I know what you thought you saw. I talked to Detective O'Connell—" another spasm of laughter "—and he told me all about it."

"You mean, about you stashing bodies in the trunk of your Saab?"

He was mopping at his eyes with his scarf. "Exactly."

"And how is that funny?"

"You know, you're gorgeous when you're pissed. And you've got quite a pair of lungs on you."

"That's it. I'm leaving."

"Rachel, it was a blow-up doll."

I paused in midstride. "A blow-up doll?"

He nodded, clearly doing his best not to burst into laughter all over again.

"A blow-up doll?" I repeated.

"Yes, a blow-up doll," he confirmed.

"So, it wasn't a body."

"No, it wasn't a body."

I thought about this. If Jonathan Beasley hadn't been stashing corpses in his trunk, then he probably wasn't a serial killer. And I'd just made an enormous scene in the middle of the Harvard Coop. It occurred to me that I should feel a bit ashamed.

But then something else occurred to me. "Would you like to explain just what you were doing with a blow-up doll?" I asked, not even trying to keep the tone of jubilant self-righteousness out of my voice.

"Actually, I have two."

"Two what?"

"Blow-up dolls."

I'd been hoping that my question would force Jonathan to admit to some sort of deviant sexual practices. It seemed only fair that he be embarrassed, too, given that I'd made a fool out of myself in front of the Geek Squad, not to mention how I'd damaged any shreds of credibility I might have had in O'Connell's eyes.

But Jonathan's explanation was neither embarrassing nor lacking in credibility, although it was creative. "I use them for role-playing exercises. To show students how they unconsciously change the way they communicate based on whether they're speaking to a man or a woman. The class gets a kick out of it, but it's a really effective exercise. And it's easier to blow the dolls up at home with my bicycle pump than to lug the pump back and forth."

"Oh." Now I was feeling truly ashamed.

"Yes. Oh."

"I guess I owe you an apology."

He shrugged good-naturedly. "Don't worry about it. At least it explains why you fled from me this morning. Besides, I think O'Connell appreciated the comic relief. We had a good chuckle over it."

"Glad to be of service." I flushed when I thought of the two of them laughing over my accusation, but I knew that I probably deserved to be laughed at.

"Listen, I really am sorry. I mean, I just didn't know what to think. When I saw the foot. And you were wearing the

scarf. But it still wasn't very nice to think that you were—
that you could have been—"

"Don't say it," interrupted Jonathan. "Or you'll get me
started all over again. I'll end up with a nasty case of hiccups."

"We wouldn't want that."

"No. Anyhow, I know how you can make it up to me."
He looked down at me, his blue eyes sparkling, and flashed
his movie-star grin. When the tingling started, I accepted it
with resignation. So much for dedicated spinsterhood.

"How's that?"

"Come have a coffee. Or, better yet—" he consulted his
watch "—a drink. It's after five."

"Okay. But I'm paying."

"Fair enough. Shall we?"

He offered me his arm and led me towards the door. The
science nerds murmured appreciatively and I heard a spat-
tering of applause as we left.

We debated a bit about where to go. He offered up his
finals club, but I refused on political grounds. The clubs were
staunchly all-male relics of an earlier age, and they controlled some of the most expensive pieces of real estate in
Cambridge. I was in no mood to rub shoulders with the current generation of undergrad male elite and whatever
alumni might have dropped by to keep the Old Boy Net-
work going strong. Besides, if we went to Jonathan's club,
I wouldn't be able to pay, and I felt obligated to make some
formal retribution for my massive gaffe. I offered up the
lounge at the Charles instead, and he acquiesced. I then spent
most of our walk to the hotel haranguing him on the political incorrectness of his affiliation with such an institution. He took it with good humor and even expressed
agreement with much of what I said. And the nice way he

helped me navigate the icy sidewalks was more chivalrous than chauvinistic.

It was only when we were nearly at the hotel that it occurred to me that it would be an awkward moment to run into Peter. But I quickly shoved that thought away. I hadn't heard a thing from him all day, and based on what I'd seen that morning, he was occupied with other matters. He was undoubtedly still at his conference unless he and Abigail had ventured out for another shopping expedition. I had a mental image of Peter helping Abigail through the snow the way Jonathan was helping me, and my heart promptly dropped into my stomach. My earlier resolution to just give up on romance now seemed like false valor. But perhaps that was only because Plan B had turned out not to be a serial killer. I resolved to forget about Peter and focus on Jonathan. After all, the tingling could only be a promising sign.

Now that most of the recruiters had vacated the premises, the hotel was much calmer. The lobby held a more usual assortment of tourists, parents in town to visit their overachieving offspring, and only a few people who looked as if they were there on business. The Regattabar threatened live jazz, so we went to Noir, the ground-floor lounge where Winslow, Brown had had its party the previous evening. When Jonathan began explaining, without any provocation from me, how much he hated live jazz, I found myself looking at him with heightened appreciation. I'd long believed that live jazz was part of a nefarious plot on the part of a shadowy anarchistic group to drive people insane.

Jonathan ordered a Guinness and I asked for a Kir Royale, a drink that seemed uniquely suited for bitterly cold winter evenings. It was still early, but there were a number of people in the lounge, clearly enjoying the cozy refuge it provided from the less than balmy weather. We sat by the window, which offered a view of the plaza outside and the un-relenting snowfall.

As we sipped our drinks I found myself able to laugh with Jonathan about my earlier suspicions, and I even filled him in on the nightmarish ups and downs of my day. His professional background made him a knowledgeable sounding board as I discussed my options for defending against the Barnetts' planned takeover. And, unlike O'Connell, he seemed to take my theory about Barbara Barnett without a drop of skepticism, only concerned curiosity, and even anger that someone so close to Sara would seek to do her harm. He seemed reassured when I told him about warning the security guard at Sara's door. Soon our conversation skipped easily to other subjects, and before long I was having a lovely time. I hadn't forgotten about all of the various things I'd been fretting about before, but I was able to put them on the back burner and enjoy myself.

I'd told Jonathan about my roommate reunion, and before I'd even thought it through I was asking him if he wanted to join us for dinner that night. He appeared flattered by the invitation and accepted after some coaxing. I had a brief twinge of regret—what if Peter showed up?—but then I reminded myself that the odds of that happening were pretty much nil. The crisp champagne with the sweet lacing of Kir washed away the sour taste this thought induced.

It was close to six when Jonathan's cell phone rang. He dug it out of his jacket pocket and checked the caller ID. "I should get this," he apologized. "I don't know who it is, and there's been too much going on lately to let it go."

He went out to the lobby to take the call, and I quickly pulled out my own phone to let Jane know that I would be bringing an unexpected guest to dinner (who, as it turned out, was *not* a serial killer) and to warn her that I expected them all to be on their best behavior. "I'm not the one you need to worry about," Jane answered pointedly when the call finally went through. I was beginning to think it was time for a new phone.

"Perhaps somebody could give Hilary an etiquette refresher before we arrive?" I suggested.

"Perhaps. Although, she's at the library right now doing some research. Apparently her interview went well, but she had some things she wanted to look up afterward. If she gets here before you do, however, I'll be sure to read her the riot act."

"Thanks. See you soon."

Jonathan returned to the table as I was replacing my phone in my bag. "That was Gabrielle LeFavre," he told me.

"Really? I thought she'd disappeared."

"She had. But she's reappeared. And she said she really needs to talk to me. I hope you don't mind, but I asked her to meet me here."

"That's fine," I said. "But I should leave you two alone to talk."

"No, stay," he urged.

"Are you sure?" Given my suspicion of Barbara Barnett, I was pretty confident now that Gabrielle hadn't attacked Sara in a fit of jealous rage, but I was still curious as to what she might have been up to.

"I wouldn't ask you if I weren't."

Gabrielle showed up less than fifteen minutes later. It was fully dark outside, but she was wearing sunglasses, and her hood was pulled up, hiding her strawberry-blond hair. She looked furtively over her shoulder as she entered and then carefully surveyed the other occupants of the lounge as she made her way to our table.

"Could we switch tables?" she asked. "I don't want to sit by the window."

It seemed like an odd request, but given that she was all

but in disguise, I guessed that she was concerned about being seen. We moved to a corner table against the back wall, which had the added virtue of being nearly hidden by a large plant. The question of who Gabrielle didn't want to see her was answered quickly enough. She required only a small amount of encouragement from Jonathan to tell her story, and it quickly put to rest any suspicions I might have once harbored as to her having a role in the attacks on Sara.

Thursday morning, Gabrielle had left for the gym early, even before Sara had left for the boathouse. She'd brought a change of clothes with her, and she showered and dressed at the gym after her workout. Then she'd gone directly to the Winslow, Brown recruiting suite where, as Cecelia had told me, she'd waited until I returned.

She turned to me apologetically. "I was a disaster when I saw you. I really was. And I'm so sorry. I was just completely in a tizzy. I was getting dinged from every bank I interviewed with, and it was making me frantic. I'd just totally lost perspective. And I felt like I was completely losing it." She'd certainly seemed to be losing it when I'd encountered her.

"It's a stressful time," I said. "It's hard to deal with all the pressure."

She nodded. "Yes. And I clearly wasn't dealing very well. Anyhow, after I spoke to you, I was pretty much at my wits' end. My mind was racing, and I felt like I just had to get away for a bit."

"So what did you do?" asked Jonathan.

"I went to the movies." This seemed a reasonable choice. I had to confess that on the semiannual occasions when I found myself at loose ends on a weekday afternoon, my first thought was to sneak into a matinee. There were always movies that none of my friends wanted to see with me, probably because they were geared toward teenage girls rather than thirtysomething Yuppies. I still didn't understand how my tastes could be so firmly aligned with a different demographic.

However, Gabrielle's choice of movies hadn't done much to calm her. The Brattle Theatre had been showing a medley of movies featuring women on the edge, and they'd whipped her into an even greater frenzy. *Fatal Attraction* and *Basic Instinct* probably shouldn't be viewed when one was already in a precarious mental state. "You see," said Gabrielle, "it wasn't just the job thing that's been upsetting me. There was a guy who I'd been really into. And for a while, I thought he might be into me, too. But then he started asking Sara out."

"Grant Crocker?" I asked.

She nodded. "It's hard, you know. Sara's got so much going for her, and she didn't even like him. *I* did. But she was the one he wanted. And I couldn't understand it. So I decided I would just ask him. Flat out. Find out why he rejected me like that."

I listened in wonder. I'd often had the urge to have similar conversations with men who'd jilted me, but fortunately those urges had never coincided with my being sufficiently drunk to act on them. Gabrielle hadn't required liquid courage, and there was a part of me that admired her for it, although I doubted it was a tactic I'd be employing anytime soon.

She'd gone to Grant Crocker's apartment. He was, not surprisingly, surprised to see her, nor was he terribly welcoming. He tried to slam the door in her face, but she was too quick for him, and managed to slide through the opening before he could shut her out. In his living room, she launched into an impassioned and prepared speech. "Then I saw it."

"Saw what?" I asked.

"He has a—I don't even know how to describe it, really—but it's like a *shrine* set up."

"A shrine?"

"To Sara." Apparently he'd dedicated a corner of his living room to a bizarre sort of installation art. There was a massive framed picture of Sara on a small table, surrounded by other pictures and various mementos. So, I'd been right after all. Grant Crocker was the Creepy Stalker.

"He'd been trying to block my view of it, but I got around him, and then he grabbed me, and we were sort of struggling. He's really strong, you know. He's sort of a work-out fanatic. But I am, too, and I've even taken self-defense courses, so I put up a good fight. He was holding on to me, but I managed to pull away, and I went crashing into his desk. There was a pile of newspaper clippings on it, and the impact made them go flying all over the room. And here's what really freaked me out."

I would have been pretty freaked out already, given the shrine, and Gabrielle had already been freaked out when she'd arrived, so it was hard to imagine what could elevate her level of panic still further. But when I heard what she had to say next, I was amazed she didn't have a coronary on the spot.

"The clippings were all about the prostitute killings. And it looked like he'd been putting them in a scrapbook. And there was a pile of stuff, too. An earring, a ring, a lipstick— none of it nice stuff. And a couple of the things were Sara's. There was a page that must have been torn from one of her notebooks—she has really distinctive handwriting—and a glove that Sara thought she'd lost."

"Souvenirs," I said, remembering Hilary's lecture on serial killers. "They frequently take souvenirs from the victims." So much for Barbara Barnett, I realized, almost disappointed. Grant Crocker was more than Creepy. He was Violent, too. And if Sara's belongings were in the pile of souvenirs Grant had taken from women he'd killed, it looked like he'd intended to kill her, as well.

"Anyhow, I saw this all in like a split second, and then he was on me again. And I punched him, hard, in the face."

Ah. That explained the black eye. "You did a great job," I said. "He has quite a shiner."

"Yeah, well, he was sort of reeling from that, but at this point he was still between me and the door and I didn't know how I was going to get out. I was looking around for a weapon, and then I realized that I had this in my bag." She opened up her shoulder pouch and pulled out an economy-size can of Aqua Net hairspray.

"I didn't realize they still made that," I said, amazed.

"Oh, yeah. It's hard to find. I buy it by the case on the Internet. Where I'm from, you learn how to do big hair early. So I gave him a good spritz, right in the eyes. It's better than Mace."

Hence the reddened eyes complementing Grant's shiner. I was beginning to think that Gabrielle might do better at an investment bank than anyone had been giving her credit for.

"I ran out," she continued. "And he was yelling after me. That I'd better not say anything to anyone, or I'd regret it. He said he'd hunt me down and kill me."

"That must have been pretty scary," Jonathan said. He'd been listening carefully, an empathetic expression on his face, and I could see why the students came to him with their problems. "What did you do next?"

"I didn't know what to do. I really thought he was going to come after me. And I was too scared to go to the police. I mean, what if they didn't believe me? Or, even if they did, what if Grant found me before the police found him? So I checked myself into a motel in Porter Square. I've been holed up there ever since, and when I finally calmed down enough, I called you. And here I am."

"You did the right thing," Jonathan assured her. "And we're going to tell the police what happened. It sounds like you've managed to find both the prostitute killer and the guy who's been attacking Sara."

"I guess so," said Gabrielle. "But are you sure he can't come after me?" She looked around the room again, her anxiety almost tangible.

"Yes. Even if they can't immediately tie Grant to the murders and the assaults, they can get him for assaulting you." He smiled. "Although, it sounds like you won that fight."

Jonathan went back to the lobby to call Detective O'Connell, and Gabrielle asked me to accompany her to the ladies' room. Although she was calmer now that she'd told her story, she was wary of going anywhere unaccompanied until Grant Crocker was safely apprehended.

As I waited outside the door for Gabrielle to emerge, I called Hilary, thinking that I'd be doing a good deed by giving her the scoop on Grant Crocker.

"Where are you?" I asked. "I have some news that you'll want to hear."

"At Widener Library. There were a few things I wanted to check into after I interviewed O'Connell. Which was great, by the way. I definitely owe you."

"You'll have to mention me in the acknowledgments. Although, after you hear this, you might just decide to dedicate the book to me."

"What?" she asked excitedly.

"I know who the killer is. And it's not Jonathan Beasley."

"That's wonderful news. So you can still go out with him. But who's the killer?"

"No, this will be more fun in person."

She didn't want to wait, but I told her I'd meet her at the library and give her the full download. "Then we can go up to Jane's together."

"Okay. But hurry. Suspense makes me cranky."

★ ★ ★

Gabrielle emerged from the ladies' room, and we met Jonathan in the lobby.

"Did you reach O'Connell?" I asked.

"Yes. He's back at the station and he suggested Gabrielle come by. Is that all right, Gabrielle?"

Gabrielle hesitated but then she nodded. "Will you come with me?" she asked him.

"Of course. In fact, I'll drive you there."

Jonathan's car was parked around the corner, and he dropped me off at the gate to Harvard Yard nearest the library. I wished Gabrielle well in her discussion with O'Connell and gave Jane's address to Jonathan.

"I'll come by as soon as we're done," he told me.

"Good. See you later. And Gabrielle, don't worry. You're doing the right thing." She didn't look convinced, but she gave me a stoic wave. I made a mental note to see what I could do about finding her a job. She still seemed like too much of a stress case to handle Winslow, Brown, but the Aqua Net incident demonstrated a level of gumption that I had to admire.

I shut the car door behind me and passed through the familiar gates.

I didn't realize I was being followed.

Twenty-Eight

Widener Library was a looming white stone edifice smack in the middle of Harvard Yard. Shallow steps led up to its pillared entrance. I'd once read that the steps were built to accommodate the hobble skirts that had been fashionable ninety years ago, when the library was endowed, but that had never made sense to me. Harvard hadn't done much embracing of women at that point in time, much less worked to accommodate their fashion needs.

Hilary had told me she'd be in the library stacks, one of her favorite haunts in college. She prided herself on having racked up a number of encounters there that hovered on the border line between NC-17 and XXX ratings, but she'd assured me that her only objective today was to dig up a couple of esoteric books about the history of violent crime and spend some quiet time reviewing her notes.

A Harvard ID was required to obtain entrance to the stacks, but I flashed my Winslow, Brown security pass to the

student at security. He was sufficiently absorbed in his reading that he didn't seem to notice the difference. Hilary had
said to meet her on the C level, and I rode the rickety elevator down two flights. My navigational abilities hadn't im-
proved since earlier that afternoon, but I remembered the
basic layout of Widener sufficiently well, having spent more
time than I cared to recall in the stacks as an undergrad on
those occasions when I couldn't afford any sort of distrac-
tions. The floors were dimly lit, but there were study carrels lining many of the walls, and you could tuck yourself
away in a corner and work undisturbed for hours, assuming
you had the foresight to smuggle in a supply of Diet Coke
and M&Ms for sustenance. Of course, what had been for
me the perfect place to power through exam prep or thesis
research had been for Hilary the perfect place for illicit sexual encounters.

Today, however, I found her alone in one of those study
carrels, surrounded by heavy, dusty texts and an assortment
of papers. My heels echoed on the hard cement floors, alert-
ing her to my arrival.

"So, tell me," she demanded. "I can't believe you held out
on me like this." She seemed to have run out of gratitude in
the last fifteen minutes. Forced patience never had a good effect on Hilary.

"Grant Crocker."

"No way. I thought he was the Creepy Stalker."

"He is. But it turns out he's violent, and a serial killer to
boot." I related what Gabrielle had told Jonathan and me. "It
sounds like a fit, doesn't it? I mean, with the newspaper clippings and souvenirs and everything."

"Absolutely. Amazing. And you used to work with him.
Unbelievable. I'll have to put you in the book, too. You can
talk about his creepiness when he was at Winslow, Bro—oh
my God!"

"What?"

"I just realized something." She began shuffling through the papers on the desk. "I'd printed out some stuff off the Internet about another uncaught serial killer. There was an article in one of the Boston papers about how the killings here were similar to a series of killings in New York City a couple of years ago. They took place over the course of about eighteen months, and then they just stopped. But they probably happened when Grant Crocker was at your firm, right? Before business school. Here, check this out." She found the pages she was looking for and handed them to me. I quickly skimmed the articles.

"The dates sound like they match," I said, my excitement nearly matching Hilary's own.

"Even better, the articles from the New York papers talk about how the police thought the killer was using a scarf to strangle his victims," she continued. "And here's the clincher." She paused, as if to heighten the drama of her revelation.

"I'm waiting."

"Work with me, Rach. This is called building tension so the climax is all the more stunning. It's a writer thing."

"Whatever. What's the clincher?"

"From the fibers they found, the police thought the scarf was red and gold."

"And how is that a clincher?"

"Those are the colors of the Marine Corps. And Crocker was a marine, right?"

I had to admit, that was a pretty good clincher. "Now that I think about it, I vaguely remember Grant having a red-and-gold-striped scarf that he seemed to wear everywhere in the winter months. That is pretty good."

"Good? It's brilliant."

"You should tell O'Connell."

"I'm going to. I mean, he must know about the New York

killings, and I guess Gabrielle will tell him what she told you, but being able to point out that Crocker was in both places and was a marine has got to be helpful. I'll go call him right now. The reception down here is lousy, so I'm going to have to go out into the main lobby. I'll be back in a few minutes, and then we can go up to Jane's together." She took her phone and strode off, the stiletto heels of her boots echoing in the empty hallway.

I took the chair Hilary had vacated and began reading more carefully through the pages she'd printed out. There had been five murders in New York during the killer's eighteen-month spree, and they did all sound exactly like the murders here in Boston. I was immersed in one of the articles when a drop of water splattered on the page. I wiped it away with my sleeve and looked up, wondering if there was a leaky pipe somewhere in the building.

But there was no leaky pipe. Instead there was Grant Crocker, looming behind me and reading over my shoulder. A few melting snowflakes adorned his crew cut.

"Hello, Rachel. What are you reading?"

I screamed. This scream was even more bloodcurdling than my earlier scream in the Coop, because the acoustics of the stacks amplified the sound. It echoed against the concrete floors and metal shelving. But no one came to see what the problem was. For once I wished the stacks were a bit more heavily trafficked. They were lonesome enough during normal hours; early on a Saturday evening they were deserted.

"What—what are you doing here?" I stuttered, twisting in my seat to face him.

He chuckled. "Well, I'd been following our friend, Ms. Le-Favre, and I was hoping to get her alone. But she drove off with Professor Beasley. So I thought I'd see what lies she might have been spreading about me."

"I don't think they're lies," I countered, playing for time.

He smiled, the sort of smile the psycho always gives in bad horror movies just before he attacks his next victim. And then he lunged for me.

Without thinking, I grabbed one of Hilary's books and swung it like a bat. It crashed into Grant's nose with a satisfying crunch. "Oof," I heard him say.

He was bent over double, holding his nose with both hands, and I used this opportunity to shove him aside and make a run for it. But while I knew where the elevator was, I wasn't eager to wait for its arrival since I doubted that I'd incapacitated Grant for more than a few moments. I needed to find the stairwell, and quickly, but with yet another sense of déjà vu I realized I couldn't remember where it was. I didn't see a soul as I tore along the hallway, looking in vain for a sign that would point me to the stairs.

I heard heavy pounding footsteps behind me, and I tried to pick up the pace, but while I'd had lots of practice running in heels, primarily while sprinting for planes, the floor was slippery and I was sliding more than I was running. I careered around a corner, only to see yet more endless rows of books and no sign for the stairs. If I got out of this alive, I vowed never again to go into a bookstore, library or other venue where books were housed without a bodyguard, attack dog and sensible shoes.

"You're not going to get away, Rachel!" I heard Grant yell, and his voice was discomfitingly close, albeit its newly nasal twang indicated that I might have done some serious damage to his nose.

I wasn't going to be able to outrun him, I realized as I skated around another corner, catching hold of a bookshelf to prevent myself from wiping out. I was going to have to outsmart him.

I stopped running, dragged a foot against the floor so it

made a squealing noise, and shrieked, as if I'd fallen. Only a couple of seconds passed before Grant appeared around the corner of the row into which I'd turned, running at full tilt.

He'd probably expected to find me in a heap on the floor, nursing a twisted ankle or a broken heel. He probably hadn't expected me to be pressed against the shelves with my foot strategically stretched into the aisle. His speed put him at a disadvantage. He tripped over my foot and was promptly airborne, sailing down the aisle headfirst. He hit the floor a good ten feet from where I was before sliding several more yards.

I grabbed several books from the nearest shelves and began pelting them at him with all of the force I could muster. But like the horror-movie monster that just won't die, he was pulling himself upright, apparently immune to the onslaught. Blood was gushing out of his nose, and combined with the black eye, he was a pretty unpleasant sight. I pulled another book from the shelf and threw it with all my strength, aiming for his head. It got him in the neck instead, but it seemed to wind him. He grabbed at his throat and opened his mouth, but all that came out was a croak. Still he kept moving toward me.

There was only one thing left to do. Something I'd always dreamed of doing. And my shoes may have lacked the appropriate traction for high-speed chases down slippery hallways, but their pointy toes had to be good for something.

I ran at Grant, closing the gap between us with a few steps. I swung my leg back, and then forward, putting all my weight into the kick. My foot connected with his groin as if it had been shot from a cannon. I won't describe what, exactly, it felt like on my end, but based on Grant's reaction, on his end it wasn't good.

His eyes rolled up into the back of his head, revealing their white undersides. Soundlessly, he crumpled to the floor.

Twenty-Nine

"Rachel?"

I looked up in relief, glad to hear Hilary's familiar voice.

Grant was curled into a fetal position, moaning, so his face wasn't visible, but she assessed the situation quickly. "Crocker?" she asked.

I nodded.

"You kicked him in the balls?"

I nodded again.

"Excellent. I've always wanted to do that to a guy."

"I know. Me, too. And I have to admit there was something sort of gratifying about it."

"I bet. I'm sorry I missed it."

"If he ever recovers, I might need some help restraining him until reinforcements arrive."

"Shall I call the police again?" asked Hilary.

"No, I'll go," I volunteered. "But keep an eye on Crocker. I don't want him to get away."

"Sure thing. Worst case, I'll just give him another little kick." Judging from her enthusiastic tone, she seemed almost hopeful that such measures would be required.

Alas, Grant remained in his fetal position until security arrived. O'Connell showed up soon after with a fleet of additional police officers. He made fast work of reading Grant his rights before instructing his team to take him into custody. Perhaps the most surprising turn of events, however, was that when Hilary invited O'Connell to join us for dinner, he agreed to come. "I'm going to need to spend some time at the station," he said, "but I'll swing by as soon as I'm done."

Hilary and I were at Jane's a little before eight, still buoyant from our crime-fighting coup. Sean and Matthew had retreated again to the basement to work on Baby Hallard's cradle, but the rest of us sat around the kitchen island, watching Jane cook. She'd rebuffed everyone's offer of help except Emma's, which was fine with me. I filled my friends in on my encounter with Beasley, leaving out the more embarrassing parts, and told them the story Gabrielle had told us. Hilary took over from there, recounting our adventures in Widener with great relish.

"And then," she concluded, "Rachel kicked Grant Crocker in the balls."

Jane gasped. "You didn't."

I blushed. "I did."

"Hard?" asked Emma.

"Really hard."

"He was practically unconscious when I got there," Hilary added.

"Was it cathartic?" Luisa asked.

I paused in order to give her question the consideration it deserved. "Absolutely," I said.

And that made everybody laugh.

★ ★ ★

I'd checked my Blackberry for messages on the way to Jane's, realizing as I did so that I was deluding myself if I was holding out any hope for a word from Peter. But it still hadn't helped to have my lowered expectations confirmed by the absence of any voice mail or e-mail from him. Think about Jonathan, I told myself. I'd learned long ago that the best cure for any failed relationship was to embark on a new one. Although the cure was becoming less effective as I grew older. Experience was teaching me all too well that the new relationship would eventually become an old one, with all of its assorted baggage and heartache. Give it one more chance, I lectured myself. And if Jonathan proved himself unworthy, then I could give it all up. I felt a fleeting moment of the euphoria I'd experienced earlier that day when I had resolved to do just that. See, I reminded myself, I did have options. If Jonathan ended up being a dud, I could pursue the idiosyncratic spinster path and have red wine and microwave popcorn for dinner whenever I wanted.

It was probably a good thing that I'd had this little mental conversation with myself before Jonathan arrived, because it prepared me for what was to come.

Meeting my old roommates was, for a potential love interest, an important test. Their reads on the various men in my life had had an unerring accuracy, and I'd learned the hard way to take their opinions seriously, sooner rather than later. I was glad that we were going to be running Jonathan through their gauntlet before anything serious had even taken place between us. I had little confidence left in my own judgment, and it would be a relief to put the matter into their capable hands. On some level, I was worried that my interest in Jonathan had more to do with wanting a Plan B than with Jonathan himself. And while my ego enjoyed ticking

off items that could be construed as evidence of his interest in me, I kept coming back to the strange way he paused,
right before each time he tried to kiss me. As if his heart
wasn't quite in it and he needed to gear himself up.

He started off strong. After all, he was absolutely gorgeous.
He apologized profusely for his late arrival, even though we
all knew that he had a good reason to be late, and he'd
brought an excellent bottle of California red. Luisa, who was
the only one of us who had an eye for such things, was impressed by his choice, which was a positive sign.

But it was all downhill from there. Perhaps he felt intimidated, but everyone was on his or her best behavior, even
Hilary, and welcomed him warmly. Still, it was only in the
presence of my friends that I started to notice what his looks
and attentiveness had blinded me to before. There was only
one way to say it, really. And Hilary, being Hilary, said it, although she waited until she was safely out of Jonathan's
hearing, which showed remarkable restraint for her.

"I've got some bad news for you, Rach," she said. The two
of us had gone out onto the porch to keep Luisa company
while she had a cigarette between dinner and dessert.

"What's that?"

"Hilary," said Luisa in a warning tone. "Be nice. Rachel's
having a really bad day."

"Damn but he's dull. Come on, Luisa. You have to
admit it."

"I was going to say bland," Luisa confessed. "And I was
going to work up to it a lot more gently."

"Immature, too," Hilary continued. "That entire faux-
threatening you in the Coop was sort of puerile. But he
thought it was really funny. He kept talking about it."

"I was thinking insecure," said Luisa.

"Boorish," added Hilary.

I had to admit, Jonathan had been less than impressive at

dinner. He'd talked at great length, and although I knew Hilary resented anybody else monopolizing the conversation, you knew you were in trouble when you found yourself wishing that she'd been doing the monopolizing. All of the embarrassing parts that I'd left out in my narrative to my friends had been included in Beasley's own narrative. And there'd been an incredibly awkward moment when Jonathan had made a reference to a poem by T. S. Eliot. Only, the poem wasn't by T. S. Eliot, it was by W. H. Auden. I'd done a double major in English and economics, and I recognized the gaffe. Jane had majored in applied mathematics, but she'd taken the same Twentieth Century Poetry course that I had, although it had been an elective for her. Still, she saw the error as well, and the teacher in her was unable to let it go uncorrected. So she corrected him, in a kind but firm way. And instead of admitting his mistake, Jonathan had insisted he was right. Fortunately, Emma had jumped in and changed the subject, but the damage had been done.

"Dull, immature and boorish," I said sadly.

"But look on the bright side, Rach. He is really great-looking," said Hilary. "You can always just use him for sex. Speaking of which, look who's here." She gestured toward the kitchen window. O'Connell had arrived. "Just in time for dessert. Let's go back inside."

O'Connell couldn't tell us everything, of course, but he did seem to be confident that Grant Crocker was the serial killer. Apparently, Grant had been ready to talk, and he'd confessed to the prostitute killings. O'Connell related the facts he could share, and he seemed more relaxed than I'd seen him before. Clearly, having solved a major case had taken a significant weight off his shoulders. He also seemed appreciative of Hilary's various charms, and she was giving him every possible opportunity to appreciate them. "You must feel great," she said, a chocolate-covered strawberry poised strategically next to her full red lips. "You've caught the killer and solved the attacks on Sara Grenthaler in one fell swoop." Then she took a bite of the strawberry and ran her tongue over her upper lip. Next to me Emma stifled a snort with a cough.

"Actually," said O'Connell, "I'm not so sure we've solved the Grenthaler attacks."

"Really?" Jonathan asked in surprise. He'd been relatively quiet since O'Connell had arrived, which was one small blessing.

"Really?" I echoed.

"He confessed to the murders, but he protested his innocence pretty vehemently when we asked him about Sara," O'Connell explained. "The guy seems to be genuinely in love."

"But what about the shrine he has set up in his apartment?" I asked. "He's obviously obsessed with Sara." It had been so nice to remove worrying about somebody trying to kill Sara from my list of things to worry about. Now that I was back to having no love life, I was loath to return a negative item to a list that was already too long.

O'Connell shook his head. "Oh, he's obsessed with her. In fact, I think that having these feelings for her, and her not returning them, has been part of what's been setting him off of late. It probably contributed to the escalation of his attacks over the last month."

"It's like a Madonna/whore complex, right?" posited Hilary. "When he's rejected by the Madonna—Sara, in this case—he takes it out on a whore. Literally."

"I'm afraid so," said O'Connell. "It's a cliché, I know, but in this case it seems accurate."

"Did you ask him about the stalking letters?" I asked.

"He said he didn't know anything about them. And given

everything else he was confessing to, I don't know why he would have held back. He was very forthright about his feelings for Sara."

"I can't imagine anyone wanting to own up to having written those letters," I said. "Wow, are they bad."

O'Connell laughed, and the conversation segued into the letters. O'Connell's opinion as to their literary merit was no higher than my own, and he entertained us with a few particularly absurd quotes from them. Soon, we were all making suggestions as to what Sara's secret admirer could write next, fueled in no small part by the wine we'd all been drinking.

"I'm thinking limericks," said Sean. "Nothing says I love you like a good limerick."

Only Jonathan didn't seem to be enjoying the tack the conversation had taken. In fact, he was not only silent, his face seemed redder than it had earlier. As if he were embarrassed, I realized. Or angry. He excused himself abruptly, asking Jane where he could find a bathroom. The rest of the party barely noticed he'd left the table.

But I had an epiphany. And it put the final nail in the coffin of Plan B.

I added it up in my head. Beasley had seemed unusually attentive to Sara, even if he was her section leader. And he was the only one who seemed to find the letters anything but nauseating. In fact, he'd described one as "sweet." He'd also been very quick to dismiss the letters as dangerous in any way, and he'd been fairly cavalier about preserving them as evidence, unconcerned with people touching the letters and soiling them with their own fingerprints. And if he was obsessed with Sara, it would explain my feeling that he was only going through the motions in his advances toward me.

Maybe Jonathan Beasley wasn't a serial killer. But could

he be a writer of truly awful love letters? And, even more importantly, had he been stalking his student? Was he behind the attacks on Sara?

Thirty

Thankfully, Sean insisted that all of the menfolk accompany him to the basement to inspect the progress that he and Matthew had made on the cradle. I couldn't understand the fascination that anything involving dangerous tools like saws and hammers held over people with a Y chromosome, but it was a convenient way to get Beasley out of the room. As soon as they were safely downstairs, I told my friends about my suspicions.

"You know, Rach, just because you're upset that Jonathan isn't Mr. Right doesn't mean that he's a crazed stalker," said Hilary. "I'm not the guy's biggest fan, but you may be jumping to conclusions—again—for the wrong reasons."

"I think what she's saying makes sense," said Emma. "I was watching him, too, and he was really getting upset when we were joking about the letters." Emma was quiet by nature, and she tended to be unusually observant, probably because she didn't spend as much time as the rest of us trying to figure out how to get a word in.

"There is something weird about him," Luisa said. "I thought he was going to blow a gasket when Jane corrected him before."

"What does that mean, anyhow, blowing a gasket?" asked Hilary.

"Most people would have just laughed it off, but he seemed to take it really personally," said Emma.

"But he's Sara's professor," Jane pointed out. "To write those letters would be really crossing a line."

"The letters do reference a 'forbidden love,'" I reminded her.

"Ick," said Hilary, reaching for a nearly empty bottle to top off her wineglass.

"Well, maybe he wrote them," Jane said. "But would he really attack her?"

"You clearly have not been watching enough Lifetime Television for Women," I answered. "Stalkers always end up trying to kill the women they love."

"How much Lifetime Television for Women is enough Lifetime Television for Women?" countered Luisa.

"Okay," said Jane. "Maybe Beasley is behind the letters. But how can we prove it?"

"I have an idea," I told them. "But I'm going to need help."

There was some debate about whether we should simply confide in O'Connell, but while I'd redeemed myself somewhat with the capture of Grant Crocker, I wasn't willing to formally make another accusation against Jonathan without tangible proof. We came up with an alternative plan and none too soon. The guys trooped up from the basement just as we were finalizing the details.

"You all look like you're plotting something," said Matthew, taking in the five of us seated around the kitchen island with our empty wineglasses. My friends talking over the remains of a drinking session was a sight he'd seen on far too many occasions not to be suspicious of what we might be hatching.

"Oh, you know, the usual. Just figuring out how to over-throw the patriarchy," said Hilary brightly.

"I thought you'd already done that."

"We're moving on to the second phase," Emma said, taking hold of Matthew's hand and looking up at him. "Beware, white males."

"We stand warned," he answered good-naturedly.

I stretched and let forth with an enormous yawn. "I'm sorry to be the first to break up the party, but I'm exhausted."

Fortunately, Jonathan offered to drop me back at the hotel. It took a while to say good-night to everyone, but we had one more dinner planned for the following night, so these weren't final goodbyes. Ten minutes later, Jona-than was unlocking the door of his car and helping me into the passenger seat. As he walked around the front of the car, I transferred my cell phone from my purse and into my left hand. I dialed Jane's cell-phone number, heard her pick up and lowered my hand under the seat, so the phone wouldn't be visible to Jonathan when he got in the car.

Under normal circumstances, this would have been an awkward ride home in a banal way. I'd realized that he wasn't for me. And I'd also realized that while Jonathan may have been going through the motions of pursuing me, he didn't really have his heart in it. Even before I'd decided Jonathan was Sara's stalker, something in the dynamic between us had shifted, and I had a feeling that he sensed it, too. The banal-ity would be due to the loss of the initial enthusiasm of which we wouldn't speak but that would tinge the drive with a stale and slightly sour quality. Tingling was a thing of the

past, and while I would mourn its potential efficacy in cal-
orie-burning, I couldn't say I would mourn its source.

But the good news was that I had more important things
to do than make awkward small talk to fill up the ten minutes it would take us to get to the hotel.

"That was a nice dinner," said Jonathan. "Your friends are
really neat."

There were many adjectives I would use to describe my
friends, but "neat" wasn't high on the list. Still, I let it pass,
saying instead, "So, Jonathan, do you want to tell me about
writing the letters to Sara?"

The car swerved into the opposite lane, and then nearly
hit a parked car when he overcorrected back to our side of
the road. "What? What are you talking about?" The note of
surprise in his voice sounded strained, and it erased any last
doubt I may have had.

"I'm talking about you being the one who wrote the letters to Sara. It's pretty obvious that it must have been you."

Headlights from behind us flashed in the rearview mirror,
and Jonathan busied himself with adjusting its angle. "I don't
know what you're talking about," he repeated through
clenched teeth. A nerve twitched along the line of his chiseled jaw. "Haven't you made enough ridiculous accusations
for one day?"

"Look, I understand why it's hard for you to admit. Writing love letters to a student is probably against some code of
behavior the business school makes you agree to or something." Harvard would likely find how badly written the letters were to be even more objectionable than Jonathan
crossing the boundaries of professional behavior.

"Rachel, I really don't know where this is coming from.
Why are you doing this?" The nerve had gone from twitch-
ing to jumping.

I carefully laid out the reasons behind my conjecture, as if

I were structuring an answer to a particularly tricky exam question, being as gentle as I could when I pointed out that both Jonathan and the letters shared a frequent habit of misquoting poetry or misattributing the poetry to the wrong poet. "When you add it up, it all points to you."

There was silence as I waited for him to respond. "You can't prove it," he said, a new and hostile tone to his voice that I smugly took as evidence of a usually hidden violent streak.

"You're admitting that you wrote the letters?"

"Yes. Not that it's any of your business." He made a sharp turn onto a deserted side street.

"Where are you going?" I asked, struggling to keep my voice level. Our plan allowed for the possibility that Jonathan might deviate from the route back to the hotel, but the speed with which he was maneuvering on the slick roads was unnerving.

"I'm driving you back to the Charles."

"This isn't the way. There's no reason to go down—" I looked in vain for a street sign so I could broadcast where we were. One flashed by, but I couldn't make out the words. Glasses, I thought. I definitely needed glasses.

"If you tell anyone about this, I'll lose my job. You know that, don't you?" He made another sharp turn onto another equally deserted side street.

"Well, I don't know how you're going to be able to do your job from jail. And are you sure this is the way to the hotel?"

"Now what are you talking about?" he exploded, jamming his foot down on the accelerator as he swung the car into another turn. The wheels skidded in the snow, and there was a hair-raising moment when we were hurtling toward a tree. I was bracing myself for the impact when I felt the wheels gain traction under us.

"Don't you think you should slow down?"

"Why would I go to jail?"

"Don't be dense, Jonathan." The reckless way he was driving was making me testy. "For attacking Sara Grenthaler, of course. And slow down already. The roads are too slippery for you to be driving like this."

"I've got snow tires."

"Snow tires or not, you're still going to jail."

"I love her, dammit! I love her! I love her," he repeated.

And then he slammed the car to a stop.

Thirty-One

Jonathan put his head down on the steering wheel and burst into tears. I looked up and realized, shocked, that we'd emerged from the tangle of side streets and were parked directly in front of the hotel.

"Um. Uh, Jonathan. Don't cry," I said lamely.

"I love her," he sobbed. "And she barely notices me. She just thinks of me as her boring old professor. But I love her."

"Um, I'm beginning to see that. But don't cry."

"I pour my heart out, and she could care less. She even gave me the letters back. As if they meant nothing to her." He picked his head up from the steering wheel and looked at me, as if I shared his anguish and his outrage. "How could she do that to me?"

Thankfully, there was a tap on the driver-side window. It was O'Connell. I turned to peer out the back. There were a couple of cars behind us: Jane and Sean's Volvo and what was probably O'Connell's unmarked police car. I was impressed that they'd managed to keep up with Jonathan's wild race through the snow-covered back streets of residential Cambridge.

O'Connell tapped on the window again and Jonathan slowly rolled it down. "Professor Beasley. I think you should come with me." The detective was holding Jane's cell phone in his hand, and it was on speaker, echoing his words back to us. I decided I could safely end the call I'd placed and pressed the off button on my own phone.

It was well after eleven, but a unanimous decision was reached that we could all use a nightcap. We retired to the lounge at Rialto, on the second floor of the hotel, once we'd ascertained that there was no longer any threat of live jazz.

"That was a nice after-dinner activity," said Hilary, tucking her long legs under her on the velvet-covered sofa.

"But it was scary hearing you trying to tease out a confession from him," Jane told me. "I mean, I knew we were right behind you and everything, but he sounded like he was really out of control."

"You know," said Emma thoughtfully, "I really believed him when he said he loved Sara."

"He does love her," I responded. "Just in a bizarre and twisted way. And it all fits. Sara went to him with the letters on Wednesday, thinking that she was going to get help from a wise and caring authority figure. Meanwhile, he must have interpreted it as her rejecting him and wasted no time lashing out. She was attacked on Thursday morning."

"What a freak," said Hilary. "And the crying! Ick. Rach, I'm glad we nipped this one in the bud before you started anything. I don't think I could handle you dating a guy who goes around weeping all the time."

★ ★ ★

When it looked like our one drink was going to extend to another round, I excused myself for a moment. I'd been wearing high heels for fifteen hours, which would have been bad enough, but my right foot was particularly sore from where it had connected with Grant Crocker's groin. I'd taken my shoes off at Jane's, but I had a feeling that the Rialto would prefer that its patrons kept their shoes on. I ran upstairs to change into a more comfortable pair.

I was all too aware that there hadn't been any messages from Peter on my Blackberry, so the blinking message light on the phone in my room took me by surprise. I listened to the message as I kicked off my heels and eased my throbbing feet into flats. It was Peter, speaking quickly and in a harried tone.

Hey. Rach. It's me. I seem to be having a hard time tracking you down, so I thought I'd leave a message here. Anyhow, I've got some great news. The client's made a decision—they've turned down Hamilton Tech's off—I mean, their pitch, and they're definitely going with us. We don't want to lose the momentum, so we agreed to stay here until we hammer out every detail. The final negotiations will probably take a while. It looks unlikely that I'll make it to Jane's. In fact, there's a chance I might not make it back tonight at all. Anyhow, I'll explain it all when I see you, okay?

Oh. And I hope you're having a good time at the reunion. Say hello to everyone for me, and tell them I wish I could be there. Miss you.

Humph. With a message like that, why even bother leaving one at all? Flimsy excuses, lame apologies—left in the last place I'd look for them and in the one place where he'd be relatively sure not to have to talk to me in person.

Who needed it? I tried to work myself up into a healthy rage as the elevator took me back down to the second floor. Surely rage was more productive than giving way to the acrid taste of rejection and its favorite dance partner, loneliness.

A fresh drink was waiting for me when I returned to my friends, and it was a welcome sight. I was already well along the path to mild inebriation, and I'd made an executive decision in the elevator that I was going to take the path to its logical end. Anything would be better than to feel the way I was feeling. Hilary was enumerating O'Connell's many merits to a less than rapt audience, and Sean and Matthew were deep in conversation in their corner, probably talking about woodworking or something similarly manly. "Anything?" asked Emma in a low voice as I picked up my glass.

"A stupid message," I told her, more loudly than I'd intended.

"What?" asked Hilary, her monologue interrupted.

"Stupid Peter. He left a stupid message. Saying he'd be locked in stupid negotiations potentially all night." I held up two fingers of each hand, indicating quotation marks around the word *negotiations.*

"Maybe he is locked in negotiations," said Jane, ever the optimist.

"With Abigail?" I said, bitterness getting the best of me. "All night?"

"It's possible," she said.

"Even after what we saw?"

"Rach, there could be an explanation that actually does explain it all," Jane persisted. "You haven't even had the chance to talk to him about it."

"Like that would help." I sighed and took a large gulp of my drink.

"I'm going to kill this Abigail person," said Hilary.

"You're just looking for ways to spend more time with O'Connell," joked Luisa. "You want him to haul you up on murder charges."

"It could be fun," she replied.

"Let's talk about something else," suggested Emma.

"Yes, Rach. Why don't you tell us again about kicking Grant Crocker in the balls?"

"I've already told you."

"I know, but it has all the makings of a classic."

"If you insist," I said, draining the last of my drink and signaling the waiter for another round.

Thirty-Two

The phone ringing the next morning felt like a dentist inserting his drill directly into my ear. I fumbled for the receiver, grunted into it and unceremoniously slammed it back down before pulling the covers up over my head. A few minutes later it rang again, insistent and shrill. "What?" I demanded, sitting up and ripping the receiver off its cradle.

"Good morning!" announced a cheery recording. "This is your wake-up call! Today's weather forecast calls for heavy snowstorms and a temperature of twenty-three degrees Fahrenheit with a blistering windchill. Have a great day!"

Swearing at a recording was useless, but I swore at it anyway. Which was a bad idea, because if the ringing phone had seemed loud, my own voice was intolerable. Somebody must have come into the room while I was asleep and pounded on my skull with an iron mallet, because that was the only possible explanation for the thudding pain that occupied the space where my brain used to be.

I moaned, but that made it hurt even more. I sat still for a moment, waiting for the pain to recede but nothing happened. I cracked one eye open, careful not to move my head. The clothes I'd been wearing the previous evening were neatly folded over the back of the bedside chair. An open bottle of Advil and an empty glass stood on the nightstand. Dimly, I could remember my friends getting me up to my room, and Jane and Emma insisting that I take the tried and true preventative measures of Advil and water before bed. However, even the best preventative measures couldn't erase the toll that my dedicated drinking had taken. I didn't want to begin to think about how much worse I would have felt if they hadn't forced me to take the painkillers. Anything that could feel worse would have probably been fatal.

Gingerly, I propelled myself to a standing position. Grasping the Advil bottle in an unsteady hand, I tottered into the bathroom and refilled the glass from the tap. I shook out two pills, reconsidered, shook out two more, and then washed all four down with a long drink of water. I could feel the cool liquid tracing its course down my throat and into my stomach, every desiccated cell in my body sucking up the moisture in gratitude. I refilled the glass again and drank until it was empty. Then I tottered back out into the suite's living room and opened the minibar in order to embark on the next part of the cure.

I reached into the refrigerator with confidence and then retracted my arm in horror.

As if the Jinxing Gods hadn't had enough fun with me this weekend. There was no more Diet Coke.

I would have cried, but I was too dehydrated.

An hour later, I'd managed to take a shower and brush my teeth. I'd considered drying my hair, but the very thought of the noise the hairdryer would make had been too much to bear, so I sat in a chair waiting for my thick curls to dry themselves. Of course, that hadn't happened, so I eventually just yanked them back into a wet knot and struggled into my clothes. Not the jeans I'd brought for my nice relaxed weekend. Oh no, lucky me had to go see Barbara Barnett this morning, to talk business while battling the hangover that ate Cincinnati, and I had to look like a grown-up, even if I drank like a fraternity pledge. At least I didn't have to worry that she was violent, now that I knew that Jonathan Beasley had been responsible for the attacks on Sara. But that thought offered little consolation as I pulled on the black pantsuit I'd already worn on Friday. I grimaced as I stuffed my still-sore feet into the high-heeled pumps that went with it.

The effort to do all this left me sufficiently exhausted that I had to sit back down to recover. Then I checked my watch. "Crap, crap, quadruple crap."

I was late. And if I had no love life, I really couldn't afford to mess up on the professional front.

My cab driver seemed to sense my delicate condition and take a cruel delight in exacerbating it by alternately slamming on the accelerator and slamming on the brakes. Despite the below-zero windchill, I had the window wide-open. The air was fresh, if frozen, and I let it wash over my face in a vain attempt to quell the nausea.

The taxi screeched to a halt in front of the Barnetts' town house in Beacon Hill. I paid the Driver de Sade, and stumbled up the front stoop to ring the bell.

The *click-clack* of Barbara's heels preceded her. She threw the door open. At ten-thirty on a Sunday morning she was decked out in a lime-green Christian Lacroix suit that probably matched my complexion exactly. "Rachel, honey, come on in out of the cold."

"Hi Barbara," I croaked. My throat was still dry.

"You sound a bit hoarse, honey. I hope you're not coming down with anything. And you look a bit peaked. Let's get you something hot to drink," she offered, ushering me into a sitting room. "Maybe some nice hot tea with honey, honey?" She paused to smile at her own joke. "That's always soothing on a sore throat. Or a hot buttered rum?"

The word *rum* made my stomach lurch. "Um, that's all right. If it's not too much trouble, what I'd really like is a Diet Coke."

"Coming right up. If you'll excuse me, I'll go get the refreshments. The maid's off today, so I'm on my own. You just make yourself right at home."

I sat on the sofa she indicated and immediately sank deep into its down-filled cushions. I looked around the room as I struggled to pull myself into something more like a sitting position. It was pretty clear that Tom hadn't had much say in decorating decisions. The room was the height of mid-eighties chic, *Dynasty* by way of the zoo. Ornate gilded furniture vied for attention with a zebra-striped throw rug and leopard-print upholstery.

Barbara returned a few minutes later carrying a tray with a fuchsia-and-black teapot and matching teacup, a crystal glass of ice, and a can of Tab. "Here we are," she announced with a cheer that rivaled that of the wake-up call recording. "I'm sorry, honey, we're fresh out of Diet Coke, so I brought you a Tab instead. Is that okay?"

I nodded mutely. Desperate times called for desperate measures. At least it wasn't Diet Pepsi. Beaming, Barbara settled herself into a chair for which some undoubtedly endangered jungle animal had given up its life. She popped open the soda and began to decant it into a glass. "Oh, that's all right, Barbara. I actually like it best straight out of the can."

I had to give her points for not commenting on my uncouth preferences. She handed me the can and I accepted it gratefully. The familiar feel of the cold aluminum in my hand was enough to still my churning stomach, and the first sip, while not my elixir of choice, tasted better than anything I'd ever drunk before. I'd gulped down half the can before I realized that Barbara was staring at me, her own teacup raised halfway to her mouth. "Why, you must have been thirsty."

I smiled sheepishly before guzzling what was left.

"So, Rachel, you wanted to talk about business?"

I collected myself, newly fortified by the dose of carbonation, caffeine and artificial sweetener. "Yes, that's right. And I really appreciate your making the time to see me. You know that I've worked with Grenthaler Media for several years now, and I advised Tom on a number of transactions."

"Of course. Tom always spoke highly of you." Her words were kind, but her voice had already taken on a more guarded tone.

Diplomacy was never my strong suit, particularly not when hungover, so I came straight out with it. "I'm concerned that your decision to back this takeover is not what Tom would have wanted you to do with the shares he left you." As smoothly as I could, I launched into my spiel, aided by the infusion of Tab rushing through my veins. I spoke passionately and at length about Samuel Grenthaler and the legacy he'd left his daughter, and how intent Barbara's late husband had been on preserving that legacy.

My eloquence bounced off her as if her Lacroix were constructed entirely of Teflon. She listened, smiling and nodding, and when I was done she seemed not to have understood a word I'd said. "Yes," she agreed, as if she were reading from a script. "It is a wonderful company. It plays such an important role in keeping the public informed about important issues. I'm so thrilled that Adam will be leading it into the future. I know he'll be able to take it to the next level."

Next level of what, I wanted to ask, but I doubted that

would be a productive direction in which to steer the conversation. I knew for a fact that her last three lines were directly paraphrased from the press release Adam had issued the previous day. "It is a wonderful and important company," I agreed. "But," I added, choosing my words carefully, "Tom and Sam Grenthaler both wanted Sara Grenthaler to be running it one day."

"You know," said Barbara, setting her fuchsia teacup down so hard that tea splashed over its edges, "Sam Grenthaler really took advantage of Tom. My late husband, may he rest in peace, worked his tail off for that man, and Sam never appreciated him." Her guarded tone had given way to much less guarded indignation.

"Why, Barbara, I don't think that's true. He designated Tom as his successor. And Tom always spoke warmly of Sam. He considered Sam to be his best friend. He loved Sam, and Anna and Sara, as much as if they were his own family."

My words, intended to soothe, seemed to have exactly the opposite effect.

"Tom was a sweet man, but he was naive. He just didn't see how Sam took advantage of him. And that wife of his, too." She imitated a Boston Brahmin lockjaw. "Anna Porter. She thought she was so classy, and she was always looking down at me over that long nose of hers when she wasn't busy making eyes at Tom. Sara's not much better, either. Spoiled brat. She thinks she's too good to have anything to do with my Adam. Well I'll be damned if I'm going to let anyone named Grenthaler continue to take advantage of my family. My son's going to get what's rightfully his."

Barbara's décor wasn't the only thing that was straight out of *Dynasty*. This little speech could have been lifted directly from the show's seventh season. Her logic was a bit faulty, but apparently I'd struck on a sore spot. I remembered Nancy Sloan's theory about Tom having carried a torch for his best friend's wife. It looked like Barbara shared in that theory, and years after Anna's death, she still wasn't happy about it. I realized, belatedly, that this takeover meant more to Barbara than just seeing her son in the limelight. In some way, she also saw it as a way to avenge herself on Anna Porter, who likely had never suspected that Tom Barnett's interest in her was anything but that of a man's friendly affection for his best friend's wife. Not to mention an opportunity to get back at Sara, who had had the temerity to reject her son. I wondered if Barbara saw herself as playing the Alexis role or the Krystle role in her own little melodrama.

"Barbara," I began, not sure what I was going to say, but she interrupted me anyhow. The gloves were officially off.

"The important thing is that Adam and I are no longer standing on the sidelines. Nothing you can say is going to make me change my mind. And unless little Sara can top our offer, it looks like this deal is going to get done." She picked up her teacup and took a demure sip. "Honey," she added, almost as an afterthought.

There was a clatter in the kitchen and a sound of breaking glass. "What was that?"

"Probably just the damned cat," said Barbara, taking another sip of tea. As if on cue, an enormous white cat waddled into the room. With surprising agility for an animal so large, it leaped upward, landing on my lap with such force that it seemed unlikely neither of us had suffered any broken bones.

"Oof."

"Krystle!" scolded Barbara, inadvertently answering my previous question. "You naughty little creature."

"It's okay," I said as Krystle began kneading my thighs. Krystle wore a rhinestone collar, and all of her claws seemed to be intact. I was glad for a temporary distraction in which to plan my next angle of attack, but it looked like the distraction was going to come at the expense of a perfectly good Armani pantsuit. A white cat and black trousers made for unfortunate results, but since Krystle's claws were busily shredding the trousers anyway, worrying about the shedding was probably not a good use of time.

I'd been debating whether or not to pull the one card I had up my sleeve. It wasn't a card in which I had a great deal of confidence, to be sure. But Barbara had pissed me off. I hadn't liked the way she'd spoken of Tom, who had been a wise and gracious man. Nor did I appreciate her referring to Sara, a woman for whom I had tremendous respect, as a "spoiled brat." And, as Janis Joplin had put it best, "freedom's just another word for nothing left to lose."

"You do realize, of course, that Whitaker Jamieson is going to have to get approval from his trustees to sink all of his assets into a hostile takeover." I was stretching the truth. Whitaker Jamieson's trust fund may have had trustees before he turned twenty-one, but now there was only one trustee, and that trustee was the Caped Avenger himself.

"Whit's a very competent businessman," responded Barbara, but I could tell that I'd rattled her.

"And the trustees might find it a bit—" I paused, pretending to be carefully selecting the right word "—*unorthodox,* that he's handing all of his assets to the son of his ex-girlfriend. And that the son in question has no significant experience managing a business of any size, let alone a large public company."

"What do you mean, ex-girlfriend?" she asked with narrowed eyes.

"Are you denying that you and Whit were an item before you married Tom?"

"Whit is an old family friend," she parried with admirable bravado. "But that doesn't mean he isn't making an in-

formed decision. He knows Adam well and is just as confident in his abilities as I am."

"I wouldn't be so sure," I responded, with equal bravado,
although mine was completely false.

"Well, your opinion doesn't matter." She fixed me with a
stony glare and then got to her feet. "Rachel, honey, I do appreciate you coming by. But this conversation is over."

Thirty-Three

Barbara showed me the door with the utmost in fake courtesy, and I was pretty sure that the noise it made when she shut it behind me could be classified as a slam. I descended the steps to the sidewalk in what could definitely be classified as a huff. The worst part was that I hadn't had the foresight to call a cab, which would have been okay if I weren't wearing heels and if it weren't twenty-three degrees Fahrenheit, not including the blistering windchill, and snowing hard.

The streets were quiet, and the chances of a taxi just happening to pass by on a Sunday morning in this residential neighborhood were slim, so I started down the sidewalk in the direction of Charles Street while simultaneously digging in my purse for my cell phone. Directory Assistance connected me to a cab company, and the dispatcher promptly put me on hold.

"Rachel?" a voice called out behind me.

It was Adam Barnett, tall and geeky in jeans and a big

down parka, the ubiquitous Harvard scarf tied around his neck. I'd forgotten about his bachelor pad on the top floor of Barbara's house.

"Hello, Adam."

"Can I give you a lift somewhere?" He gestured toward a car parked across the street. Through its blanket of snow, I could make out a bright red Porsche Carrera. If I hadn't recently been made painfully aware of Adam's aspirations to be a high-flying takeover artist, I would have thought it an odd choice for such a dorky guy. It was the sort of car I usually associated with male midlife crises.

"Um, I'm just calling a cab right now."

"It will take forever in this weather. Where are you headed?"

"Harvard Square."

"No problem. Hop in."

I did a quick inventory of my options. I could freeze to death waiting for a cab, or I could get into Adam Barnett's car. The former choice was the more attractive, hands down. However, I'd made no headway with Barbara, and while I doubted I'd make any with Adam, the puppet in Barbara's little puppet show, it did seem like I should at least take this opportunity to try, especially since all of the crazed attackers and killers I knew were safely in police custody. Besides, the sooner I got back to the hotel, the sooner I could go back to sleep, which was pretty much all I could imagine doing right now. I ended my call and put my phone back in my purse. "Thanks. That would be great."

He unlocked the car doors with a button on his key chain and I lowered myself into the bucket seat on the passenger side. He twisted the key in the ignition and the engine purred to life.

"Nice car," I said as he pulled away from the curb.

"She's a beaut," he agreed, reaching out a hand to stroke

the leather of the dash and launching into a detailed description of the Carrera's assets, using words like *cylinders* and *torque* that made my head pound with renewed vigor. I stifled a yawn while I waited for a break in Adam's enthusiastic ode to fine engineering so that I could talk to him about the takeover. He shifted smoothly from one gear to the next as the twisting streets of Beacon Hill spilled us out onto Storrow Drive. The snow was coming down even harder now, and I could barely see the river that paralleled the road.

Heedless of the snow, Adam increased the pressure on the accelerator, and the car responded by jumping forward. "Aren't you driving a little fast?" I asked, breaking into his monologue. What was it with men and driving in the snow? Didn't they realize that you were supposed to take extra caution? If I wanted to take a spin on Mr. Toad's Wild Ride I would have gone to Disneyland. And I'd always preferred the Peter Pan ride, anyhow.

"No, this baby comes equipped with antilock brakes. There's nothing to worry about. Well," he chuckled, "maybe not nothing."

The way he said this sounded so strange that I looked over and saw what I hadn't seen before. He held a gun in his left hand, and it was pointed at me.

"Oh, come on," I said in disgust.

In the past twenty-four hours I'd done battle with a serial killer and entrapped a violent stalker. I was exhausted and hungover, and all I wanted was to get back to the hotel, run a hot bath and crawl into bed.

"It's loaded," he said, indignant at my dismissive tone.

"Whatever."

"And I can shoot with my left hand. I'm ambidextrous," he said proudly.

"Right. But you still can't drive and shoot me at the same time."

"You want to try me?"

"Not especially. But can I ask why it is that you want to shoot me? I don't get it."

"How can you not get it?" he demanded, his voice rising with anger. "You're trying to screw up my deal."

"Your deal? It's your mother's deal."

"You think she had the brains to set everything up? I was the one who planned everything. I just let her think it was all her idea."

"How nice of you."

"And the deal's going to go through. There's no way it's not going to happen."

"Well, am I just supposed to sit back and let you take over Sara's company?"

"Yes!" he exploded. He jerked the wheel suddenly, steering awkwardly with his gun-laden hand while he downshifted with the other. The car skidded on the slick pavement, but after a sickening moment it straightened, and I realized we had taken the exit that led onto the Mass. Pike.

"What are you doing?" I asked, only now starting to panic. My reflexes were on some sort of time delay this morning.

"We're going for a little ride."

"Obviously. But where?"

"You'll see." He slowed the car as we approached the automated toll booth, and I grabbed for the handle of the door next to me. It was locked, of course, and Adam responded to my fumbling with a pleased snicker. With his right hand, he pushed the control that slid the driver-side window open and reached for two quarters to drop into the basket. He managed to toss the coins in and pull away from the toll without taking the gun off me.

"You know, they have cameras at the toll booth. There'll be a picture of us."

"The picture will be of the back of the car and my license plate, both of which are covered with snow. As is the camera, probably."

"Oh."

He snickered again.

"Where did you get a gun?" I asked, reaching furtively for my handbag and the phone inside. "You don't seem like the type."

"Oh, I picked it up off the street in Roxbury," he said, attempting a breezy tone as if he were, in fact, the type who would have a black-market gun. "It's completely untraceable. I planned it that way. I plan everything very carefully. Although, I have to say, this snow really helps."

"Good for you."

"You know, if I were in your position, I'd try to be a bit more polite, here."

"I'm no Emily Post, but it seems to me that pointing a gun at a person in a moving vehicle isn't exactly the height of etiquette."

"Put your phone away."

"What phone?" But it looked like my attempt at distractingly witty banter had been unsuccessful.

I heard a click. "That noise was me taking off the safety," Adam explained. "That means that all I have to do is pull the trigger and bang, you're dead."

"It would make an awful mess in your precious car," I pointed out, but I returned the phone to my bag.

"I've scheduled a detailing later today. It's part of the plan. But that was just to make sure there were none of your fingerprints or anything left over. I'd rather not have to wipe up pieces of your brain before I take the car in."

"So, this plan of yours, what is it exactly?"

"There's a park a few exits up with a nice deep ravine. I'm going to take you there and shoot you before rolling you into the ravine. It will probably be months before anyone finds you, if they find you at all."

"Um. Okay. And you're doing this because I'm messing up your deal?"

"That's right. I heard you talking to my mother about Whitaker Jamieson, and I know you met with him yesterday. It seems like it would be safer to have you out of the way if you have any influence at all over Whit."

"Nobody has any influence over Whit," I protested. "He's senile. And what do you mean you heard me talking to your mother?"

"I was in the kitchen. You must have heard me—I dropped a plate. Unless you were stupid enough to believe my mother's line about the cat."

"Did Barbara know?"

"That I was listening in? Of course not. She's pretty clueless." He snickered yet again. "She even thought Tom died of a heart attack."

"Tom did die of a heart attack," I said, confused.

"Sure he did. After I put a massive dose of my mother's diet pills in his morning coffee. She's addicted to the stuff, ephedra. It causes heart attacks and it's especially dangerous for someone with a history of heart disease."

"You killed Tom?" I asked, stunned. Although, now I had the answer to at least one question. Adam had put his plan to work before Tom's death, which explained why the activity in the stock had preceded Tom's actual demise.

"Uh-huh," he said, clearly very pleased with himself. "Mom's weight obsession came in handy for once. She has to buy the stuff online now that it's been banned, but she has a huge stash, and she doesn't seem to notice when any of it disappears."

"Jesus."

"And that's not all," he continued. He was on a roll now.

"What do you mean that's not all?"

"Well, Sara will be dead soon. I need to figure out how, but they say the third time's a charm."

"Oh my God." Stark realization washed over me. Jonathan Beasley hadn't attacked Sara. Adam had. And how dense was I? I'd gotten into a car with him. "You are a total jerk."

"A jerk with a gun," he answered smugly. "And soon to be the CEO of a pretty important company."

"That's why there was no security at the hospital on Friday night. Your mother said you'd arrange for it, but you never intended to."

"Nope. Sara was supposed to be dead by Friday night. Paying for a security guard would have been a waste of money."

"What else have you done?" I asked in horror.

"You mean, besides killing Tom? And you, and Sara?"

"I'm not dead. And neither is Sara."

"Yet. Well, let's see. Sara's parents were easy."

"What do you mean? They died in a car accident."

"That accident wasn't an accident. They lived down the street from us, so it was no big deal to slip into their garage and tinker with their brake line. And it went off without a hitch—nobody even realized there was a problem with the brakes since the car caught on fire. The only downside was having to play sick for an entire weekend. Although, after a weekend of my mother's chicken soup, I really was sick. She's an awful cook."

"Good to know. But I don't understand why you killed Sara's parents in the first place."

"You're not very bright, are you?" I assumed that was a rhetorical question and didn't bother to reply. "I thought that if Sam were out of the way, Tom would take over, and then one day I'd take over from him."

"But Tom wanted Sara to take over."

"I thought he'd come around eventually, but we had a conversation a few weeks ago in which he made it clear he wouldn't, which was a lot like signing his own death warrant. Bad things happen to people who get in my way."

"I'll keep that in mind."

"You won't have to. You'll be worm food." With that, Adam steered the car off the turnpike.

"Worm food? Who do you think you are? Clint Eastwood?"

He didn't answer.

We drove several miles down deserted, snow-covered country roads with Adam making smarmy comments the entire way that, like the "worm food" line, seemed to have been lifted from bad movies. We passed a forlorn strip mall and a couple of lonely-looking houses, but that was about it. Soon we'd pulled into the empty parking lot of a state park, identified as such by a green sign cut in the shape of a pine tree.

Adam got out of the car and walked around to the passenger side. I was digging frantically in my bag for a weapon of some sort when he opened my door, but, alas, it had never occurred to me to keep cans of Aqua Net handy. "Take your bag with you," he suggested. "I'll throw it in after you."

"Gee, thanks."

"Okay, let's go."

"Where?"

He nodded toward the woods and grasped my arm in a rough hold. "This way. There's a path to the ravine."

He pushed me in front of him. Trees crowded in on either side of us, and the path was more ice and slush than path. My feet sank deep into the snow, and I cursed my unfortunate choice of footwear. Not only would my shoes be following my suit directly into the trash bin, they weren't the most practical thing to be wearing when one had to figure out how to escape from an armed narcissist. Running was not an option given the terrain. And the gun.

"Don't you watch *CSI?*" I asked, batting a branch away from my face.

"Sure."

"Then you must know you'll never get away with this. They'll trace the gun, they'll figure out I was in your car, or they'll find your tire tracks. Or something."

"Nothing like a blizzard to really mess with forensic evidence," said Adam in the same smug tone he'd been using for the past half hour. "I'm not worried."

Besides the fact that it looked like he was actually going to kill me, his tone really pissed me off.

"You suck," I told him as he propelled me inexorably forward. This elicited a shove that nearly knocked me over. I grabbed on to a tree branch to keep from falling.

"Why don't you shut up already and keep walking."

"Okay," I said.

Then I had an idea. I looked more carefully at the path before us. "How far is this ravine, anyhow?"

"We'll be there in a minute."

Fortunately, the opportunity came soon enough. A sturdy-looking pine tree ahead of us had a nice, flexible-looking branch that protruded onto the path before us. I sized it up as we approached. It would have to do.

I pretended to slip again in the snow, and reached for the branch, grasping it firmly. Summoning up every ounce of force I possessed, I pushed it back toward Adam as hard as I could.

It hit him full in the face. The impact wasn't much—I'm a bit of a weakling—but it dislodged a spray of snow and ice that temporarily blinded him. He sputtered, trying to wipe the debris out of his eyes.

And while he was sputtering and blinded, I took a few steps back to make sure I had a running start.

The feeling of my foot connecting with his groin felt even more satisfying than when it had connected with Grant Crocker's groin the previous day. The practice paid off. The blood drained from Adam's face, and he collapsed wordlessly to the ground.

Thirty-Four

Adam seemed to be unconscious, but I wasn't taking any chances. I gave him another kick in the groin, but it didn't even elicit a grunt. He still had the gun, but it was loosely held in his limp fist, and I took it from him without a struggle. I was squeamish about handling a gun; I was about as fond of the NRA as I was of Adam himself, but I didn't want to risk leaving it there. It was heavier than I expected, and I grasped it gingerly. Now all I needed were his keys. Fortunately, he'd put them in his coat pocket, so I didn't have to rummage very deeply into his clothing, which would have been distasteful even in the best of circumstances.

He moaned, signaling that he was returning to the land of the living. I probably didn't have much time, and I wasn't willing to shoot him, so I decided to take advantage of whatever head start his temporary incapacitation might afford. I scurried back up the path with the gun in one hand, dodging tree roots and branches as best I could. By the time I got to the car I realized I was limping, and I did a quick check to figure out what I'd hurt. Bodily, I seemed to be intact, but the heel of my right shoe was missing, which accounted for my uneven gait.

The Porsche was where we'd left it, and I got in on the driver's side, enjoying the sense of security provided by the clicking of the locks but wishing I'd had the good sense to learn how to operate a stick shift. Miraculously, I still had my handbag, and with shaking hands I managed to withdraw my cell phone. Even if Adam recovered, I was safe in a locked car, with a gun and a phone. Nothing could happen before the police got here. Right?

I was freezing, and I knew how to start the car, even if I couldn't drive it, so I turned the key in the ignition and cranked the heat up to high. I opened up my phone to call O'Connell, wondering as I did if I should be concerned that I knew the number for the police station by heart. This really hadn't turned into the weekend I'd so happily planned.

I keyed in the digits and hit Send, but the call didn't go through. I looked at the screen. Not only was there no signal, the phone was emitting a strange beeping noise, as if it were angry with me.

It was an unfortunate moment for a technology failure. Especially since when I looked up, I could see Adam emerging from the trees. He was hunched over as if in pain, but then I met his gaze, and that seemed to revive him. He managed to straighten up a bit, and now I could see that he looked angry. I had to admit, I couldn't blame him.

I swore and tried to make the call again but with no luck. I told myself not to panic. After all, I was safe in the locked car. Adam reached the car and began pulling fruitlessly at the door. I smiled up at him when he started banging on the window, but that seemed to antagonize him further. It was probably a good thing that I couldn't hear what he was yelling. I leaned over the passenger seat to double-check that the other door was locked.

When I turned back, Adam was still at the window. But this time he had a large rock in his hand. I could sense a moment of hesitation—he really loved this car—but he got over any reservations. He pounded the rock into the driver's-side window.

It cracked, but it didn't shatter. Still, my nice safe feeling had evaporated. I had to get away.

Horrified, I surveyed the gear shift on the console. Why, why would anyone build a car with a manual shift when some brilliant engineer had seen fit to invent the automatic transmission? There were three pedals at my feet, and I knew enough to recognize that the one on the far left was the clutch and that you were supposed to push it in while changing gears. But that was pretty much the extent of my knowledge.

The rock struck the window again, but the glass continued to hold. Holding my breath, I jerked the gear shift into a slot and eased up on the clutch. To my relief, the car didn't stall. It rolled back toward the entrance to the park at a rapid clip.

Adam started to run after the car, but it was hard for him to run when he was in too much pain to stand up straight. He threw the rock in his hand, a last attempt to keep me from getting away. It hit the windshield, spreading a spider's web of cracks across its expanse. Which was fine, because I wasn't looking out the windshield. I was twisted around to see the road behind me. I didn't want to risk stalling the car by attempting to switch gears, so I stayed in reverse until I reached the strip mall we had passed earlier.

I backed into a parking space and turned off the engine. Then I lurched into the only open store, a White Hen Pantry, in search of a phone and a well-earned Diet Coke.

★ ★ ★

It was mid-afternoon by the time I returned to the hotel. A couple of people in the lobby turned to stare as I passed, and when I caught sight of my reflection in the elevator doors, I could easily understand why. There were sticks in my hair, my coat was covered with patches of mud and I had one three-inch heel and one missing heel. This didn't even begin to take into account the shredded suit underneath adorned with white cat hair, courtesy of Krystle, much less the fact that I still had a raging hangover.

Regardless of my hangover, the only thing that kept me moving was the vision of a stiff drink, to be sipped in a scalding bath. I walked unevenly down the hall to my room and slipped the key card into the lock.

But the door opened before I could turn the latch, and music poured out into the corridor.

I looked up into Peter's smiling face as violins played "Fascination."

"Gypsies," he said.

Thirty-Five

"Gypsies?" I repeated in disbelief.

But sure enough, there they were, in the corner of the suite's living room. A quartet of white-coated men, playing "Fascination" on a quartet of violins. The table was set with white linen and crystal and silver-domed serving platters. A bottle of champagne stood waiting in an ice bucket next to a vase holding at least three dozen red roses.

Peter was trying to take off my coat. "Just like the movie, right?" he asked eagerly.

It was perfect. I was speechless.

The speechlessness, however, lasted all of five seconds.

"WHERE. DO. YOU. GET. OFF?"

I shook my arm from his grasp.

"What?" he asked, stepping back, a look of concern washing over his face. "What do you mean? What's wrong? And why do you have twigs in your hair?"

"And you," I said in the direction of the Gypsies, who, on closer inspection, weren't really Gypsies. In fact, one was a woman and another was Korean. "Please stop playing." The music skidded to a halt.

"But, Rachel—" Peter began.

"Now, you look here. This doesn't make up for anything."

"Make up for what—"

"I can't even begin to describe the weekend I've had. I've been chased by serial killers. I've been attacked by überdork egomaniacs. And cats named after *Dynasty* characters. I've had to thwart a hostile takeover single-handedly. I had to drive stick, in the world's cheesiest expensive car, and you would think that a car that expensive would at least include an automatic transmission, but oh no, it doesn't, so I had to drive in reverse. And then there was no Diet Coke—"

"Rachel—"

"—I had to drink Tab instead. Tab sucks. And my suit is ruined, and so are my shoes. And to top it all off, you're missing in action. No, you're not missing in action. You're worse than missing in action—"

"Rachel—"

"—you're sashaying around Boston with Abigail, buying her jewelry and making out in malls."

"Sashaying?" he asked with a raised eyebrow.

"Sashaying," I said. "And have I mentioned how many people I've kicked in the balls in the last twenty-four hours? Two people, Peter. I've kicked two people in the balls. And I still have one good shoe. Maybe I should make it three. Do you want me to make it three—"

"Rachel—"

"And you didn't even call," I concluded, forlorn. "I mean, it's all my fault, because I jinxed everything, but still…"

He folded his arms across his chest. "Are you done?" he asked.

I scowled up at him.

"First of all, what do you mean I didn't call?"

"You didn't call. Oh, except for lame messages here at the hotel, where you knew you wouldn't have to talk to me in person."

"I called. But I think there's something wrong with your cell phone. For the last couple of days I call and I just get a strange buzzing noise. Except for yesterday, when you told me you'd call me back. And didn't. And then your phone doesn't even go into voice mail. Are you sure it's working?"

"Humph." A likely story. Although, my trusty Blackberry had been through a lot of late. And its collision with the wall after yesterday's board meeting probably hadn't been good for it. And I had been dropping it a lot. And there had been a strange dearth of messages, not only from Peter, but from anyone at all. In fact, its performance had been nothing short of erratic.

"And when I e-mail you, the messages get bounced back. Is your e-mail on the fritz, too?"

E-mail, too, had been strangely empty of late. I might have to learn how to stop throwing my communications gadgets at unyielding objects.

"Then I called the hotel this morning, and you grunted and hung up on me."

"That wasn't you. That was the wake-up call. And I didn't grunt."

"You grunted."

"I didn't grunt. Anyhow, that's neither here nor there."

"What does that mean?"

"It means, you've been totally AWOL. In 'negotiations' with Abigail. Nothing requires that much negotiating."

He unfolded his arms and ran both hands through his hair. "Do you want to know what I was really negotiating?"

"Yes. No. I guess."

"I—we—my company, has bought another company. It was going to be a surprise."

"Why? Why did it have to be a surprise?"

"Because they're based in New York."

"So?"

"So, now I can move to New York."

"Why would you want to move to New York?"

"Are you a complete idiot?" he asked through gritted teeth.

"If that's an apology for being missing in action for the last four days, it's not a very good one."

"Rachel," Peter said, speaking slowly and evenly, clearly struggling to keep his temper in check. "I want to move to New York so that I can be with you."

"Why would you want to be with me when you're so busy canoodling with Abigail—"

"—I thought I was sashaying with Abigail—"

"—or is she moving to New York, too?"

He took a deep breath. "Rachel, Abigail is not moving to New York. She's going to stay in San Francisco and run everything there."

"Well, good for her. I'm sure everyone in San Francisco will be very impressed by all of her new jewelry."

"Now what are you talking about?"

"You. Buying Abigail jewelry. Jane and Luisa saw you on Newbury Street. Then we all saw you in Copley Place. Coming out of Tiffany's. And making out."

"Rachel, we weren't making out," he started to say, but then he made an odd choking noise. "We weren't making out," he said again, but he made the choking noise again. Then he started to laugh.

"This is funny?"

He was laughing too hard to speak. He just nodded.

"You really think this is funny."

"Absolutely," he managed to get out between spasms of hilarity.

"That's it. I'm out of here."

"It's your suite."

"Fine. You're out of here." I threw open the closet door and pulled out his suitcase.

"Rachel. Abigail is gay."

"What?" I asked from the closet, where I was busily pulling his clothes off hangers.

"Abigail is gay."

I stopped pulling clothes off hangers. "Really?"

"Really."

Suddenly I remembered Luisa's comment from the previous day, her suggestion that maybe we were on the wrong track. Was this what she'd meant?

"But then why were you buying her jewelry? And making out with her?"

"We weren't making out. I'm pretty sure that what you saw was an innocent kiss on the cheek, viewed from the wrong angle. And we weren't buying her jewelry."

"Then why were you hitting every jewelry store in town?"

"Abigail was— Abigail has great taste. She was helping me."

"Helping you what?" I demanded, spinning around to face him, hands on hips.

"Oh, crap. This isn't how I wanted to do this."

"Do what?"

"Look, Rachel." He nodded to the Gypsies, who'd been watching our exchange in awed silence. "I had a whole speech planned."

"Just break up with me already!"

"You're impossible!"

"No, you're impossible!"
"You're more—never mind."
He sank onto one knee and the Gypsies began to play.
"Rachel. Will you marry me?"

Epilogue

I said yes, of course. I wasn't a complete idiot.

And the Gypsies played, and Peter took the lid off one of the platters with a flourish. "Whoops. Wrong one," he said, when it was revealed to be a plate of burritos. He tried a couple more before hitting on the right platter. "This is the one. I thought I'd marked it."

The ring was beautiful, a sparkling diamond solitaire surrounded by small rubies. It slid onto my ring finger as if it belonged there, as if it would always be there. We asked the Gypsies to come back in a couple of hours, and I had my hot bath, but with company. Peter was particularly handy when it came to soaping the hard-to-reach spots.

The phone rang while we were in the bath, but we were too busy to answer it. When I listened to the message the following morning, it was the Caped Avenger, calling to let me know he was backing out of the takeover. I hadn't expected that it could possibly go forward since its chief architect, Adam Barnett, was facing a long prison term for multiple counts of murder and assault. Nor was he likely to be having children anytime soon. But it was nice to know that Whit was officially calling an end to the proceedings. At our next department staff meeting, Stan Winslow announced himself to be delighted by the lengths I'd gone to to protect my client's interests and excited by the batch of new recruits who would be joining Winslow, Brown from Harvard Business School upon graduation. He also made promising noises about my prospects at the next partnership election. Scott Epson dashed out of the meeting as soon as it ended, looking sheepish and mumbling something about an incredibly important meeting for which he was already late.

Grant Crocker would be joining Adam Barnett in prison. But he managed to secure a place on the business school's much lauded list of prominent alumni, although he was a departure from the Fortune 500 CEOs and U.S. Treasury Secretaries who made up most of the list. Of course, he hadn't actually graduated from Harvard Business School, but perhaps he could finish up his degree through some sort of correspondence course.

Sara returned to class, determined to graduate in June but spending every minute of spare time she had working with Brian Mulcahey at Grenthaler Media. She and Brian had already asked me to help them identify ways to finance Sara's acquisition of another ten percent of the company. She'd learned the hard way that securing majority ownership was the only way she could be sure of never losing control of the company. And it looked like her white knight would be none other than Whitaker Jamieson. Sara expressed doubts, but I assured her that he could be quite useful when handled properly.

Jonathan Beasley, meanwhile, had been cleared of everything but writing very inappropriate letters to a student. Last

I heard, he was on "sabbatical." I could only hope that his time off included some intensive therapy and a remedial course in creative writing. And I'd introduced Gabrielle Le-Favre to some contacts at a couple of boutique investment banking firms. With some coaching, I was confident she would secure a position that would be well suited to both her objectives and her borderline personality.

Peter and I made it to the final dinner of the reunion weekend, albeit a bit late. I'd suggested that he invite Abigail to come along. It was a stretch, given that Luisa was on the rebound and lived on a different continent, but it seemed worth a try. Luisa was too self-contained to display any visible interest in Peter's colleague, but Emma told me that she saw them exchanging e-mail addresses at the end of the evening. Jane placed her hands protectively over her abdomen as Hilary and O'Connell flirted with each other. Hilary had already announced that she would need to be spending a lot of time in Boston to finish her book. "You have six months," Jane warned, "before the guest room turns into a nursery."

As for Emma, she announced over dessert that she was moving into Matthew's apartment in Boston. I turned to her, saddened that my best friend would be living in a different city. "Don't worry," she said. "It's just a shuttle flight away."

I didn't worry. I knew that we would talk just as often as we usually did. Besides, I would be busy as well in the upcoming months. Peter would be moving to New York, and I definitely didn't have enough closet space for two. We would have to find a bigger apartment to share. And I had a wedding to plan, a date to set, a venue to find, a band and caterers and florists to hire, and...

"What are you thinking?" Peter asked me in a low voice, pulling me close.

"That I'm the luckiest person in the world."

"Careful. You don't want to jinx yourself, now."

"You know what I say to the Jinxing Gods?"

"No. What?" His eyes met mine, their rich chocolate color deep and warm.

"Jinx away."

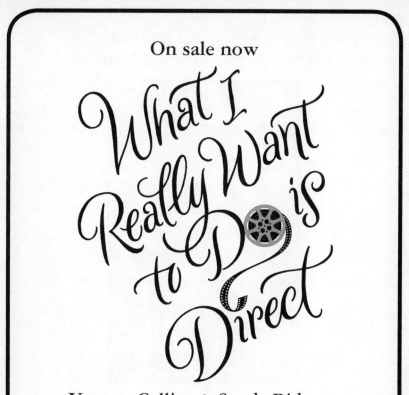

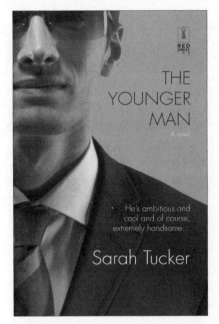

New from bestselling author
Melissa Senate

THE BREAKUP CLUB

In her most ambitious novel yet, Melissa Senate
explores life after heartbreak for four very
different yet equally memorable New Yorkers,
who have all been recently jilted and come
together to form The Breakup Club.

On sale January 2006.

Available wherever
trade paperbacks
are sold.

The Pact

by Jennifer Sturman

A mystery for anyone who has ever
hated a friend's boyfriend

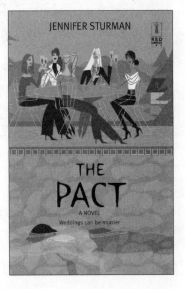

Rachel Benjamin and her friends aren't looking forward to Emma's wedding. The groom is a rat, and
nobody can understand what Emma sees in him.
So when he turns up dead on the morning of the
ceremony, no one in the wedding party is all that
upset. Is it possible that one of the five best friends
took a pact they made in university too far?

Are you getting it at least twice a month?

Here's how: Try RED DRESS INK books on for size & receive two FREE gifts!

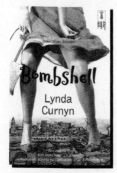

Bombshell
by Lynda Curnyn

As Seen on TV
by Sarah Mlynowski

RED DRESS I N K ™

RDI04-TR